THE CORAL THIEF

THE CORAL THIEF

REBECCA STOTT

THORNDIKE
WINDSOR
PARAGON

This Large Print edition is published by Thorndike Press, Waterville, Maine, USA and by BBC Audiobooks Ltd, Bath, England.
Thorndike Press, a part of Gale, Cengage Learning.
The text of this Large Print edition is unabridged.
Other aspects of the book may vary from the original edition.
Set in 16 pt. Plantin.
Printed on permanent paper.

LIBRARY OF CONGRESS CATALOGING-IN-PUBLICATION DATA

Stott, Rebecca.
    The coral thief / by Rebecca Stott.
       p. cm. — (Thorndike Press large print historical fiction)
    ISBN-13: 978-1-4104-2207-1 (alk. paper)
    ISBN-10: 1-4104-2207-0 (alk. paper)
    1. Anatomists—Fiction. 2. Evolution (Biology)—
Philosophy—Fiction. 3. Large type books. I. Title.
PR6119.T69C67 2009b
823'.92—dc22   2009035827

BRITISH LIBRARY CATALOGUING-IN-PUBLICATION DATA AVAILABLE

Published in 2009 in the U.S. by arrangement with Spiegel & Grau, an imprint of Bantam Dell Publishing Group, a division of Random House, Inc.
Published in 2010 in the U.K. by arrangement with The Orion Publishing Group Ltd.

U.K. Hardcover: 978 1 408 46088 7 (Windsor Large Print)
U.K. Softcover: 978 1 408 46089 4 (Paragon Large Print)

Printed in the United States of America
1 2 3 4 5 6 7 13 12 11 10 09

To Jacob

Once grant that species [of] one genus may pass into each other . . . & [the] whole fabric totters & falls.

— CHARLES DARWIN, *Notebook C,* 1838

When at the age of twenty-one I traveled to Paris from Edinburgh by mail coach, carrying in my luggage three rare fossils and the bone of a mammoth, I still believed time traveled in straight lines. It was July 1815, only a few weeks after Napoleon had been defeated by the Allies at Waterloo. War with France was over, restitution had begun, the borders were open again. Time stretched out like a long road in front of me — toward a vocation. I was to be a man of science, assistant to the illustrious Baron Georges Cuvier, professor of comparative anatomy at the Jardin des Plantes in Paris.

But fortunately for the man — or boy — who imagines he is heading in a straight line toward an illustrious future, there are highwaymen on the road, brigands in the trees, there are ambushes and skirmishes and falls to be had. If he takes a single step off the road into the undergrowth, where branchings and forkings chance along a different axis, he might begin to see the sublime contingency that is at the root of everything. He might find a different set of answers there.

And so it was that, with a night ambush on a mail coach, my voyage of discovery began. I was just one of scores of medical students traveling to Paris that summer.

She could have chosen any of us. But she chose me.

1

In the dark hours of a hot July night in 1815, sitting on the outside of a mail coach a few miles from Paris, I woke to the sound of a woman's voice, speaking in French, deep and roughly textured, like limestone. We had stopped outside a village inn whose sign creaked in the night wind. *Attention,* she said to the driver. *Be careful.*

I opened my eyes as a tall figure, her head obscured by the hood of her cloak, climbed into the seat beside me. Groaning with the effort, the driver passed up to her a large bundle wrapped in a red velvet blanket. It was a sleeping child; I could just make out a dimpled hand, the sleep-hot flush of a cheek, and a curl of dark hair. The woman spoke softly to the child, soothing it, rearranging the folds of its blanket.

"There are several empty seats inside, madame," I said in French, concentrating hard on my pronunciation.

She answered me in perfect English: "But who would want to sit inside on a night like this?"

Her voice was surprisingly low for a woman, and it stirred me. The black of the sky was already shading to a deep inky blue over toward the horizon. Mist hung over the fields and hedgerows and gathered a little in the trees on either side of the road.

"Is it safe in France for a woman to travel alone?" I asked as the coach lurched back into movement. The Edinburgh newspapers regularly reported attacks on carriages traveling at night across open country.

She laughed and turned toward me, her face illuminated by the light of a half-moon. Over to my left somewhere a rooster crowed; we must have been passing a farm or a village. "But I am not traveling alone," she said, dropping her voice to a whisper and leaning toward me. "I have Delphine. She is no ordinary child, you see. She is asleep now, of course, so it may be a little difficult for you to believe, but this child, she can fight armies and slay dragons. I have seen it with my own eyes. I have seen her lift an elephant and its rider with a single hand. *Non,* I am entirely safe with Delphine. Otherwise, of course, I would never travel alone. It is far too dangerous. What about you, monsieur? Are *you* not afraid?"

"I —"

"No, of course you are not afraid." She smiled. "You are a man."

"I have never left England before," I stammered. "I have never traveled so far or had to make myself understood in another language. Three times I decided I must take the next mail coach back to Calais . . . I've never felt so much of a coward."

She laughed, her voice mesmerizing in the darkness. "There it is. Paris. See the lights ahead . . . on the horizon? We will be there by dawn. Imagine . . ." She stopped suddenly, gazing out toward the flattened shapes of the distant hills. "Sometimes it's easier to see all that water in the darkness."

"I can't see any water," I said, confused.

She pointed from right to left. "Everything you see from there to there, the entire Paris basin, was under water thousands of years ago. Paris was just a hollow in the seafloor then. There were cliffs of chalk over there, see, where the land began. Picture it — giant sea lizards swimming around us, oysters and corals beneath us, creatures with bodies so strange we couldn't possibly imagine them crawling across the seabed. Later, when the water retreated, the creatures pulled themselves onto the rocks to make new bodies with scales and fur and feathers. Mammoths wandered down from the hills to drink from the Seine, under the same moon as this one, calling to one another."

"That's a strange thing to think about," I said.

"Oui." She laughed. "I suppose it is. But I think about it often, this earth before man. I look at the fossils in the rocks, the remains of that time so long ago, and I think about how late we came. Even the sea slugs appeared before we did. It took thousands of years for these bodies of ours to take shape, for our clever eyes and our curious brains to come to be. And now that we are big and strong, we think everything belongs to us, that we know and own everything."

"Come to be?" I said, surprised and a little alarmed. "So you think species have changed? You are a student of Professor Lamarck, the transformist?"

"I was once," she said. "Lamarck is right about most things. Species are not fixed. Everything is changing, all the time. The animals, the people, the hills — even the little things, skin, hair, everything is constantly renewing itself, taking new shapes. Just think of what we have come from — simple sea creatures with no eyes or hearts or minds — then think of what we might yet become. Doesn't that excite you?" She ran her fingers across the child's face. She — Delphine, the dragonslayer — stirred, her eyes flickering open for a moment and then closing again.

"Paris is riddled with infidels," Professor Jameson had warned me back in Edinburgh. "They are poets, these French transformists, not men of science. They dream up notions about the origins of the earth and the transmutation of species. Castles in the air. Most of them are atheists too — heretics. Steer clear."

Jameson had not mentioned that there were women who had studied with Lamarck. I wondered what he would make of this infidel sitting beside me now. I would have to record this conversation in my notebook, I thought; Jameson would want a report. He would want to know the kind of words she used, what she had read, whom she talked to. So did I.

"It will get bigger, you know," she said, her eyes shining in the dark with a touch of malevolence.

"What will?"

"The city. It doesn't look so big now, at night, but it will swallow you up. Are you not afraid?"

15

"Yes." I smiled. "Yes. Of course I'm afraid."

Paris aroused complicated feelings in me then. What did I know of cities — the sound of thousands of people moving together, the tangled dealings of commerce and trade? I had always been a country boy. I knew the insides of the cave networks and mine workings of Derbyshire; I knew the angles and curves of the hills, the names of trees, ferns, lichens, and fishes; I could tell you how the light fell across the lakes, but I knew almost nothing of cities.

Edinburgh — quiet, solid, rainy Edinburgh, hewn out of the rock and built across a ravine — where I had lived and worked for four years, had overwhelmed me as a seventeen-year-old boy arriving by carriage one frosty morning. As I slipped through the crowd of Princes Street, I could scarcely feel the beginnings and ends of myself in the roar and flow of it. So I had anchored myself, establishing daily routes between the lecture theaters, the anatomy school, the libraries, museums, and taverns. Despite the best efforts of my fellow students, one of whom urged me with mock seriousness to fall in love for the sake of my health, I had lived largely in and among books.

I had seen London fleetingly, passing through from time to time on my way from Edinburgh to my family home in Derbyshire. One day in May I walked from the inn where I was staying to the optical-instrument maker's shop in the Strand and bought a bronze-cased microscope in a velvet-lined box with money I had saved for three years. On that brief walk, London, for all its smoke and smell and noise, enraptured me. My curiosity, that shapeless thing that drove at me relentlessly, that propelled the search for origins and explanations and connections, my desire to see further and further into the insides of things that had compelled me from the day I had touched my first microscope, or turned the first page of Aristotle's *History of Animals,* or opened the encyclopedia at the page marked "Anatomy," had seemed all the more heightened in London. There were answers to be found in cities; there were libraries, instrument shops and museums and professors who knew how to pose extraordinary questions.

Now that I had graduated, I wanted more than anything to be part of what was happening in Paris — the conversations and discoveries in the debating rooms, the libraries, and the museums. The French

17

professors, given authority, freedom, and money by Napoleon, were making new inroads into knowledge. The museums in Paris were remarkable, the lectures ground-breaking. But it was also the city my father and his friends feared and loathed, the Paris of the Revolution — a city of people so hungry they had marched on Versailles, stormed the Bastille, imprisoned and then killed a royal family. I thought about the newspaper reports my father had kept that described the guillotine swallowing up lives, thousands of them; blood in the streets; mobs; children with sticks and garden tools hunting down the children of aristocrats and beating them to death; a king made to wear a red cap; bloodied heads on spikes; the grocer burned alive on a pyre made of furniture thrown from the windows of the palaces of émigrés.

Then there was the Paris of Napoleon Bonaparte. I had seen drawings of the buildings and squares and streets the Emperor had built: the vast classical perspective of the Arc du Carrousel and the Arc de Triomphe; the new bridges and water fountains; the classical façades, colonnades, marble columns — all so cool and quiet — the imperial aspirations of the Emperor laid serenely on top of fire, blood, and death.

Paris was to be the new Rome, Napoleon had declared.

Now that Napoleon had been captured, Wellington had restored the French king to the throne — Louis XVIII, they called this one; the brother of the guillotined king. But everyone was still half expecting Napoleon to rise again, like a body that just wouldn't drown. Anything could happen, and I wanted to be there to see it. Whatever *it* was going to be. There was going to be a spectacle of some kind.

"Daniel into the lion's den . . ." she said.

"How do you know my name?" The coach lurched so that my body crushed up against her shoulder in the darkness. "Pardon, madame. Have we met before?"

"A Portuguese priest taught me some tricks in a bar on the Amalfi coast," she said, turning her head toward me with a slow smile. In the lightening of the morning, I could see her face for the first time against the black folds of her hood.

She was darkly, heavily beautiful. A woman of middle years with black eyes and olive skin and thick black eyebrows that almost touched in the middle, making the shape of an archer's bow, a falcon in flight. Even in the half-light, the directness of her gaze startled me. She held me there, her eyes searching out mine, her lips forming the faintest of smiles, but I could not look back, not directly, though I wanted to. Always immersed in my studies, and growing up as a boy among boys, I had had little practice conversing with women. I felt myself blush and began to stammer. "What tricks?" I asked. "What did he teach you?"

"My friend, the abbé Faria," she said, "is a magnetist. He is half Indian, half Portuguese. He taught me many things. I put you to sleep for a few minutes, and then you told me everything — first your name, your family, your dreams . . . and then your secrets. Now I know all your secrets. Every one." She smiled.

"You didn't put me to sleep," I said. "That's ridiculous." I looked at my pocket watch. The hands were still moving clockwise at the same rate. It was half past five. I was certain I had lost no time.

"How can you be sure, monsieur?" She was no longer looking at my eyes; now her gaze had settled on my lips. Her eyes on my lips, her thigh against my thigh, her shoulder against mine. I could feel the heat of her body through my clothes. In the early-morning light, with the child sleeping in the crook of her arm, she looked like a painting. Almost sacred. Yet the intimacy of her talk and manner disturbed me.

"You must be about twenty," she said, examining me more closely. "You remind me of someone I once knew. You have the look of a Caravaggio boy — your dark curls, your skin, your coloring, your eyes."

"Caravaggio?"

"The Italian painter."

"Yes, I know who Caravaggio is."

"I think it's something about your lips. Your beauty begins there, in your lips. Some of Caravaggio's paintings are in the Louvre. You should go and see them."

"I am twenty-three," I said, exaggerating a little, while trying to steady my breathing. Could she see my discomfort, my body betraying its secrets?

She smiled. The wind had picked up. It tugged at her cloak and blew through her hair. She pulled the cloak further around the child's head. The child, disturbed, woke for a moment and sat up, black eyes wide, her black hair disheveled and wild, and said in French, as if still dreaming: *M. Napoleon, il est mort."*

"No, no, little one," the woman replied in French, "it's only a dream, just a dream. M. Napoleon is sleeping safely in his own bed. Really. His soldiers are guarding him. Now, go back to sleep. We will be in Paris soon."

The child, comforted, dropped her shoulders, closed her eyes, pulled the cloak around her, and was soon sleeping again.

The woman turned back to me, her voice low and lingering. "Your name is Daniel Connor. You are studying anatomy at the medical school in Edinburgh. You have written up your dissertation. Probably, I think, on something to do with generation or embryology —"

"The circulation of the blood in the fetus . . . How did you . . . ?"

"And now you come to Paris to study at the Jardin des Plantes, M. Daniel Connor. You think about philosophical questions. What else? Am I correct so far?"

"How can you *possibly* know that?"

My voice, when I spoke, was shaky. I was tired, I reminded myself. Just that. And this woman was a specter. Probably just a figment of my imagination, conjured in the night.

She laughed again and gestured toward my traveling bag, which sat between us on the seat, open.

"You are labeled, my friend . . . here." She ran her fingers over the letters engraved on the inside of the bag. "You see: DANIEL CONNOR, MEDICAL SCHOOL, EDINBURGH. I guessed the rest. You are easy to read."

"That is not fair," I said, relieved. "You have taken advantage of me."

"You see," she said, "I am a great investigator. We say *enquêteur*. There are many Edinburgh medical students like you in Paris now. They come to listen to the French professors of the Jardin des Plantes: Professors Lamarck, Cuvier, and Geoffroy. I like to watch them. They amuse me."

I didn't like to think of myself as just one of many, but she was right. For me and for hundreds of other medical students in July 1815, all possible roads led to — or through — the great Jardin des Plantes. Built as an herb garden on the banks of the Seine for a French king in the seventeenth century, the Jardin du Roi had, with the severing of a king's head a hundred years later, become the Jardin des Plantes, a garden for the enlightenment of the people. Twelve venerable French professors lived in the Jardin in the elegant houses built among the museums, libraries, glasshouses, and lecture halls, professors who between them knew how to formulate questions about everything in nature and would soon, without doubt, I believed, know all the answers. In a few weeks, Professors Lamarck, Cuvier, and Geoffroy would no longer be names on scientific papers or abstracts, they would become real people to me, fellow explorers and patrons. The prospect awed me.

"How long will you stay in Paris, M. Daniel Connor?"

"I don't know yet. I have six months' employment in the Museum of Comparative Anatomy in the Jardin des Plantes, working for Professor Cuvier on a new volume of his book — some illustration, some dissecting. I will be an *aide-naturaliste*. After that I have a little money. My uncle died and left me a small inheritance. I shall use it to travel."

I could see it as if I was walking through it — colonnades and staircases and hushed libraries. The universities of Europe. I saw botanical gardens and shelves stacked with glass jars of yellowing liquid preserving the shapes of rare animals and fishes. I heard animated conversation at a distance — voices speaking in Spanish, Italian, German. I pictured myself there at the center of it all: on the steps, among fountains and bougainvillea, in shady lecture halls — arguing, questioning.

Derbyshire was a backwater as far as ideas were concerned. None of the members of the local Natural Philosophical Society at Castleton, which now had a substantial collection of fossils and bones displayed in its museum, had read James Hutton or Georges Cuvier or even Alexander Humboldt. They were not philosophers but myopic collectors arguing over taxonomy, I told myself, counting angels on a pinhead. Only three men in the town of Ashbourne — the vicar, the doctor, and the judge — knew Greek. Even Edinburgh Medical School, when compared with the medical schools of Paris, seemed to be locked in the past century. I had attended all the lectures in anatomy, geology, and natural philosophy several times over by the time I graduated. The university library, where I had first read volumes of Shakespeare and Locke and Fielding and Scott as well as anatomy textbooks, closed and opened at unpredictable hours; it had no catalogue and an impenetrable shelving system. The anatomy theaters were always full to bursting, and you couldn't get a seat or see what was happening; there were never enough cadavers for us to work on.

Meanwhile the medical students I knew who had spent a winter at the Jardin des Plantes came back whispering of lecture theaters filled with the cleverest men in Europe, libraries overflowing with thousands of volumes of specialist books, museums crammed with specimens from every corner of the world, new dissection and classification techniques, and ever more powerful microscopes. Paris had become a kind of mirage in my mind — a shimmer of light on the horizon.

I had only my inheritance, but I had merit, and in France, people said then, merit still counted for something. Napoleon Bonaparte had proven that. His rise to power had been theatrical and spectacular: Corsican country boy comes to Paris during the Revolution, becomes a soldier, becomes lieutenant, becomes artillery commander, becomes general, becomes first consul, becomes Emperor of France. He was breathtaking. You couldn't not admire him. In fifteen years he had captured most of Europe, swept his way with his Imperial Army through city after city, like a high tide across mudflats, to establish himself as one of the greatest rulers the world had ever seen.

But of course, although I admired Napoleon perhaps above all men, my father would not permit my journey to Paris until the Emperor had fallen. By the time I arrived, Napoleon was already a captive on the HMS *Bellerophon,* while the Allies quarreled about what to do with him.

In 1815 Napoleon's fate seemed strangely

— inversely, superstitiously — bound to mine. Just as my journey began, his seemed to be coming to an end. As I reached Paris, he was already heading away from it. Europe had begun the process of remaking itself, redrawing its borders, and forming new alliances. The trajectory of Napoleon's power, at first relentlessly upward, like an arrow in flight, had started into its downward curve. I would follow the newspaper accounts of his journey all through that autumn, measuring my own days against his, spellbound, as I would have watched the trail of a strange comet across the night sky.

"I plan to leave Paris in the spring," I told her, "and travel down to Montpellier and then Heidelberg, then across to Padua and Pavia. My father does not approve. He thinks I should buy a practice in Derbyshire and settle down or study for the church. He says I am a dilettante. He says philosophical questions are of no practical use in this world. He does not like France or the French."

"And your mother? What does she think?"

"My mother always agrees with my father."

Over thirty years my mother had adapted to married life and a house full of large and noisy sons by retreating to her room with a vague, unnamed medical condition. *Your mother is not to be worried,* my father insisted, using her constitution as a way of ensuring compliance from his sons. Conversations with my mother were almost entirely conducted in hushed tones in darkened rooms. I remember a table of colored bottles like stained glass in her drawing room and the thick burnt-flower smell of laudanum that hung about her like incense. She had little interest in my childish obsessions with butterflies, newts, and fossils, but she taught me to draw and paint watercolors of birds and plants, which I would bring to her like offerings.

"If your father hates the French," the woman said, noticing my distraction, "why does he let you come here?"

"My professor at Edinburgh wrote to him several times pressing my case. I am the youngest son, so I think he is more indulgent with me than with my brothers." I didn't tell her how many times Jameson had used the word *exceptional* in his letter to my father or that he had described me as the finest student in my year. I had worked hard for that word *exceptional* and for his letter of recommendation to Cuvier.

"So you will take the Grand Tour."

"Well, no. Not like that. Paintings and ruins are interesting enough, but it's the natural-history collections and libraries I want to see. Knowledge, not art. That's what's important now. Advances in knowledge. We will soon discover the key to all of nature's laws. Soon we will know God's purpose and design —"

"God's design," she said. "Are God and Nature the same thing, or different? I find that a difficult question. Nature? Is she God's agent, his servant — doing his work for him, following his plan, or can she go her own way? And I wonder if they argue sometimes, Nature and God — it seems to me that they want different things."

"I don't know," I said.

She baffled me. I had never met a woman who thought about philosophical questions. The women I had spoken to at the dinner tables of Derbyshire or Edinburgh seemed only to want to gossip about people or novels or to talk earnestly about the poor. I wasn't very good at talking about those things and hadn't really listened. "You are much too serious with women, Daniel," my brother Samuel had once said. "They really don't want to know about your microscopes and your fossils and your butterflies." He was right. They didn't. I had long since given up talking about natural philosophy to women.

The horses, sensing the closeness of their destination, picked up the pace. We passed another group of French soldiers by the side of the road, wounded Waterloo veterans making their way wearily back to Paris. I had sketched several groups of soldiers since leaving Calais and had tried repeatedly to capture the details of the war-torn landscape. I had drawn fields full of ripe corn and no one to harvest it; rubbish blowing in the warm wind; half-empty villages, every second house boarded up or left with its doors and shutters flung open. I drew the white flags that peasants had suspended from windows and rooftops and trees. I sketched disoriented soldiers, some badly wounded, others being dragged on boards tied to horses, traveling home, carrying their swords over their shoulders to support bundles of clothes and food, women in uniform walking alongside them.

"It is a good plan, of course," she went on, "this one of yours to travel. But what will you do when your money runs out? Go home? Become a doctor? Marry and have children? Grow fat? Stand for Parliament, perhaps?"

"No," I said. "I have to make my own living. I'm not ashamed to say that. But I want to continue my studies, and if I'm careful with my money . . . I might —"

"You have a letter of introduction to Professor Cuvier?" she asked, yawning.

"Yes, from Jameson. And some specimens to present. Do you know him, Professor Cuvier? What is he like?"

In my mind's eye, Baron Cuvier appeared larger than life. Perhaps that had something to do with the bones he worked on — the giant bones of mammoths and megatheriums dug out from the quarries of Paris or brought to him from the canal workings or mine shafts of Europe. I imagined him walking through halls of bones, through the bellies of whales. He, more than anyone, could make them speak. He could see how they fitted together, how this joint here fitted with that foot there. He could take a single fossil toe bone, they said, and rebuild the entire skeleton of the creature from it. I wanted him to teach me to see what he saw. That's why I was in Paris. I wanted to see through Cuvier's eyes.

"He is stiff," she said. "Rather formal in his manner, but clever, very clever. A very important man in France. You seem young for such responsibility."

"Yes . . ." I hesitated. "Well, no . . . I am

one of the oldest in my year. My friend —"

"You have much to see in Paris, M. Connor. The natural-history collection at the museum in the Jardin is beyond compare. I cannot imagine what it will be like to see it for the first time. I envy you. I would like to show you, take you there."

"You've seen it?"

"Of course." She laughed. "We're almost in Paris now. Perhaps another hour or so. See how the light is lifting up the color in the fields — they are not flat anymore. The shapes are filling out and the stars have almost disappeared."

"The mammoths have gone back to the hills," I said.

"One day, when the water has retreated even more, you will be able to walk from London to Paris. There will be no more English Channel. Your country will be joined to mine."

"It will?"

"Well, perhaps not soon. It might take a few thousand years. And who knows, perhaps by then we will have wings."

In a sleeping village on the outskirts of Paris, the mail coach stopped to change the horses. A dog ran alongside us, barking. A young woman, awake in the dawn, stepped into her doorway; a small child strapped to her back stared up at us, bleary-eyed.

"I can't keep my eyes open any longer," my companion said. "I shall sleep. You should too."

I leaned against the leather side of the seat, watching the hunched silhouette of the driver beneath me, his clothes coming into color in the light of the morning, steam rising from the backs of the horses. I glanced over at the woman who had pulled her cloak around her and the child curled in sleep. I wondered why I had not asked her more questions. What else did she know? I felt the mail coach lurch one last time, and tired and hungry, I fell asleep, thinking of mammoths lumbering in the dark.

When the mail coach stopped at the Barrier of Saint Denis an hour later, I woke to find the woman and the child gone, along with my travel bag and the small case containing the specimens. She had left me only my identity papers and my wallet, which had been placed under my arm as I slept.

Two notebooks of writings and annotations. Years of precious notes on natural history taken from books I might not find again and from experiments I could not hope to repeat. A book of sketches. Letters of introduction from Professor Jameson. The cases of specimens and the manuscript entrusted to me — gone.

Startled, and still half-asleep, I turned to look for her among the ragged tangle of buildings that made up the outskirts of the city. But she was nowhere. Outrage gave way to bafflement, then a sickening sense of my own stupidity. *I had fallen asleep.* I might as well have *given* my possessions away. I climbed over to the luggage rack, turning over bag after bag, trunk after trunk, calling out to the driver for help. He was busy reining in the horses and only cursed me in French and shouted that I had better return to my seat unless I wanted to get everyone killed.

A Scottish soldier standing guard with several Prussians at the barrier called out for identity papers. The English passengers passed papers through the window of the coach below. My spirits lifted for a moment at the familiar sight of the tall soldier in his kilt.

"Sir," I called out. "My bag has been stolen."

"Welcome to Paris, my friend," the soldier called back.

"What should I do?"

"Go to the Bureau de la Sûreté and report

it. Give yourself a few hours. There's usually a queue. Want me to lend you a few francs?" He passed my papers back.

"No. I have money. She didn't take my money."

"She didn't take your money?" He turned to the Prussian soldier, mimicking sexual gestures. They laughed: a joke at my expense. "There can't be a single woman in Paris who doesn't want your money. They're not cheap, mind. Forget your bag, monsieur, and find yourself a woman. Just make sure you get what you pay for — and don't fall asleep."

The coach lumbered through the gates and into the city.

On that same hot night, in July, the Emperor Napoleon lay sleepless in a small bed on board the HMS *Bellerophon,* a British ship making its way around the westernmost point of France about to enter the English Channel. Its captain, the Scotsman Richard Maitland, also lay awake listening to the sound of the gulls and calculating how long it might take Parliament to decide the Emperor's destination. Someone had to find an island secure enough to keep the Emperor a prisoner this time. There must be no further escapes. It was a responsibility that weighed heavily on Captain Maitland. There would almost certainly be a rescue attempt.

At the other end of the ship, the Emperor lay in his bed, looking back on the trajectory of his life thus far, wondering what had happened to break the rising curve of his power. His luck had begun to falter for the first time only a year before, in 1814, when the Allies, afraid of what he might do, had defeated his armies, captured him, and imprisoned him on Elba, an island off the coast of Italy. It had been a humiliation almost beyond endurance.

But he had shown his captors what it meant to be Emperor of France. While the Allies were congratulating themselves on their victory, he had escaped from Elba and had marched on Paris a second time in March 1815. He had retaken and occupied the city for a hundred days but then been defeated by the Allies a second time, at Waterloo. Now he was a captive again, at the mercy of the British government. But, he thought, if he had escaped the clutches of the Allies once, he could do it again. His men whispered daily of rescue attempts and plots. Perhaps the British would grant him free passage to America after all.

At dawn the Emperor appeared on deck in his famous gray greatcoat. Midshipman George Home, anxious about the slipperiness of the newly scrubbed decks, offered Napoleon his arm. On the poop deck, Napoleon stood in silence for the rest of the morning. His entourage — his generals, their wives, his servants and valets — gathered around him, but he spoke to no one, keeping his eyes fixed on the lighthouse on the isle of Ushant and the slowly receding coastline of France.

2

As the coach made its way along the length of the Faubourg Saint-Denis, I looked for my thief among the soldiers in vividly colored uniforms and the men and women pushing handcarts, carrying flowers, wood, fruit, and vegetables into the city from outlying farms. Narrow cobbled roadways to each side trickled with stinking water; ancient lanterns hung from ropes overhead. All down the street, as far as I could see, haberdashers were hanging long strips of bright calico outside their shops like flags. On street corners old men clustered around smoky braziers, roasting fish and meat. I was hungry.

I tried to make out the full magnitude of what had happened. Professor Jameson, I reminded myself, seeking to build bridges between British and French science now that the war was finally over, had entrusted me with gifts and a manuscript to take to

Professor Cuvier, probably the most important man of science in France. The specimens and the manuscript were irreplaceable. The loss was not only an embarrassment, it was a scandal. This would almost certainly mean my return to the gray streets of Edinburgh, or to my father's house, shamed. Even if I went to the police and could make myself understood, even if the specimens were found and returned, the story would be the same: Daniel Connor had lost the rare and irreplaceable gifts entrusted to his care because he had dropped his guard and fallen asleep on the mail coach, seduced into a false sense of security by a beautiful woman. It was pitiable.

The mail coach turned into a wide covered courtyard, where half a dozen other coaches were drawing up at the same time. Drivers were unloading towers of luggage from roofs; porters were bustling about and attendants shouting. "Dis way, sare; are you for ze Otel of Rhin?" "Hôtel Bristol, sare!" Cards were thrust into hands; English voices jabbered. "Hicks, Hicks, take the coats and umbrellas." "Count the packages, John. There should be twenty-seven." There were nursery-maids, carpetbags, hatboxes, cloaks, and trunks everywhere. *"Enfin,"* I heard an old lady say to her daughters, yawning and rubbing her eyes with her cambric handkerchief, *"nous voilà!"*

"Hôtel Corneille," I said to the first porter who met my eye. Grinning, he lifted my three suitcases onto his handcart and set off on foot. I followed close behind, lest the man suddenly take off with the rest of my possessions. On each side of the street shopkeepers were opening up their doors to morning trade, setting up their windows and storefronts; waiters put out tables; fiacre drivers washed down the wheels of their carriages at the street pumps or brushed down their horses.

Paris was now a military encampment for the Allies. Everywhere uniforms made a mosaic of color in the morning sun — helmets, bearskins, two-pointed hats, plumes, epaulettes, sunbursts and grenade ornaments, standards, cravats, buckles, and shoulder cloaks. The British, someone had said, had set up camp right in the middle of the Champs-Élysées, their white conical tents clustered along the walkways under the plane and chestnut trees. Russian soldiers, young men with flaxen hair, round caps, and tightly tapered waists, sat about smoking and telling stories in the cafés. Prussians were in blue, Hungarians in dark green, Austrians in white, British in red, French in blue and red decorated with silver.

Was I glad Napoleon Bonaparte had fallen? No. Of course not. None of us at Edinburgh had been glad, despite what we might have said at the dinner tables of our professors or in the company of our elders. Napoleon Bonaparte, not Welllington, was the real giant killer.

Of course I had kept silent when my father muttered over his morning newspaper, saying how he would hang the captured Corsican bastard if he were in charge in Paris, how he'd make a public spectacle of him. And there was the fact that it was only after Wellington had defeated Napoleon on that battlefield at Waterloo that my father finally gave his consent to my European travels. "British order," he had declared, thumping the dinner table with his fist, "is exactly what those barbarians need. We'll show those French savages a thing or two."

Now the decadent, aristocratic atmosphere made it almost impossible to imagine the ferocity of the mobs that had so recently surged through here. A military band played music at the door of one hotel where, the porter told me, the Emperor of Austria had his quarters. Valets carried out chairs from the hotel and placed them under the shade of the trees.

My spirits began to lift.

In the rooms I had taken in the hotel in Saint-Germain, as close as I could afford to the Académie des sciences on the rue de l'École de Médecine, I washed, changed my clothes, and sat down to think. I had no idea how I was going to explain to the police what had happened. A woman thief, traveling with a child, had stolen a letter and notebooks that were useless to her and specimens whose value I could not believe she fully understood. She had not taken my money. It made no sense. A few hours ago I had a letter from Professor Jameson to Professor Cuvier commending me to elite circles of medical and scientific savants in Paris and precious gifts to present. Now everything was gone. Without Cuvier's references and support there would be no conversations in the leafy courtyards and colonnades of great universities; there would be no illustrious future among Europe's savants.

I paced the small bedroom between the window and the sink for twenty minutes or so, talking to myself, veering light-headedly between self-accusation and outrage. It was only when I bruised my right hand badly by punching the wall several times that I decided to find the Bureau de la Sûreté.

I poured water from the jug beside the sink into a basin and found my razor and the small pot of shaving cream. Since I had left Edinburgh these daily rituals had come to be important. They provided a kind of tethering, a connection to home. Rising at seven o'clock, a morning walk, breakfast, a shave. I studied my face in the cracked mirror as my skin became visible with each sweep of the razor. It was a face that seemed to look different every morning and, despite the familiar features — black curls, blue eyes, a full mouth, the tiny scar on my chin where the hair wouldn't grow — I did not recognize myself.

I was trying to remember the features of the woman's face so I could report the theft to the men at the Bureau when there was a knock on the door. A heavily built, bearded young man with bright eyes stood on the threshold of the hotel landing, clutching a bottle of champagne and two glasses. Before I had time to speak, he had stepped into my room, set the bottle and glasses down, and clasped my hand warmly.

"A fellow countryman," he said in a lilting Scottish accent. "The concierge has been talking about you for days, ever since you wrote to reserve the rooms. It's been M. Connor this and M. Connor that. She calls you *the young English gentleman.* Well, well. My name's William, William Robertson, from the Western isles. I was at the medical school at Edinburgh too — been in Paris a year. I moved into the hotel a couple of weeks ago. It's expensive but closer to work. I thought a celebration might be in order. I've been saving this." He held up the bottle. "It's not as cold as it should be, I'm afraid, but who's complaining?" He placed the glasses on the table and uncorked the bottle with his teeth. "Glad to meet you, M. Connor."

"Daniel," I said. "Daniel Connor. Mr. Robertson, can you tell me where the Bureau de la Sûreté is?"

"Actually, everyone calls me Fin," he said, "because I'm supposed to look like a fish. It's the mouth, I think." He passed me a glass of champagne and began to look over my books and equipment, which lay scattered on the bed.

"I don't think you look like a fish," I said, though I realized that he did, now that I thought about it. A big fish of course, with a large mouth.

"You might not think that a man with a

beard could actually resemble a fish," he said, peering at himself in the looking glass over the fireplace, moving his jaw around roughly, opening and closing his mouth, grimacing. "But it appears that I do. To others, of course, not to myself. It was just a joke at first — Salomon's little joke — but it stuck. I don't mind. Anyway, Daniel Connor, I'd be glad to show you the ropes. If it's ropes you want."

"I'd be grateful if —"

"You know, Paris is completely infested with medical students from Edinburgh. There's practically a colony of us over at the École de médecine, and at the lectures in the Jardin des Plantes. But there are students from everywhere else too — Romania, Hungary, Spain, Russia. You've come at a good time. Where are you headed?"

"The Jardin des Plantes. I'm supposed to start working for Cuvier, and I thought I'd sign up for the winter lectures as well. Comparative anatomy's my line, or at least it is for the moment, but —"

"Aha. A job with Cuvier? Impressive. None of that philosophy's for me. Brain just won't do it. I spend my days walking the hospitals between the École de Médecine and the teaching clinic at the Hôtel Dieu, following the coattails of Sanson the surgeon

— amputating. That's my line." He made a gesture as if he was sawing through logs.

"Amputating?"

"The soldiers are still coming in from Waterloo. Hundreds of them, laid out on mats in the hospital corridors, legs and arms black with gangrene. The smell is so vile you can hardly breathe in some rooms. Most of them are beyond saving, but we have a go anyway. All the foreign anatomy students are learning their trade with the hacksaw too. Long hours and good money. And sometimes Sanson lets you do dissection and autopsy work on the corpses."

"It's almost impossible to get hold of bodies in Edinburgh now," I said. "The anatomy professors have to make them last for weeks. They even fight over them."

"Christ. There are hundreds here every week. The hospitals send most of the corpses over to the anatomy clinics while they're still warm. Can I buy you a drink?"

The bottle was already half empty. I was thirsty and had drunk the two glasses of champagne as if it had been lemonade. I wasn't used to drinking. In Edinburgh I'd never had enough money as my father had kept my allowance deliberately small in order to ensure that I kept away from what he called "fleshly temptations." It had been as much as I could do to pay the bills for the oatmeal and potatoes, which most of the medical students lived on, and I was always hungry.

"No. I mean, yes," I said, grateful for the blurred feeling the champagne had made in my head. "Let me buy *you* a drink. I have some money here somewhere. I've never been to France before. You know, I think I might need breakfast." I tipped my bag onto the bed, searching for the French money I had exchanged, money that was now mine to spend as I chose. "I haven't worked out the coins yet."

"Your French — is it any good?"

"It's getting better. I can speak a little German too and read Greek and Latin."

"Got a good stomach?"

"I think so. What for — alcohol or dissection?"

"Both. I did three amputations last night, you know: a hand, two legs. The hand was the worst. More nerves. More blood. As soon as we've bandaged up the poor sods, they're out on the streets in their uniforms, begging — there are lines of them in the arcades in the Palais Royal. They make decent money. And the wooden-leg makers in Paris have never had it so good. They'll be out of business soon though, now that

Napoleon has been taken. No more wars, no more wooden legs."

"Embryology was my specialism," I said. "In Edinburgh at least. I don't think I'd be very good at amputations."

A flock of pigeons flew past the window, casting shadows on the whitewashed wall.

"I tell you," Fin said. "I always need several drinks after the night shift to make sure those bloody limbs don't come flying at me in my dreams."

He glanced over at the map unfolded on my bed. "You don't want to use those guidebooks," he said. "They'll only take you to the places all the English tourists go — all the bloody sights. You'll be on the same carousel as Lady Bloody Carmichael and little Georgiana and all their cronies. Just plunge in, I say. Find your bearings. I'll show you around. Be glad to. I've got the day off, you know. You are a lucky man. William Robertson will give you a personal tour of Paris. Where do you want to start?"

"The Bureau de la Sûreté," I said.

"Why the bollocks would you want to go there?"

"I'm in trouble," I said.

"There's no trouble you can't get out of," Fin said, clapping me on the back. "What have you done to your hand?" My knuckles were grazed and swollen. "A fight? Already?"

"Stupid," I said. All the connecting words were beginning to disappear.

I told Fin about the papers and the fossils. Well, I tried to explain, but of course, I couldn't. There was no logic to it. I could see the consequences though. I could see the future rolling out — or rather not rolling out — clearly enough. No chance to prove to Cuvier that Jameson was right to choose me over the rest, no way to prove that I was *exceptional.* All that work, all that time — the late nights, the exams and books — come to nothing.

"I'm sure Cuvier's a reasonable man," Fin said, taking a chair in the corner where the morning sun fell in slanting lines. "You know what I would do? I'd write to Jameson and get him to send another set of letters. That should take a week or two at most. And then you can start over."

"It's worse. I was carrying a manuscript for Jameson — a copy of his preface to an English translation of Cuvier's book. I was to give it to Cuvier for his approval. That was stolen too. And there were the fossil specimens I was supposed to give to him. Worth a fortune. Cuvier's expecting them."

"That's not good. No, that's not good at all . . . *Merde.* You *are* in trouble."

"I think I will have to go home. Explain everything to Jameson. I'll be finished of course. I feel so *stupid.*"

"First things first. You're in Paris after all. That has to be worth something. Let's get breakfast and some more champagne and have a feast. We'll wipe out your bad night and mine with a few good bottles. And then I will take you to the Bureau if you still want to go. But it won't do any good. The men there won't be interested in finding your things because there's nothing in it for them. Breakfast?"

"Yes," I said. I was too tired and hungry to argue.

"You brought your own knives, I hope," he said. "You can't get a pair of scissors or a scalpel or even a decent knife for eating with in Paris at the moment, not for love or money — and believe me, I've tried both."

No, I thought, she hadn't taken my dissecting instruments or knives — they were packed in the suitcases. That was something.

As we walked together to the first tavern, Fin threw information at me at every turn, pointing this way and that: the best place for breakfast, the safest place to gamble, the cleanest swimming spot on the river, the cheapest boats for hire, the most beautiful waitresses, the reading rooms where you could pick up English newspapers, the best laundry service.

I tried hard to remember at least some of these details but couldn't move Cuvier from the center of my vision: Cuvier, arms folded across his ample chest, looming over me, saying: "You did what, M. Connor? You fell asleep on the mail coach?" And behind him there were others waiting: Jameson, my father, my brothers. Daniel Connor was an idiot, a dunderhead; he couldn't be trusted with anything.

And so it went on. The day stretched and tautened, glittered then darkened, each step a further numbing, a fading of Cuvier's censorious gaze. Somewhere in the cloud of that first day, the dust from the road still on my skin, I saw into a city that even London could not match. They had said it would dazzle me. It did. Card tables, mirrors, glass, roulette, bar after bar, a music hall, a wax museum on the boulevard du Temple with effigies of the kings and queens of Europe; crayfish bisque at Beauvillier's; women in feathers and lace in a bar paled into an oyster feast on the quai de la Rapée as Fin and I sat above the water watching the night boats carry freight up the Seine, listening to the watermen call out to one another.

"On Sundays," Fin said, "the watermen over at La Rapée have their own show on the river in front of the Hôtel de Ville. They dive from high platforms and do triple twists. Then they have fireworks. If you sit here, you can watch them for free. It's spectacular — all the colors of the costumes reflect in the water. Céleste's brother is one of the watermen."

"Céleste?"

"My girl. Most students strike up with shopgirls here. They call them *grisettes;* I don't know why — there's nothing gray about them. With your looks you'll be fighting them off. They're not like English girls. They're much more independent and — well, how to say it? — forward. And if they like you, well, they'll show you they like you straight off. No messing about. You must meet her, Céleste. Sunday. She has some very pretty friends."

How would I behave with such women? I wondered, imagining myself trying to be entertaining in a language that was still awkward to me. I could hear those *pretty friends* laughing at me already.

"I won't be here on Sunday," I said. "I'll be heading home."

"Nonsense, my friend. You give up far too

52

easily. I told you. What happened to you, it wasn't your fault. It could have happened to anyone. You just have to go and speak to Cuvier. And send a letter of explanation to Jameson. Straighten it out."

"And then wait to be hung, drawn, and quartered? No thanks. I need sleep now," I said, suddenly overwhelmed. "You've wiped me out. I've had far too much to drink."

The water of the Seine was heavy and slow-moving. Down under the bridge a fight had broken out among a group of watermen.

"You're going to need more stamina than that, my friend," Fin said, "if we're to share rooms."

"Share rooms?"

"Well, there's lodgings up for rent on the top floor of the hotel next door. Twenty francs a month. A bargain. Much cheaper than the hotel rates. View of the street. A small stove. I spoke to the concierge about it yesterday, told her I'd find someone to share with. And then you turn up this morning right on cue. It's perfect. There's not much furniture, but we can pick up some chairs and things from the flea market. What do you think? You and me, eh? We can move in a week. Once you've sorted things out with Cuvier."

"Let me think about it," I said. "But first I must go to the Bureau. First thing tomorrow morning."

"Oh yes, the Bureau. The Bureau. Always the Bureau. Well, if you're lucky you might meet the infamous Jagot — he runs the Bureau — and that really would be worth something. He's at the center of everything in Paris. He has spies all over the city. If anyone is going to tell you how to find your thief, he will. If he likes you, that is."

"Jagot?"

"Henri Jagot. Poacher turned gamekeeper. He's famous across Europe. He was one of the most successful thieves in France until ten years ago; one of only three or four people to have escaped the prison at Toulon. Now he runs the Bureau. They say he's modeled his surveillance methods on Napoleon's secret police. He's good."

"A thief runs the Bureau? How can that be?"

"Ex-thief. The chief of police offered him a deal. He gave them information, they gave him his freedom and police protection. So he worked undercover in the prisons of Bicêtre and La Force for years — really dangerous work — he'd have been killed if the prisoners had found out he was working for the police. He's brutal, they say, unstoppable and ambitious. But he's good. He won't be interested in you, though."

"Why not?"

"Because he works on commission, of course. The price on your thief's head won't be big enough. But you must go anyway. File that report. You won't rest until you do."

3

Once inside the offices of the Palais de Justice on the Île de la Cité the next morning, I found a long line of people sitting on chairs in a windowless corridor with scuffed blue walls and highly polished floors. Most people sat staring at nothing, clutching documents; others read newspapers or talked in hushed voices. A child started to spin a hoop down the long corridor until a clerk admonished her.

Another clerk standing behind a hatch took down details from the queue of new arrivals — name, address, nature of complaint. He asked questions and crossed boxes on his form. In his questions I heard words and phrases that I had not heard spoken before: *cambriolage, un vol avec armes, un vol sans armes.* With weapon. Without weapon. Known to victim. Not known. I watched him flush with irritation when a woman said she didn't know whether her necklace had been taken from her bedroom or her sitting room. Such distinctions seemed to be important as a way of defining the type of crime more exactly.

When my turn arrived and I had answered all his questions, the clerk gave me a numbered ticket and gestured toward a chair. There was no clock here. Sensible idea, I thought, not to have a clock when people might have to wait hours, perhaps whole days. Time slips by more quickly without a clock. Instead you had to wait for the sound of the hourly bells from Notre Dame. They were especially loud in the blue corridor as we were virtually sitting in the shadow of the great cathedral.

I could hear my brother Samuel's voice as if he was sitting next to me. Samuel, the brother who was closest to me in age and who was studying for the ministry, would certainly have said that this theft was God's way of telling me I had taken the wrong path, reminding me that the pursuit of natural knowledge was always a chimera, a vanity. My mother would always nod wisely when Samuel talked like that. *Come home, Daniel. Come home,* they whispered.

Once Samuel and I had collected butterflies, fossils, and newts, dissected frogs, read the reports of the scientific societies in the local paper, shared a tutor, kept up with the latest geological theories. Now that Samuel was entering the church, he had put away his collections and his instruments, and we argued about God. When I asked him a string of rational but vaguely heretical questions about transubstantiation or the precise nature of the relationship between God, Christ, and the Holy Ghost, Samuel's answer was always the same: that if I prayed for long enough and with sufficient humility, God would show me the way. That pious refusal to answer my questions infuriated me. Samuel had given me an expensive copy of Paley's *Evidences of Christianity* for my journey to Paris in the hope that it would strengthen my faith. I had not opened it. I tried to pray there in that corridor at the Bureau but failed.

Two hours I waited — and it seemed I was one of the lucky ones.

"M. Jagot will see you himself, M. Connor," the clerk whispered, stooping to speak to me as quietly as he could. He looked impressed. "M. Jagot has taken an interest in your case. His room is the last door on the right at the end of the corridor."

Jagot's clothes seemed too small for his large frame. Thickset and powerfully muscular, though perhaps no more than about five feet six inches tall, he looked, in those expensive but ill-fitting clothes, like a fruit about to split its skin. His face was red, sweaty, and swollen, his hair dry and unkempt, his chin unshaven. His hands were square and thick, with tufts of red hair sprouting on the knuckles. He looked out of place here. He was a man of the street, not a man at ease in an expensive office. But what I remember most about Jagot, after all these years, is those eyes of his — powerfully dissecting eyes of ice blue that didn't look quite human. It wasn't easy to bear the weight of his gaze. I never saw a single glimpse of kindness or empathy there, not even curiosity, just a relentlessly assessing stare, a measuring, as if he was perpetually translating your features into notes for his files.

The room was dimly lit and largely empty apart from an entire wall of small oak drawers behind the desk — a filing cabinet that was still being built, extending around the walls, with row after row of little drawers and square brass handles. The room smelt of fresh paint, sawn wood, and glue. A map of Paris adorned another wall, the river blue, the borders of the arrondissements marked out in red.

Jagot shook my hand without smiling and gestured for me to take the chair opposite him.

"Welcome to Paris, M. Connor. You have had, my clerk tells me, some objects stolen. A woman. At night. Traveling alone?"

"Yes. That's it."

He was watching me closely. "There are many thieves in Paris now," he said, sitting back down again. "Many of the soldiers and prisoners of war who come back to the city have learned bad ways. They are all the same. A little of this, a little of that."

"I need to get my papers and packages back quickly," I said. "It's very important."

Jagot sat back in his chair and placed his hands together on the desk in front of him, interlocking his large fingers, scrutinizing me, taking his time. "Your stolen objects interest me, M. Connor. You say in your report: three letters of introduction from a professor in Edinburgh to the professors here in Paris; one manuscript from a translation of a work by Professor Cuvier; two notebooks — they are yours — yes? And some natural-history specimens, gifts for Professor Cuvier. But no money. *Pas d'argent.*" He underlined some details on the report and began to make notes in the margins.

"No. There was money in my bag, but she didn't take it."

From under his heavy eyebrows, Jagot looked up and said: "*Pas d'argent.* A woman steals from the mail coach at night, but she takes no money. Yes, that is what interests me, monsieur. The specimens — what were these things? Your report says only specimens in boxes, nothing more."

I concentrated hard to remember the words in French: "I think you would say *trois fossiles rares et l'os d'un mammouth.*"

He wrote this down. "Three fossils and the bone of a mammoth, yes. You say rare. How rare?"

"The fossil corals and the mammoth bone were part of a valuable collection from Germany. Very rare. Worth a lot of money to the right collector. The manuscript was less valuable but more important. Cream pages with a blue cover. Dark blue. It was handwritten."

I tried not to let the panic show in my voice.

"Yes, yes. I have all that. It is here in your report. It will be filed in our *bureau des objets trouvés.* If someone brings these *objets* to us, we will send you a letter. We have your address, yes? But there are no corals or bones there now, only the usual things —

umbrellas, keys, eyeglasses, and the usual *unusual* things: a violin, a wooden leg, and an expensive set of pistols. A man brought in a monkey last week, you know. He found it on the roof of a brothel in the Notre-Dame de Lorette. I said to him, Monsieur, this is not an *objet trouvé.* It is an animal. It must go to the *Fourrière des Animaux.* Did you *see* your thief, M. Connor?"

"Yes. But it was dark. She was sitting next to me. I fell asleep."

"Did anyone else see her? The other passengers?"

"No. We were the only two people in the outside seats of the mail coach. The other passengers were inside. Except for the child she carried."

"Yes, the child. Tell me, monsieur, about the child. Slowly. This was the woman's child, yes? Her daughter?"

"I assumed so," I said. "They looked very much alike." I told him as much as I could, in as much detail as I could. I left out the bit about how the child had woken up and said *"M. Napoleon, il est mort,"* with her black eyes wide and fearful. Nor did I tell him about the smell of the woman, whose name I never had asked, the slight scent of bergamot about her or the way her cheek flushed in the shape of a continent, scarlet against olive, or the dark bow of her eyebrows, or the way her lips moved as she spoke. And I didn't tell him about the mammoths lumbering or the ancient seabed she had described. Because — well, we didn't see them, not in this world anyway. It was like a dream. These things did not belong in a police record.

I tried to be as accurate as I could, but there was so little fact. I told him she appeared to be tall, but it was difficult to see her properly. I told him that the woman had mentioned a half-Portuguese, half-Indian magnetist called the abbé Faria who had taught her things. I didn't even have a name for her. I told Jagot the child was called Delphine. That she was perhaps four or five years old. Jagot asked me a disproportionate number of questions about the child — the color of her skin, eyes, and hair, the language she spoke, her precise age. I did not tell him that the woman made me feel curious, hungry, and mute; that the thought of her, the smell of her, even the memory of her voice, filled me with intense desire.

He wrote down a few words on the report. *"Bon, c'est bien."*

"She talked about unusual things," I said. "She seemed to know more than most women would."

"Such as?"

"Geology. The Jardin des Plantes. Zoo-phytes. She had an extensive knowledge of natural philosophy."

"A female savant, monsieur. Yes, that is also interesting. There are many such women in Paris."

"I am sorry," I said. "I am wasting your time."

"I am an *enquêteur,* M. Connor," he said with a sigh. "All the information you give me goes into my files. It might not be useful now, only a small detail, but it *will* be useful one day. When all the little things begin to join up."

"Are they all full?" I asked, nodding toward the neat rows of drawers that lined the wall behind him.

"My cabinet?" He turned and ran his hand over the smooth oak surfaces. "Soon all these drawers will be full, yes. Information, descriptions of faces, and histories of crimes — a card for every criminal in this country. It will be Jagot's gift to France: a *catalogue complète* of thieves. These people want to be invisible, M. Connor. They try to hide in the shadows. I make them visible. I turn the light on them. And I think you will help me."

"Yes," I said, "if I can." The resolve of this

man impressed and unnerved me. "But I don't see how."

He leaned forward.

"M. Connor, I'll tell you something. The woman you describe, who steals from you — the woman who is tall and beautiful, with the scar across the back of her left hand, the skin that is dark, the hair and eyes black, the woman who is a savant and who steals your mammoth bone and your rare fossils, that woman, she goes by the name of Lucienne Bernard. She has other names too; she once was the lover of a clever Parisian lock breaker called Leon Dufour. This woman you describe and the man she works with now — the man they call Davide Silveira — are on a special list that I keep. With these people I have unfinished business. So, Lucienne Bernard is back in Paris. That is very interesting to me. You, M. Connor, have become interesting to me."

"But what would such a woman want with my things?" I asked. "I don't understand."

He closed his ledger. "We are finished for now, monsieur. There is nothing more for us to do. But you must understand one thing: If you see Mme. Bernard again, you will come back here, immediately. You understand? And you will ask for me personally. Will you give me your word?"

I nodded, reassured. If Jagot was taking this case seriously, at least there was some hope that I might retrieve the manuscript and rescue my position. If Jagot could be discreet and quick in his investigation, the situation might yet be redeemed.

When I left the offices of the Bureau de la Sûreté, I was followed by a man in a long shabby coat who appeared to have only one arm. A fairly new recruit by the look of him; he seemed unskilled in surveillance techniques.

4

Later that afternoon I walked to the Louvre in search of the Caravaggios, stopping first at a *traiteur,* where I ordered a bowl of thick beef soup with vermicelli for fifteen sols, noting down the price and the date in one of the new notebooks I had bought. I have them still, those small black leather notebooks, filled with tiny rows of numbers, totals and subtotals. It was a habit I had taken on at medical school when my meager allowance barely stretched to give me enough food for the day. Now in Paris I was rich it seemed, at least in comparison with my former life. But I had to make my inheritance last. Everything depended on that.

I had to regulate my expenditure. The day spent with Fin had been expensive. Since entry to the Louvre was free to foreign visitors, I could spend an afternoon there and then come to a decision about what to do next. I couldn't see Jagot's man anymore, but I knew he was probably still out there somewhere. I began to feel affronted by the suspicion that being followed by a police agent implied. *I am the victim of a crime, M. Jagot, not a suspect,* I muttered to myself.

Inside the Louvre, among the columns that held up the great vaulted ceiling of gilt and white plaster over the Long Gallery, artists had set up their easels as close as they could to the paintings. On the walls, paintings hung sometimes four or five deep, frames butting right up against frames. A vast Titian was juxtaposed on one side with a Veronese, on another with a Rubens; each overwhelming square of oiled flesh and theatrical gesture and drapery, each Saint Sebastian or Venus or Mars or Holy Family hanging up there, was being copied, imitated, studied, translated by one of scores of art students. Compared with the restrained and hushed galleries of Edinburgh, it was a riot of color and movement.

The effects of the previous night's drinking still hadn't worn off. I was a mere sleepwalker in this strange gallery, my head thumping. I followed the crowds through to the Classical Gallery, where I stopped in front of the marble sculpture of Laocoön, the Greek priest, and his sons being attacked by sea snakes. It filled an entire

alcove. The naked priest's head was thrown back in agony, his sinews stretched tight in pain. The coils of the giant snakes were tangled around them all. One of the two sons, staring in mute horror at his brother and father, was trying to uncoil the snake from his right ankle.

I was trying to remember the names of the sinews in Laocoön's raised arm when I sensed her, the rustle of her skirt, the smell of her bergamot-laced perfume. I felt her hand on my arm and turned my head a fraction.

My thief, in daylight, dressed in pale blue satin. She was standing next to me.

If I was angry almost beyond words in that

moment of recognition — especially now that I knew I had been the innocent prey of a practiced thief — I determined not to show it. I kept my wits about me, focusing on only one thing — the return of the stolen objects.

"You have no idea how relieved I am to see you, madame," I said, turning to face her, each phrase tumbling over the next. "Of course . . . your bag and my bag, they were next to each other amongst the luggage, and it was dark and you were in a hurry, perhaps. It was an easy mistake to make. It wasn't your fault. Anyone might have —"

"I saw you sitting by the Seine," she said, "and I followed you in here. Isn't it terrible?" she said, looking at the Laocoön. "To make pain beautiful like that — it is a great art." That gravelly voice of hers, the slow, seductive way she spoke.

She was as tall as I was, perhaps even a little taller. Nearly six feet — unnervingly tall for a woman. In the daylight her skin was darker than I remembered and her beauty even more striking. Her black hair curled around the edges of her face. She wore no hat; instead she had twisted a swathe of blue silk around her head that matched her dress and made her look like a drawing of a famous Parisian actress I had once seen. She wore pearl earrings. I could see the colors of the squares and rectangles of paintings reflected on their convex surfaces. Jagot had called her Lucienne Bernard. She looked like no thief I had ever imagined.

I looked around for the guard and for Jagot's man but could see only other visitors standing looking at the sculptures. Everything continued as before. I felt a hot rush to my head. Until we were closer to the guard, the best thing to do was to keep her talking, I thought. I only wanted her to return the things she had taken. I didn't much care how.

"You took my papers and a package, a case, from the mail coach," I said, slowly, still trying to prompt a conversation that would lead to a restoration of my belongings. "Can we go and get them? I need them, you see. They're very important. Without them —"

"You've shaved," she said, smiling. "You look different in daylight. Younger. It's strange, isn't it, how different people look in different places and at different times of the day. As if there were many versions of us coming and going all the time."

I put my hand to my jaw, feeling the

roughness of the new growth. "My shaving mirror's too small," I said. "I cut myself this morning."

She began to walk around the Laocoön slowly, looking at it, not at me. I followed her.

"My things?" I struggled to control the panic in my voice.

"You look tired," she said softly, stopping to look at me.

She had a way of suddenly plunging into intimacy — a touch, a step too close, a question, a look held for just a few moments too long — and then, as soon as she had invoked it, she would abandon it, returning to a formal distance. And in conversation she would plunge too, from one subject to another, from distance to a seductive proximity, like a hare doubling back toward the hounds to disorient them. It was as if she was perpetually both whispering secrets and withholding them. Now she was running her fingers down a pink vein in the white marble of Laocoön's arm.

"I *am* tired," I said. "I haven't had much sleep. I've been worried, you see. Worried about the papers and the specimens you took. I didn't know how to find you. I didn't know what to do or where to go to report them missing."

An Englishwoman opposite me, clutching a catalogue to her as she would a Bible in church, ushered her two daughters out of the room, tutting. Too much naked male flesh — even in marble.

"We are some of the last people who will see all of this under one roof," Lucienne Bernard said. "In a few weeks this room will be empty. All of Napoleon's stolen art will be returned to where it was before the war."

"Before the war?" I said, disoriented by the sudden change of subject.

"Napoleon took all the statues in here from the Vatican gardens when he invaded Rome. Now the pope wants them back and your Duke of Wellington has agreed. Vivant Denon, the director of the Louvre, is procrastinating, but without Napoleon's protection he will have to give them up. Wellington will send his soldiers if he doesn't. The Prussians want their paintings back too. It won't be long."

I was estimating the distance to the door and, to the guard, trying to calculate the likely consequences of anything I might do. "Please," I said, my words sharpening. "Don't play games with me. It's not fair."

"Now all the empty monasteries and the houses of émigrés in Paris are stacked high with the paintings and statues and collections that Napoleon took from the palaces of Europe —"

"Madame," I said. "I have been polite. I have been in earnest. I have pleaded with you. Entreated you. But you seem to want to talk only about art. Please. I have no time for conversation about these things. I am expected at the Jardin des Plantes. You took my belongings. I trust you still have them. We have only to arrange for me to pick them up. I will send someone. Please give me an address, and I will do the rest."

"Your notebooks —" she said.

"You've been reading my notebooks?" I said, my voice constricted. No one had read those notebooks. They were full of speculations, ideas about species and strata and comparative anatomy, mixed with poetry, drawings, and observations about people, women I had seen, private feelings.

"Your work on homology is very good," she said, "very interesting. You have insight and curiosity. But you are reading the wrong books."

"You shouldn't have looked at my notebooks."

She saw me glance toward the guard. We were both waiting for me to do something. Her black eyes, now very close, glittered. Was she daring me?

"And if I refuse to return them?" she said, leaning up against a marble pillar with that maddening flicker of a smile that seemed to hover about her mouth whenever she talked to me. "What then?"

Fragments of conversation in several languages reached us from men and women crossing and recrossing the space, the sound of shoes on marble, the keys of a guard, the creak of a door. Somewhere far away, a gunshot.

"I have money," I said.

She laughed. "I don't want your money." I watched the guard begin his walk down the gallery.

"I'm going to have you arrested," I said, grabbing her arm. "I shall call the guard."

"And what will you say to the guard?" she said, her face suddenly close to mine. "How will you prove that I am the woman you saw in the dark on the mail coach? I will deny it of course. My French is better than yours, and I have excellent identity papers. It's all about evidence, you see. I shall tell the guard that you accosted me. That you are a little drunk. That I have never seen you before. I think you had better take your hand off my arm."

"I will take you myself to the Bureau de la Sûreté."

"*Take* me?" Her black eyes flashed. "You propose to take me by force to the Bureau?" she whispered. "Do you think a man like you can force a woman like me to go anywhere and not be stopped? If I call out, people will be concerned for my safety. It is quite a distance from here to the Île de la Cité."

She had paralyzed me a second time, I thought, like a wasp with its prey. I let go of her arm. I had stepped into a spell, across a threshold. Curiosity had prevented me from calling out when I first saw her, and the delay had been critical. Her talk. Her voice. I had wanted her to talk to me. I began to plead like a child.

"Yes, yes, I will give them back to you," she said, "but come. Walk this way. I want to show you something. If you have time, of course, M. Connor. I know you are in a great hurry."

She turned away from the Laocoön toward the door to the Long Gallery, where scores of fashionably dressed visitors crowded in front of paintings by Veronese, Titian, Rubens, and Raphael. We walked through arches of light falling slantways from the tall windows onto the marble floor, easing our way between groups, slipping in and out of hushed conversations. I watched her black slippers appear and disappear beneath the blue silk drapery of her skirts, offering the occasional glimpse of white lace.

"Taking me to the Bureau will not get your things back. That will do nothing for you. And it will be bad for me. I think you had better sit down, Daniel. You are pale." She gestured to a marble seat in an alcove. I sat down, my hands and legs shaking. She took the seat next to me.

"Jameson will never trust me with anything again," I said. "Without those things I have no job, nothing . . ."

She didn't respond. She was watching a woman dressed in gray who was sitting nearby. Her long cloak, fastened at the neck, was thrown back from her arms, and one beautiful ungloved hand pillowed her cheek. Her white bonnet made a halo around her braided dark brown hair. She was not looking at the paintings; her large eyes were fixed dreamily on a streak of sunlight that fell across the floor.

"What would you have me do?" I asked.

"You need do nothing now. I wanted to show you the Caravaggio boy, that's all," she said. "Look. There he is." She gestured up to a painted boy. "He is the image of you. See? The hair. The eyes. The flushed face. He has just stolen something for himself, don't you think? Look at the pleasure in his face. As if he has lost his virtue for the first time." She turned to look at me and said, "First you are pale, and now you are flushed."

"I am angry . . ."

"You will have to trust me, I think."

"What do you want?"

She hesitated for a moment and then said quietly, "I need something from you. There is something that only you can get for me."

"I won't make deals with a thief."

"No," she said, and sighed, "I didn't think you would."

The bells of Notre Dame struck out across the city, marking four o'clock.

"I must go now," she said, standing. "I will keep your papers and your bones for the moment. Then in a few days I will come and find you and explain. Wait for me, Daniel Connor. I will bring your things back. I promise you that. And then perhaps you will do something for me."

And, yes, I let her walk away. Some unaccountable instinct made me trust her. I watched her disappear down into another hole in the city, back into the shadows.

I said nothing to Fin that night; I did not return to the Bureau and ask for Jagot. I kept my secret, biding my time, conscious that I was tied to this woman by an invisible thread and that I was already complicit in something I did not understand.

I walked back to the Caravaggio boy that afternoon. From high on the crowded wall he stared down at me, his face knowing, goading me, his pleasure in his own transgression palpable. What had she seen there in the face of that painted boy that she could also see in me?

That night I dreamed of Laocoön. I was entangled in the coils of the snakes, but they were flesh, not marble. They were in my mouth and around my ankles, so that I couldn't stand. And somewhere in a darkened and empty Louvre, where Titian women walked and Caravaggio boys took off their clothes, a seated woman in a blue satin dress leaned toward me and said, "Daniel, I have a confession to make. All this time we have been talking, I have wanted to kiss you. There is something about your mouth, I think, that makes me want to . . . kiss you."

I woke and sat up, sweating, shaking, aroused, and saw Fin sleeping there on the pallet bed I had made up for him on the other side of the room, in the moonlight. He was breathing heavily, lying on his back, sprawled, as if all those long and heavy limbs of his had fallen from some great height. I dressed and took myself out into the Paris night and walked, through labyrinths and alleyways and in and out of the lost colonnades and stone staircases of imagined great universities, until I no longer wanted to kiss her back.

5

The following day the sun disappeared and a gray sky settled over the city. The concierge brought me a package that had been delivered to the hotel that morning. Inside, an unsigned note said only: *I have been called away. I will write again in a few days. Wait for me.* She knew where I lived, then. The package also contained an ornate shaving mirror, considerably bigger than my own, and a copy of Rousseau's *Confessions*.

She was no longer on the map. But, I was sure, my papers and the specimens were. Somewhere in a hotel room or atelier in the city. Was she watching me now? I wondered as I folded up her letter and put it away. I walked to the window and looked down into the street: children playing with ninepins; the fruit stall on the corner and the lemonade stand. No thief. No woman with a false name looking up, waiting for me to come down.

I bought myself a little time that day, sending Cuvier, under Fin's direction, a short formal letter, pleading illness to explain the delay. I told Cuvier that as a consequence of my illness — about which I was vague — a short period of convalescence would be necessary before I took up my position. I petitioned his tolerance. I would, I promised, be with him by the last week in August. I also wrote once to my father, assuring him that all was well and that I was taking care of myself, and extolling the virtues and beauties of the city.

I told no one about my encounter with Lucienne Bernard in the Louvre. Despite Jagot's revelation of her criminal life, I had persuaded myself that her reappearance depended, at least for now, on my silence, patience, and discretion. I gave her three weeks. After that, I determined, I would resign my position at the Jardin and return to England.

On July 29, six days after I had arrived in Paris, Fin and I moved into the new lodgings on the top floor of the hotel next door, where, beyond the pigeons who occupied the window ledge, you could see the turrets of Notre Dame. The concierge told us not to feed the birds, but we gave them our stale bread just the same, and so our flock became a feathered multitude, pushing and shoving one another behind the cracked glass. In the afternoons the light seemed to have feathers in it.

We found furniture at the flea markets to supplement what was provided by the concierge: old pieces that had seen better days. I bought two chairs, their gilt flaking off, a desk with a missing drawer, and a mahogany table gouged along its sides, which we covered with an old velvet curtain and stacked with our growing library of books and my microscope. We bought linen, worn but still white and stiff, which we threw across the horsehair mattresses. Fin spent his allowance on a chaise longue in purple velvet, an antique glassware set, and an inlaid cupboard to store wine. I wrote all the expenses down in my notebook and tried not to think about money.

This shifting, edgeless life of ours was quite unlike any I had known. I had been used to austerity. Now, if we wanted to preserve candles, we went to the Palais Royal. Wine was cheap, and there was entertainment on every street corner. I preserved what I could of my previous ways, reading through the volumes of anatomy books Fin owned, but any routine I established was quickly eroded by Fin's sudden impulses and whims. The lack of order alarmed me at first, but I told myself it would all fall back into place once I had taken up my desk at the Jardin des Plantes. This was an in-between time. It did not need to be accounted for. I had only to wait.

At night we watched the occupants in the building opposite move about in their candle- and lamp-lit boxes behind frayed curtains — other students like us bent low over desks piled with books, an ancient violinist who played what sounded like Russian Gypsy music from eleven at night until well past midnight, two young women who hung their underwear from their balcony and waved to us as they did so. Fin called them *les dames aux sous-vêtements.*

"Now if we can find a few women, we can have our very own salon," Fin said, admiring the view, waving back to *les dames.* "You can't have a salon without women in Paris. It's too civilized otherwise, much too tame. How about Wednesdays at midnight? We'll have to think of a signature, something to make our salon different. Some stuffed animals and a few skins might do it. Then we can call ourselves the Salon of Dead Things — it sounds much better in French: *le Salon de nécrologie.* I will invite Mme. de

Staël to join us. She's moved into a house only a few streets away, apparently, back in Paris from England at last; though she's very old now, they say she talks as well as she ever did. She'll be here at the drop of a hat, of course, once she knows she has such illustrious neighbors, once she knows who we are."

"Who are we?" I said, "that Mme. de Staël should want to call on us?"

"*L'Amputator* and *l'Homme qui a perdu ses choses,*" he said. "You know, I think I will write a little poetry today. *Poetry from the Salon of Dead Things.*"

While I waited for Lucienne Bernard's return, the days swung into grooves, filled with domestic pleasures. Early in the morning, before he left for the hospitals, Fin bought bread and cheese and fruit — grapes, figs, apples grown in country orchards — from the stalls at the end of the street. I kept the rooms tidy and carried our dirty clothes to the laundress, collecting them again a few days later. I read all day, studying, and taking notes from books borrowed for me by Fin's friends from the library in the Jardin des Plantes, books and geological and zoological papers by Cuvier, to improve my French, so that when the papers and parcels had been returned, I would be ready to engage in informed conversation with the great man. I prepared and honed the questions I wanted to ask him about homologies and extinction. And in the afternoons, in the cafés along the Left Bank, I read Lucienne Bernard's copy of Rousseau's *Confessions*. Her penciled annotations hung around the margins of every page.

A few days after we moved in, Fin put up some shelves to hold the wax anatomical models he had bought cheaply when the wax model maker's shop closed down and for the scratched glass domes of the stuffed curlew and fox he had bought from the flea market. Now *le Salon de nécrologie* was open for visitors, he announced, draping a gold cloth across a life-sized torso.

Several of the anatomy students Fin brought back to our rooms that first night were students of Lamarck, the transformist professor at the Jardin des Plantes. Francisco Evangelista and Louis Ramon were zealots and reformists; they called themselves the "advance guard of the people." Lamarck's ideas about species shaped and defined their politics. Simple forms of life, Lamarck claimed, were being created continuously all the time by spontaneous generation — spores, germs, flecks, maggots crawling out of mud or soil or pond water. Over thousands or millions of years, as they adapted to their habitats, growing a longer neck here to reach for higher leaves or losing a no-longer-needed leg there, these simple organisms became complex animals — maggot became fish, fish became lizard, lizard became mammal, mammal became man. Everything was improving, Lamarck claimed. Striving toward perfection. And for Fin's friends this meant the principles of the Revolution — liberty, equality, fraternity, and the overturning of the authority of the priests and the kings — were enshrined in nature's laws. And of course, in Lamarck's world life on earth had been established over a much longer period of time than the story the Bible told, immeasurably longer.

"Imagine an arm," Ramon said, slightly drunk, stretching out his own arm. "According to the priests, human history starts out with Adam and Eve in the garden up here on the shoulder and reaches down to the tip of the finger — the present — where you are now. Here's Herodotus near the shoulder, and here's Napoleon down toward the end of the index finger. But the real truth is that *all* human history can be contained on a single fingernail. All of this, all of this from the shoulder down to the fingernail here, is *prehuman* history. So now you have to look for Herodotus and Napoleon with a microscope. And us, well, where are we in all of that abyss of time, and where is now? Time doesn't stop for us. *La marche.*"

La marche. Lamarck's slogan. It meant forward movement. March. Walk. It even sounded like him: *la marche; la mark.* For the anatomy students like Ramon and Evangelista, this idea explained everything. *La marche* meant throwing off the past, marching forward.

While the others talked of transformism, Céleste, Fin's girl, talked to me about Rousseau. She sat curled into the purple chaise longue under the shelf of wax heads, sweeping back her long blond hair, which was always escaping from the knot she tied at the back of her head. "There may be a new king back on the throne of France," she said, "and the priests may be buying new robes, but they can't simply put everything back the way it was. There's a new spirit in Paris. They will try to pacify it, but it will be back. You will see, this isn't the end yet. Paris hasn't had the last word."

For the anatomy students who came to

Fin's salon that night, Cuvier was considered clever, even brilliant, but wrong; he was a conservative protector of the old order. In his repudiation and mockery of Lamarck's transformist ideas, Ramon said, Cuvier was maintaining the status quo, reinforcing the old values. In stressing that animal species were hierarchical and fixed, he was talking about social hierarchies, they said; he was really saying everyone had his place in society and should stay there. For Fin's friends, Lamarck's world of change and flux and progress was revolutionary, a world of horizontals and possibilities, whereas Cuvier's was a world of fixed and vertical hierarchies. Politically, they were absolutely opposed ways of seeing.

Despite my loyalty to Cuvier, or perhaps because of it, I kept my own counsel; I hedged around the subject of transformism when asked for an opinion. Besides, I told myself, my French was not yet good enough for me to hold my own in such heated and fast-moving arguments. I would only look a fool. I resolved to watch and learn. *Know your opponent,* Jameson used to say at the student debating societies. *Understand the way he thinks.*

"It's what's in front of us that matters," Céleste said, looking at Fin, her eyebrows raised in that way she had. "If we stick with the fathers, the autocrats, the husbands, the priests — all of you men who want to keep the past at the center of everything because it suits you — if we listen and obey, if we do everything exactly as our fathers tell us, then we're acting against nature. That's why the Revolution must go on. It must not be allowed to stop."

"Transformism is an act of dethronement," Ramon said. "A bloody, brilliant dethronement of man. And once man is dethroned, we're just one more organism among all those others. Larger and more powerful, yes, but it's always the small organisms that make the long-term difference. The *people* will make the future, not the kings anymore."

"Lamarck teaches that?" I said. "Lamarck is a *republican?*"

"Of course not. He's only interested in science, not politics, but if you think about it, it's brilliant. If you accept the principles of transformism, you *have* to think differently, put yourself in a different kind of picture — one where everything's moving and changing, where there is no high or low. *La marche* is a political liberation, not purely a scientific one. And Céleste is right — we have to burn the old books. Only then can we step into the future."

I had overheard fragments of conversations about transformism in the coffee-houses and taverns of Edinburgh, where the medical students talked politics. Most of us had read that chapter in Erasmus Darwin's *Zoonomia* in which he claimed that species had started out as aquatic filaments, but Erasmus Darwin was mostly ridiculed by the students in Edinburgh; there was a whole set of jokes about whether we had descended from cabbages or oysters.

In Paris they called all of this transformism. In Edinburgh it was transmutation or sometimes the development hypothesis. For Jameson it was heresy. And for Cuvier, it was nonsense. Fin's friends talked openly about transformism, and rationally, not speculatively or apologetically, but as if their hypothesis was beyond question. They — the heretics and infidels of Fin's salon — now fascinated me.

Jagot's one-armed man in his dirty coat came and went. Sometimes I glimpsed him at the corner when I left the house in the mornings. Sometimes when I looked down on the street at night watching for the arrival of Fin's friends, I could see the gray shape of him in the alleyway opposite.

Jagot's man maddened me, but Fin was delighted with our police shadow.

"Damn it, Daniel. Half of Paris is being followed," he said. "Never before have so many surveillance reports been written on so many people. It's brilliant. Everyone is being paid to watch everyone else. They are compiling reports on all the infidels and radicals in Paris. Anyone with an education is a suspect. Every student is listed as part of a conspiracy to invade the city or to bring Napoleon back. Someone told me yesterday the police actually believe that Napoleon has already escaped and is hiding in the quarries under the city with a large army. Paris is a powder keg. Jagot's man isn't interested in you, my friend. It's Ramon and Evangelista he'll be watching. They'll put all the radicals on an exile list eventually. Make a clean sweep of it."

"Are you saying I'm not part of the intelligentsia?" I said, feigning hurt pride.

"Yes, of course you are, but what kind of danger do you pose, my friend? Really? Daniel Connor is hardly a threat to national security. Believe me, it's Evangelista and Ramon he's after."

But Fin changed his mind, when, on August 4, I received a letter from M. Jagot written in a fine sloping hand, asking me to meet him at the Jardin des Plantes at three o'clock the following day.

"*Mon diable,* Daniel," Fin exclaimed. "A personal summons from Jagot. I have seriously underestimated you. You *are* on the surveillance list after all. That must mean that your thief is more important than I thought. Let me come with you? I'll buy dinner for the rest of the week if you let me come. Daniel, it's my chance to meet Jagot. You can't rob me of that."

But, I pointed out with some relief, Jagot had insisted I come alone.

Shamed by my blunder, I had not yet visited the Jardin des Plantes. But now with my appointment there, I was impatient to see with my own eyes everything I had dreamed of and read about. And I was full of hope. Perhaps Jagot had news. I stood on the Austerlitz Bridge looking across to the famous wrought-iron railings of the Jardin; the gates were open, the magnificent trees towering beyond them. I watched visitors spilling out of fiacres, gathering in groups with tour guides, clutching guidebooks and parasols, their servants following along behind with picnic baskets.

Visitors came here to see the museums, the bones, the animals in the menagerie,

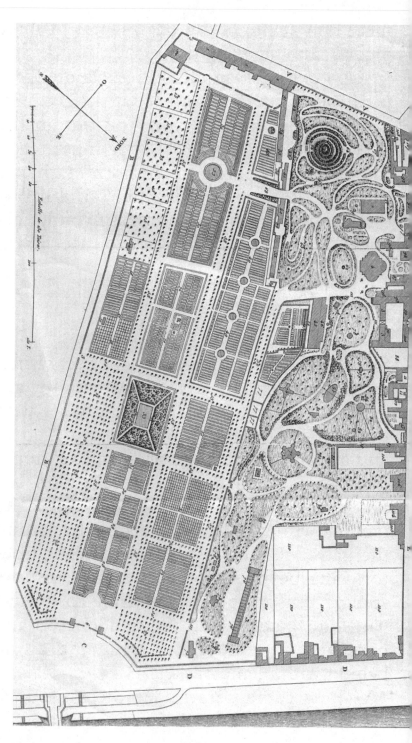

94

the glasshouses, the collections of exotic trees and plants; they came for assignations, for trysts, for stolen kisses; they came because the sun was out or because it wasn't. I came to see what I had lost and hoped to regain, a utopia, I thought, passing through the gates, handing over my coins. The center of a new world.

Daniel into the lions' den, she'd said. I remembered that remark of hers as I stood just inside the main gate, looking down the straight sand-colored paths through the classically arranged flower beds, a series of lines that ran all the way to the Museum of Zoology ahead of me, its yellow stone flushed with pink in the afternoon light. This museum of bones had once been the palace of a king.

Between the gates where I stood and the Museum of Zoology there were at least ten flower beds, each as big as an English field, planted with carefully labeled botanical and medical specimens from all over the world, every conceivable green in every possible texture: spiky, arched, fanned, and feathered. Explosions of late-summer flowers in reds, golds, whites, and oranges. Beyond them light glinted on the panes of a dozen glasshouses that lined the east and west sides of the rectangle like mirrors.

More than fifty families lived within the walls of the Jardin, Jameson had said. The professors lived alongside their assistants and families in the elegant houses that flanked the high walls. Hundreds of students attended the lectures or worked in the museums or libraries for the professors, producing scores of books and hundreds of papers on botany, chemistry, comparative anatomy, taxonomy, or mineralogy, or sorting, preparing, and mounting the thousands of bones, plants, fossils, pinned and boxed insects and butterflies, preserved snakes, and stuffed birds that were sent to the Jardin every year.

Daniel into the lions' den. There were lions in the Jardin des Plantes over to my right, in the menagerie. Paris was a kind of Babylon, I thought then, but Daniel Connor . . . he was no biblical Daniel. That Daniel, the other one, was a kidnapped Jewish boy forced to live in the court of pagan Babylon on the banks of the Euphrates; that Daniel was the boy who remained steadfast, true to his principles, even among those seductive pagans. When they threw him in with the lions, the animals didn't touch him. He was protected by his own virtuous edges.

My edges were disappearing.

No, I was not that Daniel. I was another

one, not so steadfast or sure. I imagined the lions would finish me off without hesitation. *Paris will swallow you up,* she'd said. *Are you not afraid?*

I found Jagot sitting in the palm glasshouse on the north bench under the blossoms of a scarlet rhododendron. He had taken off his jacket and had fallen asleep, his hands tucked behind his head. When my shadow fell across his face, his eyes snapped open like the eyes of a crocodile.

"M. Jagot, you have recovered my things?" I asked immediately, shaking his hand.

"*Non,* monsieur," he said, stretching and yawning. "I am sorry to say, I have not. But I have other news. Certain information has come to me, M. Connor."

"About what?"

"About you, monsieur. About your comings and goings. Also about Mme. Bernard. She has been asking questions about you. I have reports." He opened up a notebook.

"Mme. Bernard?" I said. "Who is Mme. Bernard?"

"You know who Mme. Bernard is, M. Connor," he said with a sigh. "You know her. She knows you."

"What questions has she been asking?" I said, taking the seat beside him. "And if you have reports about her, you must know where she is. And if you know where she is —"

"She has disappeared again. We have no trace. That is of great annoyance to me. But my men tell me that before she disappeared Mme. Bernard was asking questions about you, M. Connor, about where you lived. It seems she has developed an interest in you. Do you know why that is? Can you help me to explain that? Have you seen her again?"

"No, monsieur, I have no idea why she has taken an interest in me. And I really can't be sure that the wretched woman I spoke to on the mail coach *is* the same woman you're looking for. It might be a mistake," I said quickly, remembering the shadowy and tentative allegiance I had made to Lucienne Bernard in the Louvre and trying my best to extricate myself from the apparently dangerous place I seemed to have taken in Jagot's investigation. "I think it is best if I withdraw my statement . . . It was dark. I can't be certain what she looked like . . ."

Jagot leaned close to me, then reached out and cupped my chin in his hand, turning my face toward his for a moment. He spoke slowly. "You are a handsome man, M. Connor. And you have expectations. You have . . . promise."

"Monsieur?" I was sweating now, profusely. Jagot's acrid smell mingled with the sweet and overblown perfume of the rhododendrons.

"Life is short." He sighed. "Sometimes these investigations take a long time. My men, they get impatient. They like results, they like the files to close, they like rewards. Impatient men are difficult to control." He paused, nodding toward the end of the path. The one-armed man stood there leaning against the glass. "Have you anything to tell me, M. Connor? Something perhaps you might have forgotten?"

"I have seen her only once," I stammered, understanding the threat implicit in his words.

"Yes," he said. "I know that. You saw her at half past three on the afternoon of July twenty-third. In the Louvre, I understand. I looked for your report of that meeting in my file, M. Connor, yesterday, but I did not find it. Perhaps I did not look carefully enough."

"I didn't think it was —"

"Let us say that your report has gone missing. We will call it a bureaucratic error. We will say it is not important. Of course the next report you write for the Bureau will not go missing. And now, M. Connor, I must ask for your identity papers — your passport?"

"My passport, M. Jagot? Why do you need my passport?" I reached into my jacket pocket.

"We have rules in Paris, monsieur, and those rules say that a man or woman who is part of a police investigation cannot leave the city. Your papers will be safe with me, M. Connor. You have my word." He took them from me and folded them into a silver case.

"For how long?" I stuttered. "I mean to return to England."

"Until we know what is what, M. Connor. And how long does that take? Who is to say? Of course, if we find Mme. Bernard, or if someone brings her to us, then we close the files. We say this is finished business. But until that moment, it is unfinished business. You may go now, monsieur, but you must not speak of our meeting. Not to anyone, you understand? It is a private matter."

I stood up. "M. Jagot —" I began to remonstrate.

"*Au revoir,* M. Connor."

The one-armed man did not meet my eye as I passed him. He spat into the undergrowth.

Furious at Jagot's veiled accusations and threats and conscious of being tangled up in a web that was as thick as a forest and over which I had no control, I resolved to walk in the Jardin until I had seized on a plan. I slipped into the lecture hall in the amphitheater between lectures, waiting until a group of students talking animatedly to a professor I did not recognize had spilled onto the gravel path outside. The empty lecture hall, curved seats raked high behind me, smelled of furniture wax and heated bodies; on the blackboard a chalked diagram of a cuttlefish, tentacles sprawling, had been marked with arrows and letters, all its parts labeled; over to the left on the same board someone had pinned a drawing of what looked like a crocodile. On the lecturer's podium a series of monkey skulls had been arranged in a row.

Despite everything, I reasoned with myself, this particular knot would unravel in a few days, when Jagot had tracked down Lucienne Bernard and recovered my things. He would come to see my innocence. I might have gone to see the British ambassador to plead my case, or found a lawyer to petition for the return of my passport, but my story was now full of embarrassing kinks, each of which undermined my claim to innocence. Why had I not called the guard in the Louvre? Why had I failed to make a report to Jagot despite having given him my word? Why had I fallen asleep on the mail coach with objects of such value and consequence? No matter how you looked at it, it didn't look good.

On the fourth of August, the HMS *Bellerophon,* which had been anchored off the coast of Torbay for almost a week, finally set sail, heading for deeper waters. Beyond the gaze of the English journalists, who had positioned their telescopes at all the seaward-facing windows of all the lodging houses of Plymouth hoping to catch a glimpse of the famous greatcoat, the Emperor of France was about to board a new ship, the HMS *Northumberland,* a forty-four-gun ship of the line. The *Bellerophon,* for all its fighting glory, for all the mythology of its name, was not fit or young enough, the admirals said, to take the Emperor the full distance to Saint Helena, an island in the Atlantic Ocean, thirteen hundred miles from the nearest landmass. On board, the Emperor, his spirits low, began a new game of cards.

Two days before, when the state official had read out a letter from the British government announcing that the prisoner of war was to be exiled to the island of Saint Helena and permitted to take with him only three officers, his surgeon, and twelve servants, Napoleon had protested violently. "What am I to do on this little rock at the end of the world?" he roared. "The climate is too hot for me. No, I will not go to Saint Helena. Botany Bay is better than Saint Helena. If your government wishes to put me to death, they may kill me here." But within a few hours, his anger had dissipated and he had returned to the deck to show himself to the large crowds who had gathered in boats in the bay to catch a glimpse of him.

On the morning of August 4 when the *Bellerophon* set out to sea to make its way to the *Northumberland,* the number of boats in the bay had increased to dangerous levels. Every boat in Devon had been commandeered by tourists it seemed. In the chaos, a cutter that had been circling the *Bellerophon* to keep away the large crowds ran down a boat full of spectators. Several people, including two women, died in the waves.

"Be it so," the Emperor said to his secretary, Comte Las Cases, later that evening. "On this desolate rock we will write our memoirs. We must be employed — occupation is the scythe of time. After all, what must a man do but fulfill his destiny? Mine is yet to be completed."

6

I felt her always, her presence in the shadows, like Jagot's man. I imagined that she watched everything I did. If, a few days before, I had been confident that she would come and find me, now I feared that she would, knowing it would only implicate me further in Jagot's eyes. At night she twisted in and out of my dreams, down labyrinths and alleyways, in and out of sight, tormenting me.

After Jagot's threat in the Jardin, I found it increasingly difficult to concentrate on the course of reading I had assigned myself. Unable to leave Paris and now dependent on the success of the investigation, I began to sleep through most of the days, turning into a nocturnal creature, the companion of the night visitors Fin brought back to the salon: medical students with black rings under their eyes who talked of autopsies and typhus and skin diseases, and the philosophically minded ones who talked about transformism and taxonomy and homologies, and the artists' models, shopgirls, and dancers. Mme. de Staël never appeared. I dared not think about what my father would say about this life I was now living. I told myself, still confident that order would be restored, that he might never need know.

I was walking home alone after a night spent drinking with Fin in the first week of August, down an alleyway off the rue de Chartres near the back entrance to the Théâtre de Vaudeville. It was dark and I was walking like one already asleep, one foot after the other, my footsteps echoing deep into the shadows. Two wooden cellar doors in the street were flung open. Out of the hole that opened up in the cobbles, three men dressed in women's clothes — wigs, pearls, feathers, satin, and silk in red and gold and orange on black — lit from below, flurried up into the night like giant moths shaking out their wings. Man-moths, I thought, their faces turned to the moon, scaling the sides of buildings, eyes all pupil like hers, an entire night unto themselves.

I think sometimes, with the vantage of hindsight, that we were the lotus-eaters, Fin and I, Odysseus's sailors resting on the peninsula of the African coast, intoxicated by the lotus flowers of Paris nights. The edges of dream and reality had shifted and I couldn't say where they were anymore. The world of the Jardin des Plantes, with its taxonomies and classifications and labels, had receded, and the heady scientific and political conversations of the salon had filled the hole like an incoming tide. And in those dream nights, listening to Ramon and Evangelista and Céleste talk, I was coming to see certain things as if for the first time. The evidence they used to support their transformist ideas — fossils, strata, intermediate species, extinctions — was persuasive. The edges of time had stretched in that atelier in Saint-Germain — not my time, not this little life of mine, but the time that, in my mind, until now, had stretched back through history books, in straight lines, through kings and queens and wars and tribes, Romans and Britons, and then back through the fragments of Herodotus I remembered, to a garden where God made a woman from the rib of a man. It's not that I hadn't wondered about origins before, just that I had known only this one with the rib and the apple and the snake, and the spirit of God moving on the face of the waters. And that version was still unassailable. It was in the Bible.

In Derbyshire I had been taught that questioning the truth of the Bible had eternal consequences. At the age of seven, sitting in the family pew in my Sunday clothes in the chapel in Ashbourne, my father on one side, my brothers on the other, I had listened to the preacher deliver a lurid sermon about the various tortures of damnation. During the silent prayer that followed, I had seen Satan, or thought I had seen him, out of the corner of my eye, at the door of the vestry. He was a thing of scales, a malevolent creature; his hooves made a scuttling sound on the stone flags of the church. He had grinned at me. I did not sleep for days.

When Céleste asked what I'd been taught about God and I told her about seeing Satan at the vestry door and that as a child I had worried about eternity and how long it might be, she'd said that's how the priests worked — through fear and trembling. It's enough to send a child mad. You don't have to believe it, she said. Just because they tell you there's a hell, you don't have to believe it. But then, I reminded myself later that night, my brother would say that Céleste was on Satan's side. She was a heretic, after all. So she *would* say that.

■ ■ ■ ■

When I saw Lucienne Bernard for the third time, actually saw her, in flesh and blood, not in my dreams, it was the night of August 10, in the crypt of a former Capuchin convent near the place Vendôme. Fin and Céleste had taken me to the Fantasmagorie — a distraction, Céleste said, for *le garçon perdu,* the lost boy, as she called me. A Belgian illusionist named Étienne-Gaspard Robertson had built a theater inside the crypt as a tourist attraction. They called it the theater of the dead.

I protested but I went. I was curious, of course.

It was seven o'clock. Dusk. The first dimly lit rooms of the convent, beyond the craggy door studded with metal, were arranged like a museum of scientific curiosities and optical illusions, small in scale and rather tawdry in the stony dank caverns of the convent. Beyond, in the curtained darkness of the refectory, a woman called *la Femme invisible* addressed us in English, her voice as loud as if she was standing right next to us but she was invisible, a voice without a body, a mechanized ghost. I looked for an auditory apparatus in the walls, some kind of speaking tube, but could find nothing. She challenged us to ask her questions.

"And where will my friend find the woman who stole from him?" Fin asked.

"In the Palais Royal," she said, "for if he has enough livres to pay, he can have the woman steal anything he likes, from wherever he likes."

Each room became darker as we descended, following a single candle flame down stone steps through more curtains into the dampness of the crypt itself — the Salle de la Fantasmagorie. Here, once we had taken our seats, the assistant extinguished the guttering candle. I could hear muffled cries and laughter from Céleste and Fin, gasps and whispers from other members of the audience, but could see nothing, not even my hand in front of my face. Then the sound of wind and thunder came at us from all directions and on top of that the sound of a glass harmonica, invisible fingers tracing the curved lips of invisible glasses somewhere offstage. Robertson spoke in French and English by turns — murmuring something incoherent about immortality, death, and superstition. Despite myself, I could feel the hairs on my skin rise.

Then a succession of ghostly figures seemed to be flung into the air above us;

luminous shapes, some close enough to touch, flew out over our heads: glimmering sea creatures swimming in dark seas, an Egyptian girl, the three Graces flickering into the shape of skeletons, Macbeth, a nun, witches at Sabbath, the severed head of Medusa, Orpheus looking for Eurydice. I searched for the telltale light of the magic lantern behind the side curtains but found nothing. The phantoms moved in every direction, lunging at us, too quick to trace.

It was in the midst of that incessant flickering of smoky lights, the spirit illusions lunging across our heads, that for a moment, just for a second or two, I saw Lucienne Bernard, her head among the other heads in the audience, only three or four rows away. Her face, lit briefly by the glare of the lamps, stared back at me, her eyes dark. I saw surprised recognition on her face, then alarm, even, perhaps, fear. But though I stood to try to find my way to her, stumbling among the seats, Robertson extinguished the lights, and when he lit them again to illuminate the next spectacle — the skeleton of a young woman arranged on a pedestal, holding a champagne glass — Lucienne had gone, her seat empty.

"Remember the Fantasmagorie," Robertson's voice boomed, plunging us into darkness again. "Remember thy end."

We went straight to the bar in the Palais Royal after that for brandies, losing ourselves on the way. I said nothing. I was not sure of what I had really seen among the shadows and the specters. I kept looking out for her though, down the streets that ran off the place Vendôme. I was sure she was close by, watching, perhaps even following us. She would show herself, I was certain. But she didn't.

"These damned alleyways and cul-de-sacs, they drive me mad," Fin complained. Take any of the names of the streets at random — say, see, on your map here — the rue Croix-des-Petits-Champs. That's the Street of the Cross and the Little Fields; the rue Vide-Gousset, that's the Street of the Pickpocket, of course, which leads to the passage des Petits-Pères, presumably a nickname given to a monastic order; here's the rue des Mauvais Garçons, the street of the Bad Boys, the rue de la Femme-sans-Tête, the Road of the Headless Woman, and the rue du Chat qui Pêche, the Road of the Cat Who Fishes. *Alors*. It's bric-a-brac. Nonsense. A bit of this, a bit of that . . . all cluttered together with no logic, no plan —"

"You are a philistine," Céleste taunted

back. "I am glad you're not in charge in Paris. You would number and file everything. It's beautiful. I like the old house names too, so much better than the numbers — Star of Gold and Name of Jesus and Basket of Flowers or Hunting Box or the Court of the Two Sisters. They're like a poem."

Céleste was right of course, though I wouldn't have agreed with her then. Later those streets disappeared in the renovations and the planning reforms to make way for gaslights and arcades and order. All that time, as Fin and Céleste talked and argued, the reality of my situation was becoming clearer with each step. The fact that Lucienne had left the Fantasmagorie and had failed to reappear meant only one thing: She had no intention of coming to find me or of returning my things. And if Jagot couldn't find her, no one could.

"Paris is an ocean," a lawyer called Honoré said to me in a bar on the place Vendôme later that night. We were very drunk. "You can take as many soundings as you like, but you'll never reach the bottom of it. You can survey it, draw it, describe it. But, however thorough you are, however careful and scrupulous, something is always just beyond your reach. There will always be another unmapped cave, monsters, pearls, things undreamt of, overlooked by everyone else."

"If only I could go to church," I said. For a moment I longed to be able to pray for help and to have the confidence that salvation would be granted.

"Go to church," the lawyer said. "But it won't help you. Kill or be killed. Deceive or be deceived. That's the law in Paris. God has given up on this city. He has given up on you, my friend."

I had not been to church since I arrived in Paris, despite the promises I had made to my family. I knew where the four Protestant churches were on the Paris map; I had even walked past two of them — Sainte-Marie on the rue Saint-Antoine and Saint-Louis on the rue Saint-Thomas-du-Louvre. Both times I had stopped, looked up at the stone façades, and walked on. I had felt a guilty sense of liberation in that drift into the glitter of the city; my soul was no doubt in grave danger, I thought, and then I confess I forgot about the condition of my soul.

In Edinburgh there had been rumors the previous summer about a student called John Rivers who had gone mad after several months studying anatomy in the hospitals of Paris. He had given himself up to the seductions of the infidels, Jameson had told us. He spent too long listening to the lectures of the materialists and the atheists. An English pastor had found him wandering the streets of Paris at dawn, scarcely dressed and raving about his soul. God abandoned me in the dissecting rooms of Salpêtrière, he'd said. I am already in hell. Then, once his family had sent him to an expensive sanatorium in the Alps, Rivers went completely silent for seven long months. It was a form of catalepsy brought on by overwork and spiritual conflict, Jameson said. I glimpsed John Rivers once on his return from Paris, wandering around Edinburgh in the rain, scratching at his face.

I went to church the following day hoping to find some solace and with a new resolve to untangle myself. First I walked to the Protestant church on the rue d'Aguesseau where Bishop Luscombe's sermon sent me to sleep so that I woke up shivering in an empty church. Then I went to the church on the rue Bouloi where Mr. Newstead, the pastor, preached about redemption and grace to a congregation mostly composed of English dissenters. Afterward, in the churchyard, I tried to talk to the pastor about redemption, but I was no longer sure what I wanted to be redeemed from.

■ ■ ■ ■

A few days later, Jagot climbed out of a fiacre outside our lodgings just as I was leaving. He was dressed as a laborer in dusty clothes flecked with paint and mud, a cap pulled down low over his forehead. This was one of his famous street disguises, I presumed. I came slowly down the steps, my hands in my pockets, feeling his eyes taking in details — my height, posture, clothing, even the color of my shoelaces, turning me into a report. Jagot must know everything there was to know about me by now, I thought. My name. My address. The birthmark on my back. Was there a card for me yet? What would it say?

"I need to ask you a few questions, M. Connor," he said.

"Do you want to come in?" I asked.

"You will come with me a little way, perhaps," he said, opening the door to the fiacre. The driver looked down at me, his eyes blank. I climbed in reluctantly, fearful for my safety. Jagot took the seat next to me, closed the door, and pulled the blinds halfway down. The fiacre smelled of oranges, stale coffee, and sweat. Jagot picked up a pile of papers and a notebook inside his pocket. As the carriage lurched into movement, he pulled up the blind at the back of the fiacre and adjusted a small mirror that was fixed to the side so that he could see through into the street more easily. He thumped the roof once, and we slowed to a walking pace. He had someone in his sights, it seemed.

"You are in Paris for three weeks now, M. Connor. You see many interesting things. You talk to many people. You move in interesting circles. Have you seen Mme. Bernard again?" He looked closely at me as I answered.

"No, monsieur, I have not," I said, determined not to confess seeing something I may only have imagined.

"You have heard the name Silveira spoken by any of your new friends?"

"Silveira? No, monsieur. I have never heard them use that name."

"It seems," Jagot said slowly, "that he too is back in Paris."

"With respect, M. Jagot, what has this Silveira to do with me?"

"M. Silveira is a very dangerous man. He is the banker for the Society of Ten Thousand. I had him in my hand five years ago, but he disappeared from Paris. I sent one of my men to look for him in Leghorn and

Marseilles, where he has other houses. I paid that agent to look for Silveira for three months, but he didn't find him. But now Silveira is back in Paris, my men say. None of them has seen him yet, but he is here somewhere. And I will find him."

"Society of ten thousand?" I asked.

"The Society of Ten Thousand is the thief aristocracy of Paris, M. Connor. These rich men and women take on a job only if it is worth more than ten thousand francs. Silveira is a *Portugais*. A Jew. A dealer in diamonds. They call him *'Trompe-la-Mort.'* The man who cheats death."

"It sounds like you need more men," I said.

"Yes, monsieur. I need more men. But first I must catch Silveira. Then they will give me more men."

"I still don't understand why this has anything to do with me," I said.

"Davide Silveira, M. Connor, is a friend of Lucienne Bernard. Lucienne Bernard is a friend of Davide Silveira. If I have one, I have both. You understand? And Lucienne Bernard is a friend of Daniel Connor. Or perhaps Daniel Connor is the accomplice of Lucienne Bernard. You see how one thing leads to another."

"Accomplice?" I protested. "That woman

stole from me. How can you possibly think I am her accomplice?"

He smiled as if he were testing me, scrutinizing my reactions. I had a headache.

"I did not say you *were* an accomplice, M. Connor. I said *perhaps*. I must consider all the possibilities. Mme. Bernard is looking for you and I don't know what she wants. Victim? Accomplice? Innocent, guilty? Who can be sure?"

Jagot thumped on the roof of the fiacre twice, and we came to a stop.

"In Paris everyone is someone else," he continued, his eyes bright. "You see that man there?" He put his finger on the mirror and beckoned for me to look closer.

"The one in black? The one we've been following?"

"*Oui.* That is Pierre Coignard, jewel thief. I shared a cell with him in the prison at Toulon in '88. He escaped into Spain and became head of the Catalan bandits. Then he meets a woman in a bar called Maria-Rosa. She steals her master's papers when he dies, and so Coignard and Maria-Rosa became the Comte and Comtesse Sainte-Hélène. Coignard even fought as the comte in Napoleon's armies in Spain. The king received him at court only a few weeks ago. He has done very well for himself."

"Why are you following him?"

"Someone he knew in Toulon recognized him. Blackmail. Coignard refused to pay and yesterday we found the dead body of Coignard's valet in the quarries. Now, of course, Coignard wants revenge. One thing follows another unless we put a stop to it. And now with Silveira back, things will grow worse. In Paris you stop one thing and another opens up."

He was climbing out of the fiacre. "Excuse me, M. Connor," he said, "I must speak with M. Coignard. The driver will take you back. Keep listening, M. Connor, and if you hear the name of Silveira spoken, or if you see or speak to the woman Bernard, you come and tell me. You will be Jagot's eyes."

He closed the door and disappeared almost instantly into the street, camouflaged like a leopard in dappled light.

But Lucienne Bernard did not appear and I came to detest my own languor. Five days later, August 20, upon waking after a troubled night, my money almost gone, time disappearing, a career lost, almost a month since I had arrived in Paris, I resolved to go to see Jagot, plead for the restitution of my passport, and return home. Paris had already changed me. Soon I would become like one of those half-human creatures in Ovid, I thought, human skin transmuting into leather or claw or hoof. I would no longer know myself.

I packed my bags carefully, leaving them stacked near the door, gathered what money I had left, and went to find Fin at the Palais Royal. I walked past the guards at the entrance, their muskets cocked, through the arcade of shops selling jewels, china, prints, books, flowers, and ribbons, through the hazard and billiard tables, the restaurants and taverns. I climbed the dusty staircase to the second floor, walking past the apartments advertising lectures on every branch of science and philosophy on the hour every hour.

Babylon, I thought. It was time to redeem myself.

Walking there, through the aisles of expensive trinkets and drunken gamblers, I felt things begin to take shape again. Evil on one side. Good on the other. True. False. Now that I could see again, I thought, everything would be all right.

I found Fin on the outer row of a crowd of fifty or sixty people who were watching a card game. Keeping to the edge of the room, I moved closer, avoiding the light of the chandeliers. Smoke from the candles, oil lamps, and cigars thickened the air, interspersed by shafts of light. I thought of Coignard, the comte, and his comtesse, and wondered how many others in the Palais Royal were dissembling, living someone else's life.

"Just in time, my friend," Fin said without taking his eyes from the table. "This is a very good game. Very good indeed. Watch and learn."

"Fin," I said, "I need to speak to you."

"Later . . . just let me watch this."

Through the thicket of standing figures I could see only fragments of the card players' hands: white fingers, rings, a bony, yellowed, crablike hand stretching out to clutch a heap of coins. Then a face or two: the large, gaunt face of a man with deep-set eyes and grizzled eyebrows; a dry-lipped woman prematurely old, withered like her artificial flowers; a man who resembled a respectable Edinburgh tradesman I had once known, blond and soft-handed, his sleek hair neatly parted. And then a face I recognized. A half profile.

It was her, Lucienne Bernard, but not her, for *she* was now a *he,* sitting at a table playing cards only a few feet away from me. Her face but not her body. It was Lucienne, but it wasn't.

I pushed through the spectators to get closer. Yes, it was her, seated at a card table, dressed as a man: green silk frock coat, silver waistcoat, neckerchief arranged artfully around her throat. And no one seemed to notice. It was like a tableau, frozen in time, a tableau of a card game in the Palais Royal. I was in it too, reflected in the mirrors behind her.

She was winning magnificently and, judging from the gasps of the crowd that had gathered in the smoky candlelight, unexpectedly. As her fingers, delicately gloved in pale gray, adjusted the coins that had been pushed toward her in order to pass them back again to the winning point, she looked up. Her black eyes met mine, and she smiled suddenly with what seemed to me a flush of unguarded pleasure — even relief — before she dropped her gaze to the cards in her hand and continued to play. Each time her stake was swept off the table she doubled it. Many people were watching her now, but I felt certain that the only eyes she was conscious of were mine. When she looked at me again as the crowd applauded her final hand — a full house, fanned out in triumph across the green baize — she appeared to be amused.

"A striking man, don't you think?" Fin said. "All that green and silver. Good facial structure."

"Very."

"You're in a strange mood today. What's wrong with you?"

"His mouth . . ."

"The mouth?" he said. *Did he not see? Did he really not see?* Her lips were a smoky crimson, rich, full, and slightly parted. She was beautiful. Not a man at all.

"A touch too complacent, perhaps?" Fin said. "Is that what you mean?"

"Arrogant."

"Good card player, though. I don't think I've ever seen anyone win so much in a single afternoon. And he's not short of money, I'd guess. From his clothes I mean."

As the game finished, I watched her stand and look for me, preparing, I imagined, yet another escape. I clenched my fists, feeling the nails dig sharply into my skin.

Fin turned. "You said you wanted to speak to me?"

"No. It doesn't matter now," I said. "I'll find you at home later. There's something I have to do first."

Suddenly the desire to return to Edinburgh receded; there was hope, if only I could stop her from disappearing again.

One last chance, I thought, making my way as stealthily as I could toward the patch of sea-green silk that was being swallowed up by a crowd of congratulatory admirers. This time, I determined, I would take her to the Bureau, whatever the outcome, however much she protested. This time I would not be afraid of making a scene. Then at least I would know I had *acted.* I would have some measure of self-respect to return with even if the manuscript and specimens were irrecoverable.

But then, as the crowd fell away and she walked slowly but directly toward me, looking slightly nervous, her brow furrowed. "Don't give me away," she whispered. "Jagot's man is here, I've seen him, but he hasn't recognized me."

I was silent. I could scarcely breathe.

"Where have you been?" I muttered. "You promised. Everything is much worse for me now."

"Where have *you* been?" she said, virtually dragging me into a window seat in an alcove and drawing a red velvet curtain across to shield us a little. "I sent letters; I called, but the concierge, she said you had left the hotel. I looked for you in the Jardin, at the lectures. But then things were dangerous . . . I had to leave Paris for a while.

126

Where did *you* go?"

"I moved out of the hotel and into lodgings with a friend," I said. "It's cheaper. I left word."

"Of course. So the concierge," she said, "thinking I looked disreputable, wouldn't give me your forwarding address. Of course. *Quelle idiote.* I should have known."

"But," I said, "you were at the Fantasmagorie that night. You saw me. You could have spoken to me then."

"Jagot's man was sitting right behind you. I saw him the moment you saw me. I had to take the back staircase out through the crypt. Listen, Daniel," she said, her voice barely audible. "I want to give you back your things. Taking them was a stupid idea. I regretted it as soon as I thought about the price you would have to pay for losing them. Two hours," she said. "I need just two hours. Meet me in the alley that runs off the passage des Petits-Pères at seven o'clock. Under the third lamp from the east. Exactly seven o'clock, you understand? And when I leave here, you mustn't follow me, because Jagot's man will follow you. Do you understand? You *must not* follow me."

She pushed me hard, as if shaking me from some state of stupefaction. I wanted to embrace her. Her promise to return my belongings, the turning back of time, the prospect of starting again, acted like a strong draft of laudanum. I didn't think about Jagot or about how I was going to account for the recovery of the stolen goods. It didn't even matter if her story was true or not. I was light-headed with expectation and relief.

"Thank you. Yes, I understand," I said. "Seven o'clock. Passage des Petits-Pères. Third streetlamp from the east."

"Now let me buy you a drink," she said. "I need to steady my nerves, and it will throw Jagot's man off the scent. He doesn't recognize me dressed like this."

I followed her to the bar, watching her broad stride, her slight swagger, marveling at the woman's body moving in the man's clothes. Lucienne ordered two glasses of champagne and took a seat on a high stool at the bar next to a man with white hair who was smoking a cigar. I sat to her left. The white-haired man had cast down a calf-skin copy of Byron's *Childe Harold's Pilgrimage* and was slumped across the bar, intent on maintaining his flirtation with the barmaid. He seemed to have drunk rather too much brandy. Lucienne leaned toward him. "*Bonjour,* Alain," she said.

The man stiffened and, putting out his

cigar, turned to look at her. "Excuse me, monsieur, but you are mistaken," he said, looking ashen and disoriented. "My name is Thomas. Thomas Gutell. This young lady here will tell you. It's Thomas Gutell."

"Forgive me, M. Gutell. You look remarkably like an old friend of mine, Citoyen Alain Saint-Vincent. He reads poetry too." She picked up his book and opened it, running her eyes over the words. "Yes," she said, "Byron. Yes. I like this. My friend Saint-Vincent would like this too. But, sadly, he is no longer in Paris. He was exiled for speaking out against the king. He has left the country, they say. Perhaps I should send him a copy of this book."

"Please, I assure you, it's not a problem. It was an easy mistake to make." The man who called himself M. Gutell took another gulp of his brandy. Lucienne stood up and passed a few coins to the barmaid, preparing to leave.

"You have had good luck today, monsieur, at the card table?" Gutell seemed to want to keep the conversation going a little longer.

"Yes. Very good." She smiled and passed him back the book.

"Can I buy you a drink?"

"I don't like the brandy here."

"Might I recommend the Café des Invalides?" he said. "The best time is around six o'clock, when the orchestra plays. The brandy there is very good."

"Six o'clock? Thank you, monsieur, for your recommendation. Enjoy your afternoon." She nodded in my direction. "*Au revoir,* M. Connor," she said. "Until later."

I glanced at the clock. It was half past five.

7

I did follow her, despite the promise I had made, because in leaving the Palais, I took care to lose Jagot's man. But I hadn't lost him; he had only made himself invisible. After all these weeks of waiting, I couldn't simply let her disappear again into that unfathomable city. I was elated at the prospect of a reprieve from my sentence of exile from the Jardin. But I still didn't trust her.

I followed her through the crowd, down the stairs, and out into the arched cloisters of the Palais Royal gardens, where Russian and Austrian soldiers stood among groups of women dressed in grubby white and pale yellow chiffon dresses that clung to their thighs, buttons undone. The women were soliciting, goading, beguiling, pointing to the upper rooms of the brothel. *Racolage.* Money and sex. Soldiers roamed the cloistered courtyard with glistening eyes, selecting the women with the finest skin or fullest figures, as if they were choosing fruit from some stall. It disgusted and fascinated me. The prostitutes in Edinburgh, thin and cold, lined up along the streetlamps down by the harbor, looked nothing like this. These men and women reminded me of the strutting and preening peacocks in the menagerie of the Jardin, with all the plumage and fur that adorned the soldiers' helmets and the women's headdresses. Small ornamental dogs played among the furls of trousers and skirts.

I watched Lucienne slipping through the groups of men and women in the cloisters. One or two of the women greeted her. The prostitutes parted to let her pass. She was known here despite her disguise. Respected, it seemed. What curious history had produced that respect, I wondered.

My passage through the cloisters was different. The women rose from both sides, stepping toward me from behind the arches with rouged faces and shining eyes, taunting me, rousing me, and yes, my body betrayed me with every touch. Warm fingers brushed against the insides of my thighs as I passed; painted mouths whispered profanities. A few steps farther a blond woman with a missing tooth took my hand and pressed it to her breast, where I felt a nipple harden beneath chiffon.

I kept my eyes resolutely forward, focused them on a series of arches above my head; I concentrated on reading the faded letters advertising the wares of the numerous shops to left and right: CHANGE DE TOUTES SORTES DE MONNAIE, OMBRES CHINOISES SÉRAPHINE, CAFÉ AMERICAIN, CABINET DE CONSULTATION À L'ENTRESOL. I watched her slip through an arch and step out into the bright late-afternoon light.

She stopped to look around her, then walked toward a woman in a white dress who was sitting on a bench under a plane tree, reading a book to a small dark-haired child. The seated woman's hair was gathered into a knot on the top of her head with a twist of purple silk in a way that reminded me of Grecian statues. She was small and neat, elegant. Delphine, the child from the mail coach, was sitting on the woman's lap, her eyes fixed on the book. She seemed to be struggling to stay awake.

Lucienne stood very still a few feet away, watching the woman read to the child, until the girl, glancing up, saw her, clambered off the woman's lap and ran across the grass toward her mother. Lucienne took Delphine in her arms and swung her up into the air and spun her around, the soft burnt-orange cloth of the child's dress fluttering up around her. Then the three of them, animated and laughing, sat down under the plane tree in the long shadows and Lucienne tipped out the gold coins she had won at the card table into the grass for the child to play with. It was a pretty picture.

Only a few hours before, I had decided to return home. Now I was watching Lucienne Bernard sitting in the Palais Royal gardens dressed in the clothes of a man, with the child Delphine and another woman, who might be a cousin or a friend.

What if her promise had been a ruse to throw me off? I wondered, considering how quickly I had believed her. I had already begun to question whether instead of following her, I should be sending word to Jagot to bring his men. But I had no choice, I reasoned. I would follow her to her lodgings, make a careful note of everything I saw or heard, and then, if she failed to appear with my belongings in the passage des Petits-Pères at seven o'clock, I would go straight to the Bureau. Then Jagot and his men would go and retrieve my papers, the corals, the mammoth-bone specimens, and the precious manuscript pages, and arrest Lucienne and her associates. And I would go to Cuvier and start again. Properly this time. Almost a month had passed, but the work on Cuvier's book would be there just the same. *I need an army of assistants to complete my great work,* he had written in that letter to Jameson. He would still need me.

Lucienne walked with the woman and the child into the warren of streets lined with brothels and gambling dens. At a fork in the road they separated, Lucienne walking in one direction, the woman and the child in the other. When Delphine glanced back over her shoulder for a moment, she saw me. Her black eyes lingered on me, and she smiled.

I found, to my relief, that Lucienne had been distracted by the shops and the people passing her. I followed at a distance through crowded streets, watching for the scrap of sea-green silk and the head of sleek black hair moving out there in front of me. Black like crow feathers.

We entered the gilded passage des Panoramas. Storefronts displayed their wares behind polished glass; some goods spilled out onto the marbled walkway: fabrics, umbrellas, boots, flowers, cashmere shawls, books, prints, musical instruments. I ran my hands over cheap knickknacks, requisites in walnut shells, ragpickers' baskets, Vendôme

columns and obelisks containing thermom-
eters. I was trying to disappear, to make
myself look like any of the men and women
captivated by the glittering cornucopia of
the arcade.

I followed her out into the boulevard
Montmartre and down into the boulevard
des Italiens, where she stopped at the Café
des Invalides and took a seat at the window.
I stepped into the dark corner of a shop
doorway across the street. The reflections of
carriages clattering by and parasolled
women swam through the glass like fish. I
crossed the road to see better and leaned
against a wall just a few yards to the left of
the window. It was six o'clock.

Gutell arrived from the other end of the
street, entered the café, and joined Lucienne at the table. She stood to kiss his
cheek; he returned the kiss, looking around
anxiously. They were clearly not strangers.
Through the frame of the café window, I
watched him offer her a cigar and Lucienne
wave it away. As they talked, the smoke from
his cigar curled up and around them. He
had the air of a dandy, despite his evident
agitation.

Twenty minutes or so later they left the
café together and I followed them down
narrowing streets until finally they turned

into a darkened alleyway, the passage des Petits-Pères, under lines of washing strung from the windows of upper lodgings. I waited at the corner, listening for their footsteps on the cobbles. I heard a bolt being pulled back, the creak of a large door opening and then closing. I glanced down the alleyway. It was empty, except for a cat and three mangy kittens that were chewing over some rotting bones. The two figures had disappeared. My heart began to pound.

Venturing down the alley, I saw only one door large enough to have made the sound I had heard; it was made of dark wood, intricately carved, with two unpolished brass lion-head knockers, their manes rippling outward. It appeared to be the side door of what once must have been a building of some importance. There had been a sign here, but it had been wrenched off; I could see the holes where nails had been torn away, leaving a square of unblackened stone behind. I looked up. The windows were boarded over.

I sat on a wooden crate outside the door, under the third streetlamp from the east. Perhaps Lucienne would honor her promise after all. Those things she had stolen from me were probably in there, behind that door, in that very building. Despite her explanation, it made my blood boil to think of the damage she had done; how close I had come to losing everything. And so I waited, watching the washerwomen come and go, listening to fragments of their conversations, the humming of flies, and the intermittent screech of swallows gathering on the rooftops.

8

When the door to the street opened and she came out alone, something broke inside me. All my careful strategies collapsed. I pushed her up against the wall, unconscious of anything except the need to stop her from disappearing again. She did not struggle. I felt the sea-green silk of her jacket against my hands, felt the muscle and bone of her shoulders under my grip. I smelled the faint scent of her sweat, noticed the flushed skin that took the shape of an island on her left cheek. She kept quite still, tilting her head backward slightly, as if she was expecting me to hit her. Suddenly, with my face up close to hers, her mouth there, like that, I became confused and disoriented.

"Everything," I said, "is ruined. I have no money, no job, and no prospects."

"M. Connor. You are hurting me."

"You have destroyed everything for me." But I let her go all the same. She brushed her hands along her shoulders, smoothing down the folds of her jacket.

"I *told* you," she said. "I tried to find you. You broke your promise." She glanced nervously up the street. "You said you wouldn't follow me. You have no idea how dangerous that was."

"Dangerous?" I could hear the sneer in my voice.

"Dangerous for *me*. Yes. But then that doesn't matter to you."

"That's not fair," I said. "How long was I supposed to wait for you? Weeks? Months? What are you doing? Is this some kind of game?"

"Don't," she said.

She walked away from me a little. I kept close.

"I know who you are," I said clumsily, "and what you do. I know all about you."

Suddenly, afraid she would slip away again, I lunged toward her but stumbled, falling against her, pushing her hard. She fell toward the wall, tripping over some boxes and hitting her shoulder; then, regaining her balance, she turned, stepped toward me, and hit me across the face with her fist. The sound of the blow, her knuckles across my jaw, echoed against the walls. A caged bird was singing above us, repeating its refrain over and over.

"You know nothing. You are blind," she said, rubbing her hand, "as blind as it is possible to be, monsieur. You have no idea. You see nothing beyond yourself."

I kicked the wall several times. Everything else around me in the gathering twilight seemed to be turning to water.

"Merde," I said. "Damn. Damn. Damn. That hurt. I hate this. What do you want me to do? I agree to anything. Everything. I will do . . . whatever. I am tired. I just want to —"

"What? What is it you want?"

"I came to Paris to make something of myself. You have no idea how hard I have worked or how long I have waited to get this position. You have no idea how difficult it was to persuade my father to let me travel here. And in a single night you have ruined everything."

"And what does that something look like, Daniel, this thing that you will make of yourself?" She was leaning against the wall next to me. "The Grand Tour, then home for church on Sundays, a practice, a spell on the town council, conversations with ladies taking tea in the afternoons? What will you make of yourself, M. Connor?"

"If I had gone to Cuvier in the first place,"

I said, "or done anything halfway sensible, I might have been able to salvage something. . . ." I closed my eyes and watched the small pinpricks of light puncturing the darkness.

"But then there would be no now." Her voice had softened. "Keep your eyes closed," she said, moving closer to me, putting one hand on my shoulder. "Now tell me what color you see when I do this."

I saw blue when she kissed me, there in the darkening alley. I could not open my eyes, afraid that if I did, I would wake up back in my room, or somewhere she wasn't, where there was no smell of bergamot mixed with old beer and something like crushed herbs from the cobbles, somewhere not blue.

"Blue?" she said when I answered her. "I see purple."

When I opened my eyes, the street was darker; the edges of everything had softened; the colors had drained away. Down at the end of the alley the lamplighter lowered a lamp on its rope pulley, lit it, and pulled it back up into place.

"I have no plan, Daniel," she said. "I am making this up as I go along. I make mistakes. Everything about this — about you — gets under my skin. The Caravaggio boy, the coral fossils, the clever questions you ask in those notebooks of yours, your beautiful drawings. I have dreamt about you — I was trying to talk to you, but you were shouting. But . . . there are other things. Things you don't know about and . . . you are —"

"Don't," I said.

"Don't what?"

"Don't tell me you don't trust me."

"Shhh," she said, and kissed me again. I could feel her breath, see her eyebrows thick and dark, the crow's-feet around her eyes. I closed my eyes again, and in the darkness I could see flowers opening infinitely slowly, rust-colored petals against dark blue, stamens dusted gold.

"*Doucement,*" she said. "Come inside. There's always someone listening. Everywhere." She looked up and down the street, pointed toward white sheets that billowed in the wind like sails. A shutter banged shut.

"But the man in the café? Gutell."

"Saint-Vincent?" she said. "His real name is Saint-Vincent. He's gone. There's no one here."

She unlocked the door in the wall and led me into a courtyard. Untended trees, banana palms and figs, had grown up against the side of the building, arching over to

143

make a jungle of moving shadows; an urn here and there that had once held flowers now filled with nothing but bare earth and a scattering of cigar butts. An old folding table had cracked and fallen onto its side; chairs lay scattered about like the limbs of something long dead.

We crossed the courtyard and I followed her up a flight of stone steps covered with leaves. They led to an open door, the glass in its panels fractured in several places, and we entered a dusty hallway lined with doors, most boarded up. I translated the trades listed on the plaque in the hall: a printer, a knife grinder, an ironmonger, a linen trader, a locksmith, a dealer in curiosities. The house was silent except for the faint cooing of pigeons from an upper floor.

"It was once very grand here," she said, "before the Revolution. Then they divided it up to make workshops and lodgings, and now, well, there's almost no one left. There's Sandrine, the linen merchant, Pierre, the ink maker, both of them on the ground floor, and there's me on the second floor. We share the building with the cats. Sandrine has five cats. If I were here more, I'd do something about the courtyard and mend a few things. What do you smell?"

"Cats," I said. "I can smell cats and damp."

"Yes, it belongs to the cats now, finally, and the pigeons. We are the trespassers."

At the top of an ornate cast-iron balustrade that swept upward around a staircase that spiraled to a skylight perhaps a hundred feet above me, I could see the flurried shapes of what looked like pigeons. We climbed the stairs to the second floor in the dusty half-light. If I had thought I had a plan only an hour before, I abandoned it now. I had decided only to trust her.

I had no idea what that would mean.

On the second floor she stopped to unlock a door. A small painted sign on the wall read SERRURIER. Locksmith. Jagot had said that Lucienne's lover had been a lock breaker or a locksmith, called Duluc, or Duford. No, *Dufour.* Leon Dufour.

We stepped into a dark room lined with shelves and all the paraphernalia of a locksmith's art — metal saws, metal presses and molds, boxes of screws and levers. The air was thick with the smell of metal and dust. Cobwebs hung heavy from the tables and walls. Some cupboards had been draped with grimy sheets, encrusted here and there with pigeon droppings. A fragment of song drifted up from a street seller below.

"The locksmith, Dufour . . . ," I said, imagining him and his tall lover, here in the striped light of hot afternoons, and then I tried not to think about that. "Is he here?"

"He died," she said. "Dufour is dead."

"Who was he?"

"A friend. Someone who lived here once. A locksmith and a poet. He left me all of this, so sometimes I am Dufour, the locksmith." She gestured at her clothes. "Today I am Dufour the locksmith. Tomorrow I am a linen dealer or a botanical illustrator or a printer's assistant. In Paris I am many people. Dressed like this, I can come and go as I please."

I felt a stirring, a heat spreading through my body. Yes, I thought. *I would give you anything if you would just kiss me again.*

"I'm not used to having guests here in the atelier. Can I offer you some wine? I have a bottle of Burgundy here somewhere, I think. Come."

I was not prepared for what came next. Behind the room of locks and keys and dust, the locksmith's workshop, was another room.

"My cabinet," she said.

It might have been a cave beneath the sea. The last of the evening light fell onto shelves covered with spiraled shells, the intricate branchings of red corals, and the fanned shapes of sponges. Shelves covered every wall and in the center stood cabinets, with drawers of different lengths and widths, among packing cases from which dried seaweed spilled out. A stuffed crocodile hung suspended from a rafter; giant conch shells lay on the floor. A long table covered with dusty books and papers ran almost the length of the window, scattered with small cream-colored labels threaded with red silk.

"My specimens," I muttered. "They're here? You stole them. For this? A collection?"

"Yes, they're here somewhere. I'll find them for you. But first you must have some wine." She reached for a couple of glasses and a bottle of wine from a cupboard and blew the dust off them, uncorking the bottle a moment later.

"I've never seen anything —"

"It's nothing," she said. "You will see larger collections than this even a few streets away. The comtesse de Sévignon —"

"May I, can I look?" I asked, opening a drawer of coiled and netted and tentacled white corals arranged against dark blue velvet. "How long have you had all of these? Are they all stolen? How long have you —"

"Most of them are the remains of my grandmother's collection. She left it to me when she died. Some are from the Red Sea. Others are new. All of them are rare and worth a great deal of money. Some, yes," she said with a smile, "have been *acquired.* Stolen. It is more than a collection to me. It has a certain history, of course, which gives it importance, but I am also writing a book."

She opened a drawer and lifted out a black fan coral, running her fingertips along its delicate netted fibers. She passed it to me, telling me how it had been plucked from the bed of the Red Sea by a diver from Alexandria, who later sold it in the port of Al Quşayr to a Dutch sailor who was buying up corals for a ship's captain who knew something about corals and collectors. In a London auction room leased by a Russian prince, the novelist Horace Walpole procured it for his friend the Duchess of Portland, who placed it in the museum she'd built for her coral and shell collection at Bulstrode Park in Buckinghamshire. That's where it stayed, until her death in 1786, when her entire collection — the birds' nests, the corals, the snuffboxes, the paintings, the china, the birds' eggs, the fossils — was sold to pay off the duchess's debts.

"My grandmother sent her agents to London to buy the duchess's corals," she said. "The trouble was, half of the other coral collectors in Europe were there and the prices were impossible. She had to sell three paintings to get the pieces she wanted, and this was one of them. This little piece of black coral from the Red Sea. She sold a Rembrandt drawing for this."

Lucienne Bernard was an aristocrat, then, or at least her family had been. How had someone from such a background ended up as a common thief hunted by Jagot?

"Why, though?" I asked, handing her back the coral. "Why did she go to such trouble? Why do you?"

"My grandmother collected corals because she loved rare and exotic things. It's different for me. My interest is philosophical. The corals know things we do not know," she said.

"What do you mean *know?* They don't have minds or eyes or souls. They can't know anything."

She placed the piece of coral on the table and wrapped it in thin white paper; she marked the paper with some symbols and letters, tied it with red silk, and put it in the packing case deep in the dried seaweed. She took another coral specimen from a drawer and did the same.

"They know how old the earth is," she said. "They know how life on earth began. They know how animals have changed down there on the seabed, the way bodies have mutated and transformed from fishes to reptiles. They've seen it. They know it."

"That's ridiculous." She talked like a poet, I thought, not at all like any natural philosopher I had met.

"Alors," she said. "Perhaps they can't *tell* us, but we can read them, like we read a book or a clock and find out. The corals are a clock to tell us how old the earth is."

"But we know how old the earth is," I said, "or at least how long it is since the last great catastrophe that wiped everything out. Three thousand years. Cuvier has settled that."

"But Cuvier is wrong, and it's easy to *prove* he is wrong. If a coral reef grows at the rate of an inch a year," she said, making the distance between her forefinger and thumb, "and some reefs are a thousand feet thick, how many years would it have taken them to grow?"

I did the calculations. "Around twelve thousand years," I said. "That can't be right."

I was supposed to be taking the corals

back, I reminded myself, not listening to her criticism of Cuvier's work. But, despite my intentions, I was rapt.

"*Oui, c'est vrai. C'est merveilleux, n'est-ce pas?* Think about it. The reefs are even all the way through, which means they can't have been disturbed. It means there have been no catastrophes, no boiling seas, no eruptions or tidal waves or angels of the apocalypse for *at least* twelve thousand years. Cuvier's wrong — he just has to look at the corals properly to see that. But he won't."

I nodded toward the packing cases, almost afraid to ask the question. "You really *are* going then? Leaving Paris?"

"I came back to Paris to move my collection," she said, "to take everything back to Italy. Nothing is safe here now that Paris is occupied. But it has taken much longer than I expected. I need to leave quickly — in a few days." She passed me a glass of wine. "I wanted to give you your things before I left. To apologize. You had fallen asleep and I was curious to see what you were taking to Cuvier, and, well, once I had seen two coral fossils from the Ambras collection in your box, they were more than I could resist. Did you know that they once belonged to Ferdinand II? Still, I shouldn't have taken them, and now I can give them back."

"Italy?" I said, my voice shaking. "You're going to Italy?"

"Yes, that's where I live."

"The child," I said. "Delphine?"

"She doesn't want to leave Paris."

"Where is she?" I had looked for signs of a child in the atelier — toys, books, shoes — but saw none.

"She is staying at a convent on the north side of the city. The nuns run it as a school. It's not safe for her to be here with me in the atelier. Not anymore. I see her almost every day — she is not far away."

The heat in the room was stifling. I eased off my jacket, and when she stepped toward me and kissed me again, I felt an unbearable longing, softer and darker than the seabed.

"It is too hot," she said. "You know, you were lucky to see the paintings in the Louvre when you did. The walls are full of gaps now. The Prussians took their paintings two weeks ago, and Wellington sent a hundred and fifty riflemen in today to reclaim the Italian paintings. They took them down in less than two hours, except for the ones that Denon has hidden away, the ones he can't bear to part with. Come through and let me light some candles. We can't sit in here. Soon it will be too dark to see."

"The Louvre? You were there . . . today?"

"Yes. I was looking for you," she said. "When the soldiers came up the main staircase with guns, Denon simply stood and watched. He's getting used to it. A few weeks ago, when the Prussian soldiers went to take back the marble columns that Napoleon had removed from Aachen Cathedral, Denon told them that if they took them, the Louvre roof would fall in."

I followed her through a low doorway into a room that was empty except for a mattress on a rugless floor, covered in crumpled sheets, a pale, blue silk nightdress lying like sloughed skin. She carried in a candleholder and placed it on the floor near the head of the mattress.

"When . . . do you leave?" I asked, my words breaking up as she began to unbutton my shirt.

"Soon. There's so little time. I wanted to ask you about your notebooks. There are questions you are asking that . . . there are books you could read . . ."

"I can stay in Paris now," I said, "if you return my things. You could stay too, perhaps." For a second I wondered whether I should warn her about my conversations with Jagot, tell her that there seemed to be a high price on her head, but when she pulled her shirt over her head and her hair came loose from its ribbon, catching the light from the candles, I forgot about that too. Underneath the shirt, her chest was bound with strips of white linen.

"You will have to help me with this," she said.

As I reached to untie the white bands that bound her body, I tried to keep my mind on the soldiers in the Louvre. I imagined them climbing the ladders to reach the highest pictures, passing down paintings by Rubens, Caravaggio, and Titian, taking the canvases from their frames and rolling them up. If I kept my mind in the Louvre, I thought, my hands might stop shaking.

Without thinking, I leaned forward to kiss her in that hollow where her shoulder curved toward her neck as she slipped off the rest of her clothes. "You can change your mind," I said. "You could stay."

She was naked now except for her silk drawers, white against her dark skin.

"You are flushed," she said as she turned to face me, smiling. She reached for a sheet and draped it around herself. As I let the last strips of linen fall to the floor, she touched me, her fingers reaching for the skin beneath my unbuttoned shirt. "Wellington has told the Venetians they can have the horses back."

"He has?" I tried to keep my mind on the empty white spaces on the walls of the Louvre as she took off my shirt and slipped the belt from my waist. "The horses? What horses?"

"The four bronze horses that Napoleon took from Saint Mark's Square and put up on the top of the Arc de Triomphe." She lowered herself onto the mattress, pulling me down beside her.

"The horses coming down," she whispered, "that will be something to see." Lying on her side facing me, her head propped on her hand, she traced the lines of my thigh and hip with her fingers.

"I can see purple now," I said, my eyes closed. I pressed my mouth to hers, my hand on her breast, underneath the sheet.

"Paris will never be like this again," she said. "It's all changing. You will be here to see it all, even when I am gone. You will see everything."

On the night of August 20, Napoleon, having walked eight or nine times the length of the deck of the HMS *Northumberland,* had taken his usual seat on the second gun from the gangway on the starboard side. He was dictating his memoirs to his secretary, Las Cases, recalling on this particular night his childhood in Corsica — the smell of the houses in Ajaccio, his first military uniform, the history of his family, who were émigrés to Corsica from Italy, and the fact that, as he had been born prematurely, his mother's nurse had placed him on the bedroom floor, on a carpet woven with scenes from the *Iliad,* while she attended to his mother. Those scenes from Homer were the first pictures I saw, he told Las Cases: Menelaus and Achilles in battle and Hector's body being dragged around the walls of Troy.

For days the Emperor had stared out from the deck toward an unbroken horizon or watched the distant landmasses slip by: Cape

Finisterre on the northwestern corner of Spain, the dazzling bird-nested cliffs of Cape Saint Vincent on the southern coast of Portugal, down past the Strait of Gibraltar where merchant ships gathered to pass from the Atlantic Ocean through to the Mediterranean Sea, the boundaries once known as the Pillars of Hercules. The HMS *Northumberland* and the warships that accompanied it continued to tack slowly down the coast of Africa toward Madeira and beyond Madeira to the equator. It would be at least another month before the Emperor would set foot on solid land, thousands of miles from Paris.

The heat was so great that Napoleon could not sleep; he complained of swollen feet from lack of exercise. For hours every day he and Las Cases pored over maps in the volumes of the *Historical Atlas* Las Cases had published a few years before in England and had brought on board for the Emperor's amusement. By night, after his walk on deck, the Emperor played vingt-et-un or chess with his generals, Las Cases, and his valet, then retired to his cabin. Only that day he had received word that Wellington had allowed the Louvre to be sacked by Prussian soldiers. Where would it all end, he wondered, now that vultures circled the imperial city? If you would

only find me a musket, he whispered to Las
Cases, then we might do something.

9

The cats woke us that dawn with cries like human screams that echoed from the roof-tops outside her window. We lay listening to the rain, the first we'd had in weeks.

"Stay a few more days," I said. "I want to see you again. I want —"

"What does Daniel Connor want?" she asked, half-asleep. "It's dangerous for me in Paris," she said, her head heavy against my chest. "You keep forgetting."

"I have forgotten everything outside this room," I said, running my fingers through her hair, reminding myself she was no apparition. "There is nothing outside."

"There is Henri Jagot," she said. "He is always there. He doesn't forget."

"What can Jagot possibly want with you? It must be a mistake."

I remembered Jagot's suspicions about Silveira and what he had said about Dufour. Lucienne was not a woman who chose her friends wisely, I thought. For a moment I imagined what my father might say about such a woman — he would call her fallen — but then perhaps he would use the same word for me now. It was a hollow word. It meant nothing to me anymore.

"It was a bad mistake," she said. "There was a gunfight in an old warehouse in Montmartre six years ago. One of Jagot's men died."

"Did *you* kill him? Jagot's man?" The thought seemed ridiculous.

"No, I didn't. But Jagot arrested me and some other people — it was mistaken identities, you understand."

"So he wants revenge. Saint-Vincent, the man in the Palais Royal. Was he arrested too?"

"Yes. And Manon. Four of us escaped from the Bureau, but my friend Dufour, he did not escape and was sent to Toulon. Jagot never sleeps and he never stops looking. Eventually he will find me even in Italy. Wherever I am. You are a beautiful boy, Daniel Connor, but even for your beauty and your cleverness and your questions that never stop, I cannot stay in Paris."

"Just stay to see the Venetian horses come down," I said. "It will only be a few more

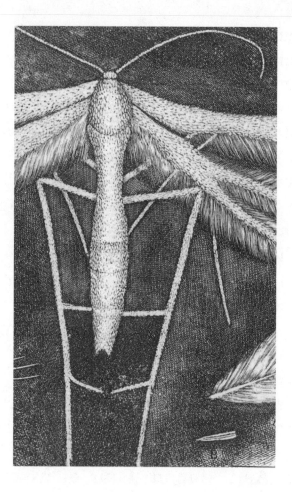

days. Stay for five days. At least five more days."

And so it began.

I traded the coral fossils that morning for five of her days, taking only the mammoth bone, the manuscript, and the notebooks from the locksmith's atelier. A few hours later, I stepped out into the rain, as if into a new time, a new air. I'd find a way of explaining the disappearance of the corals, I thought. I would tell Cuvier they had been delayed in London and would arrive later in the year. I had become reckless.

I could hardly believe the reversal of my fortunes. Only the day before, utterly dejected, I had determined to resign my position and go home. Now that Lucienne had returned Cuvier's manuscript and the mammoth bone, anything was possible. The doors were open, and not just the anticipated ones — the Jardin, the lectures, the job — but a new corridor of doors I never even imagined existed, and behind each of them was Lucienne Bernard, the beautiful savant, the thief, the woman who dressed as a man and who understood the language of corals. I felt as if I had been given the keys to the city.

If only we'd known. I had traded the coral fossils for five of her days. If I hadn't been enraptured, if she hadn't wanted to see the Venetian horses' flight from the Arc, if Jagot's man hadn't followed me to the atelier as she had suspected he would . . . she might have gone. And she might have gotten away.

I knew there would be no hiding anything

from Fin. I had not slept in my bed that night, and for Fin that would mean only one thing. I would have to have a story prepared. When I let myself back into the lodgings the following evening, he was ready for me. He had come home early from the hospital, tidied the rooms, and then arranged himself on the chaise longue with a medical textbook. Despite his overwhelming curiosity, Fin had clearly intended to maintain, at least to start with, an apparently casual indifference to my reappearance. He failed.

"*Bonsoir,* M. Connor," he said, his eyes scrutinizing me over the top of the book.

"*Bonsoir,* M. Robertson," I replied. "You're home early."

"And you're home late, my friend, by a small matter of an entire night."

"It's a fine evening out there. I passed a group of Prussian soldiers swimming under the Petit Pont, and there were circus performers on the quai. We should go out."

"Where have you been?" he asked.

"I stopped off at the bathhouse on the river on the way home."

"I mean before that."

"Lunch. Before that, breakfast at the café on the rue de Rivoli. I had soup and cheese and half a loaf of bread. Then I went to the barbers in that little alleyway near the Tuileries this afternoon and had my hair cut."

"Connor, I am losing my patience. You didn't come home last night."

"Yes, I know," I said. "I stayed somewhere else."

"*Mon Dieu.* So Daniel Connor finally got lucky? Did you find a girl who was good enough for you? Will you see her again? What does she look like — blond, brunette, tall, short?"

"I'm going to dress for dinner," I said. "Then I think we had better go out. We have some celebrating to do."

I placed the wooden box containing the mammoth bone and the travel bag on the table, stepped into the bedroom, and closed the door.

A few moments later he called out, "*Mon diable!* Is this what I think it is? It's a bloody mammoth bone. *Merde.* Did you find *her* as well? The beautiful thief? And she just gave it all back to you? Just like that? You *must* have been good."

"I'll tell you later," I said, grateful that he couldn't see the flush on my face. "Fin, you know what this means?"

"I do indeed. Daniel Connor got lucky. *Mon diable* — it's about time."

"It means I'm back in the Jardin. It means

I'm in time. I told Cuvier I'd start work at the end of August. I can now. I can start over —"

"Weren't there other specimens apart from the mammoth bone and the manuscript?" Fin asked. "Fossils?"

"Yes, but I can find a way of explaining those. Look, Fin. This means I can start work at the Jardin. I will have money. I can pay the rent. I don't have to go home. I can stay in Paris."

"And her? Tell me about her — *immédiatement.* There is no time to lose. Fin is curious. Fin must not be kept waiting."

I had composed a story that would protect both Fin and Lucienne if Jagot came by asking questions. So as we walked toward the first bar, the sky fading from dark blue to pink on the horizon, the smell of garlic and spices heavy on the air, I told Fin that my thief wasn't a thief at all but a widow called Mme. Rochefide — Victorine — and that she had taken my luggage by accident. I had seen her at the Palais Royal that afternoon, and she had taken me back to her lodgings to return my belongings and eventually one thing had led to another. Well, it was almost true. I felt slightly ashamed at the ease with which I could turn the philosopher-thief into a mysterious widow with a life story all of her own. Now all I had to do, I thought, was remember it.

"It was your first time, wasn't it, Connor?" Fin said drunkenly, sometime in the early hours of the morning, propped against a seat in the Café des Deux Chats. "That's something to drink to. You know there's no shame in that. I'll tell you a secret — Céleste was my first too . . . my first and only. There are not many people I would admit that to, you know. But you, my friend . . ."

He was asleep before he had finished the sentence.

Two days later I found Lucienne sitting on the steps of the Louvre, reading a newspaper, waiting for me. I stood nearby in the shadows watching her, remembering. I watched her for as long as I dared, my heart beating, sure she would disappear again, or turn into something with wings and fly up to circle the square.

The streets of Paris were hot and dusty; foreigners in holiday spirits made their way to the gallery to see the latest gaps in the walls. Everyone was talking. Wellington's name was whispered everywhere. Defeating Napoleon at Waterloo had made him a kind of god. Now he had become the puppet master who controlled the strings in Paris.

They said he had given the authorization for the Prussian army to enter the Louvre. Wellington was playing it slow, as diplomatically as he could, but he was lighting matches over a powder keg, the English papers said, sending soldiers into the Louvre like that.

The Parisians were incensed. These trophies Napoleon had brought back to Paris were for them, for France. They were theirs: their paintings, their Venetian horses, their sculptures. They belonged to Paris. And of course, everyone still half believed that Napoleon would stroll back into Paris as if nothing had happened and send all the ambassadors and diplomats and soldiers packing.

That day, against the stone steps, Lucienne was only a man, in a gray-green coat, slightly worn, brown breeches, and boots. This masquerade of hers was carefully put together, I thought, so that she would not stand out. She looked like a thousand artists or writers in Paris. She wore her hair falling straight around her face, in the way I had seen artists do. Would I have noticed, I wondered, if I hadn't known, if I hadn't uncoiled her in candlelight? Would I have been able to pick her out from a crowd in a coffeehouse or bar, nudge my companion, and say: *That is a woman dressed as a man.* Almost certainly not. She used no tricks. There was no false hair. She was only a very tall woman dressed as a man, and thus, understood to be so. And she was only one of many masqueraders in Paris, women who passed as men, men who passed as women, thieves turned police agents, thieves turned counts.

"Imagine the crowds there must have been here in the square," she said, pointing down the place du Carrousel to where the four bronze horses made black muscular shapes against the sky on top of the Arc De Triomphe. "It's seventeen years since they brought the horses to Paris — on carts in a long procession, flanked by animals from the menagerie — ostriches, camels, gazelles, and vultures — soldiers and a military band."

"You saw it?" My shoulder brushed against hers. We both sat looking down the street to the Arc, its stone gleaming in the sun after two days of rain.

"No. I was in Egypt," she said. "I read about it in the French papers there."

"You went to Egypt?" I heard the incredulity in my voice, my own boyish awe and envy. "In Napoleon's campaign?"

Napoleon had taken savants with him to Egypt — archaeologists, botanists, astronomers, doctors, and engineers. I knew that. He took them with him so that they might study Egypt and bring ancient knowledge back to France. That story of Napoleon and his savants and soldiers in Egypt was glorious to me. It seemed a uniquely imperial act. Jameson had read the newspaper descriptions of the expedition out to us in a lecture, describing with transparent envy the boatloads of scientific equipment and books that had accompanied the 167 savants. And for me there had been two men in particular who held my attention — Étienne Geoffroy Saint-Hilaire and Marie Jules Savigny. Geoffroy, then just twenty-six and already a professor at the Jardin des Plantes, was put in charge of all the vertebrate investigations, and Savigny, only twenty-one, the invertebrates.

"I was in Egypt when the horses came to Paris," Lucienne said, "yes, at the end of July 1798. I went out as one of Geoffroy's assistants. They made us wear uniforms. It was incredibly hot."

"They made women wear uniforms?"

"I went as a man, of course," she said, laughing. "They wouldn't let women go to Egypt except as camp followers and I didn't

170

want to be a camp follower." I pictured bright uniforms against white sand, thousands of men and boys a long way from home. Yes, I could imagine her there in Cairo's streets, a French soldier moving through crowds of Mamluks, camels, and dancing girls.

"Geoffroy was collecting new species of fish," she said. "So I went out with the fishermen on the coasts and rivers, or visited the fish stalls of remote fishing villages. Sharks, rays, puffer fish, lungfish, I brought them all back to Geoffroy, packed in cases of ice and straw. You can't imagine all the different fish out there where the desert meets the fertile land, and fresh water and seawater join."

"What was it like working with Geoffroy? Is he as brilliant as they say?"

"It was frustrating more than anything," she said. "He worked so hard he made himself ill. He found a fish in the waters of the Nile that he decided was a *chalnon manquant* — how do you say that in English?"

"A missing link," I said. "A fish?"

"When Geoffroy dissected it, he found bronchioles that looked like the lungs of a human. It changed everything for him. It made him see that we've all come from one form. I kept telling him it was the Red Sea

171

corals we should be looking at. Further back. They're the key, Geoffroy, I'd say, not the fish. But he wouldn't listen. He could not see anything beyond that fish of his, not even when the British were camped right outside Alexandria."

Now, as well as the drawings and descriptions of the Egyptian campaign I had seen or read in Jameson's yellowing newspapers, I saw another world out there, one in which men quarreled over microscopes in brightly lit rooms with shelves of glass jars full of dead sea creatures. And corals in a red sea. I wasn't stupid. I knew, even then, that the Red Sea wasn't red, but that's what I saw when I closed my eyes: tentacled cream- and pink-tipped corals swaying in red water. And I saw her in the water among them, her hair undulating like sea snakes, her skin bare like the pictures of the half-naked Japanese pearl divers I had seen, diving like birds of prey.

"Look, see the soldiers over there, looking up," she said. "They're wondering how to take the horses down." A group of English soldiers on the other side of the square were looking up at the Arc and pointing. "Just a few more days perhaps."

"So Napoleon's war trophies will go back to Venice, where they belong," I said.

"They've been war trophies for a thousand years, at least," she said. "Passed back and forth between emperors and invaders. Napoleon took them from Venice but before that the Venetians stole them from Constantinople. And before that the emperor Constantine took them from Rome, and the Romans had stolen them, or copied them, from the Greeks. So where should they go back to? Venice or Constantinople or Greece? Only they know where they began."

"They're made of bronze," I said. "They can't *know* anything."

"You are so literal, M. Connor," she said, laughing. "Where is your imagination?"

I wondered what we must look like — two men sitting together under the Arc looking up. We must have looked like brothers or friends. But we were lovers. I wanted to touch her again. The memory of her body tormented me.

"Where is Jagot's man today?" she asked suddenly, looking up and down the street.

"He's gone," I said, trying not to show my satisfaction. "I lost him."

"No one loses one of Jagot's men," she said. "Trust me. Jagot must have called off his surveillance for some reason . . . I wonder what that means." She hesitated, calculating. "That will make things easier," she said. "For the moment. Until I get out of Paris. What will you do now that you have your things back?"

"I've written to Cuvier and sent him the letters from Jameson. He wrote back yesterday. It was easy. I have an appointment with him at three o'clock on Monday, and then on Tuesday I start work. I wish it was sooner. There are so many things I want to discuss with him."

"A week today," she said. "*Bon.* A new beginning for Daniel Connor. Yes, that is good. Where will you work? For how long?"

"Seven hours a day. Monday to Saturday. In the Museum of Comparative Anatomy. I have my own desk. I am to go to Cuvier's own study for the appointment. He writes that he is overwhelmed with the work for his new book."

"Bon," she said. "That's very good. You are lucky. You will learn many things in Cuvier's house."

"He is writing a catalogue of the whole animal kingdom," I said, "which will include a description of every species in the world. No wonder he is overwhelmed. It's the most ambitious project since Buffon's *Historie Naturelle.* Just think — all the species on earth will be collected in those pages." It thrilled me to imagine my own name listed among others on the title page of one of those volumes.

"All the species that have been *discovered*," she said. "That is not the same as all the species on earth. It seems a strange thing to be cataloguing species when there are so many important questions to be answered — like how life began or why species change. Cuvier still wants to prove that species are fixed."

"I am to work on the bird volume," I said, slightly offended by her disparagement of Cuvier's work. "That is where I will begin. With the birds. The volume is progressing, but it is behind schedule, apparently. He needs more assistants." Although I was beginning to question everything I had ever known, even the definition of species, the full implications of transformism still alarmed me. Without belief in order and structure and providence, where would we be? The imagined godlessness of such a world frightened me.

"And by the time you begin your work with the Baron," she said, "I will be back in my study in Italy, among my books and papers."

"The end of the summer," I said. In an instant, thinking of the loss of her, what had seemed important dulled into insignificance.

"Stay in Paris till the end of the summer. Till the leaves have fallen. Jagot can't find you. He has too much to do and too few men. You are not in danger now."

And Lucienne smiled that slow smile of hers that said she knew better. But she promised to stay just a little longer, and in that last week before my work began in the Jardin, as the days shortened and the gardeners tended late-summer roses, she showed me the Paris she remembered — her Paris: rooftops, hidden coffee shops and bars by the river, *traiteurs* that sold the best fish in Paris for a few sous, abandoned pleasure grounds and old palaces. One afternoon we lay in the bottom of a boat under a willow tree for hours in the sun talking about the circulation of the blood, spontaneous generation, and the colors of the corals on the seabed off the coast of Egypt.

Fin and Céleste never tired of asking me about Mme. Rochefide, the beautiful widow — what she wore, whom she saw, what she did. When I could, I made things up, though doing so made me feel uncomfortable. I'd never been much good at lying. But I had no choice. I was always vague about the street on which she lived. Eventually, Fin began to goad me, persuaded by my evasiveness, saying that Mme. Rochefide was not a widow after all, and that there must be a jealous husband waiting in the wings.

10

On August 27, in a new sky-blue coat I had bought for the occasion, I stood outside Cuvier's house in the Jardin, clutching the mammoth bone in its case and the manuscript, waiting for the bells to sound out the hour of my appointment. All the shutters were closed against the hot afternoon sun. A family of French visitors had laid white tablecloths across picnic tables in the shade of the plane trees. Women in straw bonnets passed children plates of small cakes and poured glasses of milk from earthenware jugs. Beyond them and beyond the latticework wooden fence that surrounded all the enclosures in the Jardin, a gardener pruned white roses.

The woman who opened the door introduced herself as Cuvier's stepdaughter, Sophie Duvaucel, a tall, handsome, but tired-looking young woman who worked as Cuvier's assistant and one of his many illustrators. From the hallway I glimpsed a series of rooms with polished floorboards, full of books, vases of flowers, and richly colored rugs.

She took me up a flight of stairs. I followed her through a long library broken up into a suite of rooms, each containing works on a single subject — osteology, law, ornithology — and then to the door of Cuvier's studio. This was his famous sanctum sanctorum where he wrote his books and thought his thoughts and solved the puzzles of time and origins.

"No one is allowed in here," Sophie whispered as she pushed the heavy door open, "except by invitation. Not even the *aide-naturalistes.*"

The room — dark and shuttered and with eleven desks arranged around the walls — was scattered with bones, books, and papers. Cuvier sat behind his desk like an eastern sultan receiving a dusty foreign envoy in his inner chamber. Yes, I had traveled a long way, I thought, with these gifts. More than he could know.

It was a little hard to breathe.

Cuvier was impressive: his bulk, his bearing, his clothes, even his head of thick, loose curls, flecked with gray. He had the bearing of a man of state; his dark blue tailcoat was decorated with medals.

If the short welcome speech seemed rehearsed, I did not mind, but I did mind the fact that in the full ten-minute interview, Cuvier barely looked at me. I knew I was one of many scores of *aide-naturalistes* who had stood where I was now standing, but I had persuaded myself that, as a protégé of Jameson, as the Edinburgh student specially selected and commended most highly for his skills of dissection and observation, who had been sent bearing gifts for the great French professor, I would be regarded as a particularly important arrival. It seemed it was not so. Cuvier was distracted, a little impatient, although he managed a certain degree of warmth in his welcome and in his handshake. He spoke in French with a pronounced German accent. His voice was tight, a little constricted, a small voice for such a big man.

"I trust your health has returned in full?" he asked, looking at me warily for signs of weakness. "Mlle. Duvaucel says you have been quite ill since you have been in Paris. We need young men who have strong constitutions. Your eyes are good, I trust."

"I am entirely well again, monsieur, I assure you," I said, hoping my manners were good enough when translated into French.

"I am eager to begin work. To be of use. And my eyesight is excellent."

"Yes, yes," he said. "Good. That is good. Jameson speaks highly of you."

I had prepared a short speech on behalf of Jameson, but once Cuvier had asked about the reception of his new book, *Discours préliminaire,* in England, made a few complimentary remarks about Jameson and inquired about his health, he dismissed me. When I hesitated, holding out the case containing the mammoth bone, muttering a phrase or two about comparative anatomy, Jameson, and the new relations between France and England, he even waved me away. Sophie gently took the case from me, laid it on the table nearest her, and opened the door.

"Don't take it personally, M. Connor," she whispered, as we walked back through the library. "My stepfather is a very busy man. You won't see much of him. He has a great deal to do for this new book, and he has many responsibilities in France now that the king is back. So you must never take anything personally. All of us who work with him have learned that. The work is good. It brings its own rewards . . . The blue jacket," she added, "it's very fine. But the professor prefers his assistants to dress in more somber colors. Black or brown is fine." She smiled.

And so it was that, the following day, I finally began work as *aide-naturaliste* to Professor Cuvier in the library of the Museum of Comparative Anatomy in the Jardin des Plantes. The work was painstaking and laborious and seemingly without end. There were ten of us working that summer on the bird volume of Cuvier's *Règne animal;* eleven, if you counted Sophie Duvaucel, who worked alongside us. We worked at desks arranged in a long row in the library near the windows. The other *aide-naturalistes,* apart from Sophie, were all young men in their twenties, but it was with Achille and Joseph that I dined in the Jardin café every day. Achille Valencienne had been born in Paris and had published a paper on parasitic worms; Joseph Risso, from Nice, had published a book on the ichthyosaurs of the region and had begun a study of the natural history of oranges. Neither of them was particularly interested in birds, but they were Cuvier's assistants and so they did what they were told.

Being Cuvier's *aide-naturaliste* was an apprenticeship. And it was competitive; we were all under pressure to perform. What

Achille and Joseph both wanted was a posting out to India or up into the Himalayan mountains or to Sumatra to collect specimens for the museum. However, no one was assigned to fieldwork until they had done the graft, learned the craft, earned their spurs, or so they said. And in the autumn of 1815, because of Cuvier's new volume, earning your spurs meant birds — bird illustration, bird description, and bird taxonomy. Alfred Duvaucel, Cuvier's stepson and Sophie's younger brother, was next in line for a posting, according to Achille and Joseph. He was going to Chandannagar with Pierre-Médard Diard. These two young men had finished working in the library and were now learning taxidermy in the laboratory on the other side of the Jardin. They would have to be able to stuff birds out in the wet heat of India, on the banks of the Ganges. They were a good deal farther down the line than Achille and Joseph.

I longed for a conversation with Cuvier about embryological questions, but I barely saw him. As a newly appointed councillor of state he had many official engagements that took him away from the museum, and as Achille explained, mocking my optimism, it was not Cuvier's way to have conversations with his assistants about anything, even if he had had the time to do so.

"You are merely an illustrator and a scribe, M. Connor," Achille postured, imitating Cuvier's German accent. "A humble foot soldier in the long march toward knowledge. You must not get ideas above your station. And you will leave the philosophical questions to the professors. Facts, M. Connor, facts are what is needed. We will have no speculation here."

I carried on honing my questions just the same, and when the work was particularly laborious and myopic, I reminded myself of the important part I was playing in shaping Cuvier's magnum opus; I hoped eventually to attract the notice of the professor, not only through my diligence but also through the precision and speed of my descriptions. I imagined that one day I might ask him a question so dazzling that he would be bound to summon me into his office to *talk*.

I began to work longer hours than the other assistants. Despite my impatience to see Lucienne, I was often the last to leave. The trouble was that now I couldn't separate Cuvier's taxonomic questions from Lucienne's speculative ones. The hours I spent on bird taxonomies ensured that. Why, I wanted to ask, are there so many minute variations in the claw structures of birds from very similar subspecies and from close but distinct habitats? The facts would not stay as facts; they kept transforming into difficult questions about divergence and variation. I took those questions to Lucienne Bernard's bed in the locksmith's atelier, where I was given more controversial answers and rather different scientific books and papers to read than Professor Cuvier might have given me.

Not long after I began work at the Jardin, and when I complained that I knew nothing of her friends, Lucienne Bernard took me to the Café Zoppi in Saint-Germain-des-Prés. Manon Laforge, the woman I had seen in the Palais gardens, and Alain Saint-Vincent were playing cards in an alcove behind a curtain, and it was here, she said, that Rousseau had once played cards with a famous widow whose name she had now forgotten.

The first thing Alain Saint-Vincent said to me was: "M. Connor, *je suis un homme mort.*" That was typical of Alain, I later discovered. He was theatrical and melodramatic. *I am a dead man.* He meant only: *I am losing at cards.*

"Not yet, Alain, not quite yet," Lucienne said, glancing at his hand.

"Well, well," Alain replied, tucking his cards into his top pocket and reaching over to shake my hand. "One of Cuvier's protégés. That is one for the books. Lucienne, can you lend me two thousand francs? Manon has stripped me of my very last coins. She has no compassion." He pulled out a chair for me to sit on. "You play cards, M. Connor?"

"No, I don't. I'm sorry."

"I will teach you. Never trust a man who does not play cards. Let's play on."

"Impossible, Alain," Manon said. "You know the rules. No money, no cards."

Lucienne leaned forward and pushed some notes into Alain's top pocket.

"Enough?" she said.

"Yes. Are you sure?"

"Of course. You'd do the same for me if it was the other way around. We owe you."

"You've paid it back a thousand times."

Alain Saint-Vincent smoked too many cigars and drank too much whisky; he had a cough that sounded painful. He looked older than both Manon and Lucienne and he had a high forehead with fine lines, and expressive eyebrows. His clothes looked expensive and were brightly colored; his shirts had fine lace cuffs. Although he was charming and verbose, he liked to pick fights. He was supposed to be in hiding, but he did not seem to know how to hide or to make himself invisible.

Manon Laforge was short, slim, and muscular, more like an acrobat than a dancer. Her black hair was cut short, but sometimes she wore a turban in the fashion of the day, and bangles, I remember that. There was something of the Gypsy about her, with all that jewelry and the silk around her hair. Yet she was quiet and untheatrical.

Manon didn't like me much. I could see that from the start. She didn't trust me, and she didn't like that Lucienne trusted me. She didn't like it that I stayed in the atelier. Clearly she thought that was a mistake. When she talked her eyes flickered back and forth to Lucienne. The two of them shared secrets, and I didn't like that. They were kin. They lived together in Italy. They traveled together, cooked together. They told each other jokes; they laughed at the same things.

"How old are you, M. Connor. Fourteen? Fifteen?" Saint-Vincent asked. I refused to rise to the provocation.

"Twenty-three."

"And such a charming English accent. Twenty-three. You don't get much younger than that. Or prettier."

Manon kept her eyes fixed on Lucienne, who looked nervous, edgy. Lucienne took a cigar from Saint-Vincent, lit it, drew a few breaths, grimaced, and stubbed it out in an ashtray.

"Time was when we didn't have to pull the curtain across in the Café Zoppi," she said.

"You have a bad memory, Lucienne Bernard," Alain said. "It's been like this for the past twenty years. Since when have you minded? At least you have only Jagot to watch out for. I have to look out for Wellington's spies as well as the French royal guard. *Banishment.* The shame of it. Who are they to say that I am expelled from France? Who has the right to say that?"

"You backed the wrong horse, my friend." Lucienne drew up a chair for herself. "Banishment? That's the worst of it? What about Saint Helena, the countess, the three Corsican brothers . . . shall I go on?"

"I was right to speak out against the restoration of that fat, good-for-nothing king and his fat, good-for-nothing government. I'm just not lucky, that's all. I have not been lucky, no."

But Lucienne would not let him off the hook. "It might have helped if you hadn't criticized the new king so publicly. What were they supposed to do with you after that? Eh? *Quoi?* Ignore you? And don't go claiming political heroism. You've been switching sides for years. You were a royalist until Napoleon marched on Paris this spring. You can't have it both ways."

"It doesn't look good, Alain," Manon jibed. "M. Connor, does this man look like a political hero to you?"

"I wouldn't know," I said. "I've never met one."

"I am a war veteran," Alain said. "An esteemed scientist. No one in the world knows as much as I do about marine botany or algae. I am a former director of the Department of Maps and Records in the ministry. I was wounded in the Battle of Austerlitz."

"Keep your voice down," Lucienne hissed.

"Did you know that the bastards have canceled my war pension?" Alain had taken a knife to an apple and was peeling it in one continuous spiral, slowly and carefully. Now he jabbed the blade into the fruit, cut off a quarter, and put it into his mouth.

"That's the law," Manon said. "Exiled botanists don't get pensions."

"Why didn't you leave Paris? It's been two months since they banished you," Lucienne said. "I bet there's a woman in the story somewhere."

"What are you implying?" Alain looked hurt.

"And where is your wife?" Manon asked.

"In Bordeaux. I can't even go there."

"The decision to put you on that list was made high up."

"Cuvier or one of his cronies," Saint-Vincent said. "He had a word with the authorities, didn't he? Now that he's councillor of state he'll find a way of exiling everyone who has ever challenged him."

Lucienne, aware of my presence, changed the subject before I had a chance to question Saint-Vincent's allegations about Cuvier.

"Davide?" Lucienne asked. "Have you found him? Have you asked at the curiosity dealers?"

"Not yet," Manon said, her face darkening. "He'll find us before we find him. Did you read about Coignard? They found his body in the Seine yesterday morning. He'd been tortured and his hands and feet had been cut off. People are saying it was Jagot — an old score. They say Coignard was supposed to be a lesson to the others on the list. Lucienne, we have to leave Paris."

"I know," she said. "I know. We will. We'll be long gone before he catches up with us."

■ ■ ■ ■

"Tell me something no one else in the world knows about you," Lucienne said as we lay in her bed that night. "A secret."

So I told her about the carved boat my father had bought for my older brother when I was ten and he was twelve, and how I wanted it so much that I had thrown it out of the window into the nettle patch, where no one would find it. I told her about the day I had stolen a key to open my father's desk and look among his papers in the hope that I would find letters from my real parents. I told her that I had always been sure that there was a secret in the house, something everyone, including the servants, covered up, and that I often went looking for it — whatever it was — whenever the house was empty.

I told her that, in looking for this one secret about me, I had found out all sorts of secrets that belonged to other people — that I had once seen my older brother touching one of the maids in a way he shouldn't have; that I discovered from hiding in the butler's pantry that the servants had ways of keeping the younger maids out of my brother's reach; that my mother didn't really have an

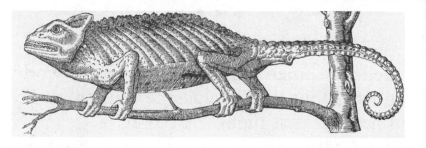

illness because I had seen her walk perfectly well when my father was away on business, and that I had once seen her kiss a man who was not my father. I told her that, to me as a child, the world had seemed full of astonishing secrets, and that I had even kept a notebook in shorthand full of the secrets I had collected.

Lucienne laughed. "And no one knows any of those things?" she said. "Only I know that the toy boat is in the nettle patch? And that your mother sometimes kisses a man who is not your father?"

"Yes," I said. "But I only saw her do it once. It was my father's brother. My uncle. She still writes letters to him. I was shocked, of course, but now it seems rather ordinary. I wonder how many secrets there are in Paris. Now tell me something about you that no one knows. A secret."

"A secret?" she said. "There is a man who comes to my bed —"

"There is?" I said, sitting up suddenly.

"He has black curls and a scar on his chin and he looks like a Caravaggio boy, except that when he gets serious, or cross, or jealous, he doesn't look like a Caravaggio boy at all. When he talks to me, when I see how the world looks to him, how full of expectation and curiosity and ambition he is, I can see the world as it looked to me twenty years ago, when everything seemed possible, when I thought I could find all the secrets too and solve all the mysteries. Before the Revolution. But, you know, the secrets, they just multiply. One question answered just makes another in its place."

"And am I a secret?" I said.

"I think Manon might know," she said. "Manon knows everything, whether I tell her or not."

I wanted to ask about Delphine's father, the locksmith Dufour, but I didn't know how, so I began to approach the question from another direction. "Delphine," I said. "Will she go to school?"

"Absolutely not. She does not need to go to school. Manon and I have raised her in the spirit of Rousseau. We live in the country and we teach her and she teaches herself. She has no tutors. Even at the convent the nuns give her the run of the library. She has no lessons. My grandmother raised me the same way; she read Rousseau's *Émile* when it was first published, so I was lucky. I was very free. I had a library and a garden and the finest microscope in Marseilles. Delphine is five now and she asks even more questions than you do. Even more than I did at her age. And now most of her questions are about Napoleon."

"Why Napoleon? It seems a strange passion for a child."

"She met him once at the ambassador's house in Florence. He played a game of vingt-et-un with her and let her win. I think she believed he was invincible until Waterloo, that he was a kind of god. It is a hard lesson for her to learn. She still thinks he's going to be rescued."

"Perhaps he *will* be rescued," I said. "We don't know. There are hundreds of miles of ocean to be crossed before he reaches Saint Helena."

And as we began to talk of who might rescue Napoleon, that important question of Delphine's father was lost again.

On August 22, the HMS *Northumberland* and the nine other warships accompanying it came within sight of Madeira. Two of the boats tried to anchor in the port in order to bring in supplies for the squadron, but a storm blew in. The sea was rough, the sky obscured by thick, low clouds, and the wind was full of stinging sand from the deserts of Africa. The Emperor was now dictating his memories of his Egyptian campaign and describing the dromedary-mounted armies that had proved so successful in the desert skirmishes. Riding a camel, he told Las Cases, is a little like the sensation of being aboard ship.

The Madeira storm made it impossible for the supply boats to reach the port. The boats tacked backward and forward waiting for their chance to drop anchor, but the storm continued for two days. Napoleon wrote several new letters to the empress and his four-year-old son who were living in exile in Vienna.

What the English admiral called a storm, the English consul at Madeira called a hurricane. All the vintage had been destroyed, all the windows in the town broken; it had not been possible to breathe in the streets for the sand in the air, and the heat.

Two days later, after another long, sickness-bated night, some supply boats reached the ship from the shore, carrying several oxen and crates full of other provisions: cases of Madeira wine; oranges, which the Emperor declared to be unripe; and peaches, which the Emperor declared to be bad. The figs and the grapes, however, were excellent, and the Madeira wine he declared passable. The boats also brought mailbags and news of the latest decisions made by the Congress of Vienna. The printers in Paris are redesigning the maps of Europe, he told Las Cases. The empire of France is being redrawn by politicians with rulers and set squares. They are not men. What do they know of campaigns and mutinies and battles?

The sky remained obscured by low clouds for days as the squadron made its way back out to open sea. The Emperor began another game of chess. There were no fish to be seen, and the trade winds, usually so predictable at this latitude, were blowing from the wrong direction, making progress slow. It was an ill omen, the sailors declared. No good would come of it.

11

In the library of the Museum of Comparative Anatomy, my days disappeared into the minute tangles of Cuvier's handwriting, which I copied out, page after page, or into the delicately inked lines that traced the plumage of birds, wing after wing and beak after beak.

After a week, once I had adjusted to the life of the museum and had come to know the assistants better, I took great pleasure in my work, especially when, after two or three weeks, Cuvier began to gave Sophie Duvaucel special assignments for me, because I was quick and my drawings were accurate. He had said, she told me, that I had a talent for the concise phrase when it came to describing the body parts of birds. It didn't seem like any special kind of talent to me, I told her, and after all, given that she checked my French so carefully, any credit for my success belonged to her. Despite her evident pleasure in my remark, she told me that the Museum of Comparative Anatomy had more than enough sycophants and there were no vacancies for any more.

We were only, of course, a small part of the production line of Cuvier's ambitious cataloguing and taxonomy project, *Le Règne animal.* We were only the illustrators and the scribes. Behind us a web of adventurers and field naturalists and missionaries and explorers stretched out to every corner of the world. On the front line, in the wet heat of the jungles of Sumatra or Madagascar or the East Indies or in the scrubland of New South Wales, Cuvier's field assistants were hunting, shooting, and stuffing every new species they could find.

Missionaries and civil servants, diplomats and ambassadors sent Cuvier stuffed birds from every port in the world. The specimens came in by the boatload every few weeks, delivered to the Jardin gates by barges carrying crates of labeled boxes. The birds were of every color and shape imaginable, and each arrived with carefully recorded details of where it had been found and the contents of its stomach, and usually an anatomical drawing.

Cuvier's praise of my work sometimes made things difficult for me with the other assistants. They said I was climbing the ladder more quickly than was fair. But when the pressure rose in the weeks leading up to the Dutch ambassador's expected arrival in Paris — Ambassador Brugmans, they said, was going to take a large number of the stuffed birds and skeletons we were working with back to Holland — we all benefited from any special accuracy or efficiency, as Cuvier's temper and impatience increased by the day.

From time to time Mme. Cuvier appeared in the library with her eleven-year-old daughter, Clementine, who liked to watch us or to sit and draw the stuffed birds lined up near the window. Clementine was a pious, even austere, child, dressed always in black, an enthusiastic member of the Ladies' Bible Society and, with her governess, a regular visitor at the Hospital for Aged Women. She was already a talented anatomical illustrator and scribe. Her father had seen to that.

Mme. Cuvier had had a difficult time of it, the other assistants said. She was already a widow when Cuvier married her in 1803. Her husband, General Duvaucel, had been sent to the guillotine, leaving her with four children and no money. And of the four children Cuvier himself had then fathered after their marriage, all of them except Clementine had died. The first, a boy, died a few days after he was born. A second, George, had died at the age of seven in 1813, and Anne had died in 1814, at the age of four. One of the Duvaucel boys had died too, caught in the cross fire when the French army had retreated from Portugal in 1809. So Mme. Cuvier had buried four of her eight children, and Cuvier still had no natural male heir, and male heirs were important among the dynasties of the Jardin.

There was, therefore, an air of protracted and strained mourning about the place. The work we did was mostly carried out in complete silence, following Cuvier's instructions, except for the days on which both Cuvier and Clementine were absent from the building; then Sophie Duvaucel allowed us, even encouraged us, to talk while we worked. Sometimes she would even sing. Just for the sake of it, she said. Just to break the silence. I admired her energy. No one else could have kept us working for such long hours.

The assistants imitated Cuvier's pronounced German accent, and behind his back they called him Herr Kufer, for, German by birth, he'd been christened not

Georges Cuvier but Johan Kufer, the German word for "cooper," a maker of barrels, buckets, and vats. Achille told me to keep quiet about that, since Cuvier didn't like people to know. Apparently, it was when the young Johan Kufer, promising student at the university in Stuttgart, was appointed tutor to the twelve-year-old grandson of the Marquis d'Héricy in Normandy, that he had renamed himself Georges Cuvier in order to fit in to provincial French society.

Sometimes I even heard Sophie calling him Herr Kufer under her breath, usually when he was at his most despotic. She was very respectful, but I don't believe she much liked her stepfather, although she admired him; sometimes she would raise an eyebrow just a little when Cuvier began the stories about his life that he so loved to tell his protégés. Those stories rather paled in repetition, and Cuvier always talked about his life as though he was dictating his memoirs.

In Normandy — Cuvier's sycophantic secretary, Charles Laurillard, never tired of telling this story — Cuvier had been discovered by the brilliant local surgeon, Antoine Tessier, a Parisian abbot living in disguise in the countryside to escape the guillotine. Tessier, the story went, was so impressed by the young tutor's extraordinary knowledge of natural history that he wrote excitedly to his friends in the Jardin des Plantes: "I have just found a pearl in the dunghill of Normandy." Cuvier was summoned to Paris and appointed assistant professor at the Jardin.

And then there was Joseph Deleuze — old man Deleuze we called him — eccentric and obsessive, who joined us in mid-September in order to speed up the production of the bird volume ahead of Brugmans's arrival. Deleuze had lived in the Jardin, in lodgings next to the museum, for twenty years. He led a kind of double life. In the Jardin he was a senior botanist who classified, catalogued, and illustrated plants. But outside the Jardin he was the president of the Magnetic Society and the author of *A Critical History of Animal Magnetism,* volume 1, which, he told me with pride, was enjoying some success in the expanding world of Parisian animal magnetists.

"Not enough of you young men take magnetism seriously," he said when I smiled at the idea of a Magnetic Society. "You have closed minds. I was young when I saw my first magnetism, and like you, I was a skeptic. But there's nothing occult about it. If we learn to harness magnetism properly, it will revolutionize medicine. You must come along to one of our meetings on the rue Rivoli. Or perhaps you would like to borrow some of the society journals?"

I liked old man Deleuze. However much he proselytized about magnetism, he knew everything there was to know about the Jardin.

Meanwhile, after several weeks in which Jagot's man had not appeared, Lucienne was becoming increasingly reckless. Certain that the success of her disguise was the reason Jagot had called off the surveillance, she continued to dress as a man outside the atelier, but she walked in daylight down the streets with me, and even came to meet me at the Jardin.

As Lucienne's recklessness increased, so did my sense of foreboding. For me, Jagot's absence was considerably more troublesome than his presence. I didn't know what it meant and he still had my passport in his office. Although I knew I should petition for its return, I did not want a further conversation with the man. I resolved I would not need the passport until I left Paris, and I had no immediate intention of doing that.

Despite my protestations about her safety, Lucienne and I took a boat to the Jardin des Plantes on one of my rare holidays from the museum. It was a fine early-September morning. Our waterman picked his way among barges, colliers, and small trading boats, looking over his shoulder every few minutes to avoid rusty chain cables, floating wood, and buoys. Brown-green water slapped along the side of the stone quais and reflected river light played across brick walls and the underside of the arched metal bridges, where pigeons sat in rows.

"What happens next?" Lucienne asked the waterman.

"Pardon, *citoyen?*"

"Now that the emperor is gone?"

"I can tell you one thing, monsieur, for free: The new king will never do what the emperor did for Paris. Look at all the bridges, slaughterhouses, covered markets, the Canal de l'Ourcq, the covered passageways along the Right Bank. Paris needs him back." Others in the boat nodded their agreement. A woman moved her child onto her lap, pulling her cloak about them both. *"Vive l'empereur,"* she said.

Walls and trees and the hulls of boats seemed to disappear below the scum and oil of the water's surface. We sailed past the yards of boatbuilders and ship breakers, rusty anchors sticking up out of the mud, we heard the sounds of hammers against metal saws and clashing engines; watermen shouted to each other over the bulwarks. Gradually the gates of the Jardin came into view.

"Hanz and Marguerite, they called them," she said, when we had disembarked and were standing among the tourists looking down the long garden to the natural-history museum. "Hanz and Marguerite, yes. The elephants they brought from the Netherlands, from the stadtholder's menagerie."

"I think they're dead now," I said.

"That's sad," she said. "They were famous all over France. You had to line up to see them. The keepers brought in musicians from the Conservatoire de musique to play to them and persuade them to mate."

Lucienne handed a few coins to the man in the kiosk at the entrance to the menagerie, and we walked through the turnstile. At the top of a series of stone steps, men, women, and children were gathered around the bear pit, leaning forward over the railings to watch a brown bear climbing a tree trunk. Three other bears paced on the stone flagging below, swaying slightly.

To our left a crowd collected outside a large round building surrounded by a railed enclosure. Behind the black shiny hats and parasols a large gray mass moved back and forth, its elephant trunk reaching toward the crowd, who clapped and roared each time it swung in their direction. For a second I caught a glimpse of a large wet eye.

"It's all so tight," she said as we squeezed past a group of Englishwomen standing by the flower borders taking notes for their gardeners. "This place. *C'est un jardin militaire.* Everything grows in straight lines. Everything is trained, and clipped. It makes me think of corsets and whalebone."

"Surely a garden has to be managed," I said. "Or everything goes to seed."

"My grandmother had a garden in Marseilles . . . ," she began. "I spent my summers there."

As she talked, one garden opened up inside another. She spoke of peacocks and hares, a grotto lined with shells, and borders full of hybrids and flowers allowed to throw their seeds wherever they wanted. And inside the house, she said, her grandmother's collection of shells, fossils, and corals filled most of the downstairs rooms so that there was never anywhere to sit.

"My grandmother let me take the corals from the drawers on special days, then, while I arranged them in patterns on the blue velvet cloth, she would tell me where each of them came from, and she would show me on her map and talk to me about the sea and all the undiscovered creatures that lived there. She told me that when the ships' captains talked about seeing mermaids and mermen, they were really describing a race of humans that hadn't yet found their way onto land. They didn't need to, she said, because they had everything they needed under the sea."

Lucienne talked as if she was dreaming. I imagined a dark-skinned child running through large shuttered rooms, sleeping among giant snuffboxes and bones and ammonites, chasing peacocks.

During the Revolution, her grandmother's collection was requisitioned for the republic, she told me, for the enlightenment of the French people. Cuvier had made a list of the important natural-history collections in the great houses of France and handed it to Napoleon, who in turn had handed it to his generals.

"My grandmother's collection was only one of hundreds on Cuvier's list," she said. "When I went back to Marseilles after the first years of the Revolution, everything was gone; the soldiers had killed all the peacocks and the animals in the menagerie; they'd walked over my grandmother's gardens and dug up her botanical collection. Inside the house, all the drawers and cabinets were empty except for a few shells and fragments of broken pottery. All the paintings had gone . . ."

"And your family?" I hardly dared ask. I knew something of what had happened to wealthy families such as Lucienne's. Even out on their provincial estates the rich were not safe from the fury of the people. Cuvier might have made a list of notable natural-history collections, I told myself, but he wasn't responsible for that fury or for what the French soldiers might have done in the name of the republic.

"It was 1794," she continued. "I came to Paris to find them — my parents and my grandmother. I was your age. I saw things no one should ever see. People called it *la Terroir.* The Terror. Robespierre called it *la Justice.* He thought he was doing the right thing for France. Purifying his country. Imagine that. Thousands of people dead in just a few weeks. It wasn't justice. It was a massacre."

"The guillotine."

"Yes, there was the guillotine, but what happened in the streets was worse — people with pickaxes, kitchen knives, scythes. I saw

one woman and a child cut to pieces limb
by limb . . . trying to crawl to each other. I
still see them in my dreams."

"Enough to send someone mad," I said. "I don't know how you stop remembering things like that."

"You don't," she said. "It just keeps on coming back."

We were climbing up through the labyrinth now, taking paths to the right and left through low hedges. Ahead, I could see the golden pavilion and the dark horizontal branches of the cedar where birds sang.

I was still trying to understand how Lucienne Bernard had come to be, how the child of slaughtered aristocrats had become the philosopher-thief. I was looking for causes and effects and straight lines; instead there were only loops and spirals and tangles.

Below us the Jardin stretched away in avenues of lime trees flanked by neatly bordered rows of flowers and small shrubs. Beyond the garden the Seine made a horizontal line of blue before the city rose again, all spires and domes and towers, on the north bank.

"I wish we were inside," I said. "I wish we were in your bed. I can't stop thinking about you. Do you know how much I think about you?"

"Yes," she said, smiling. "Yes, I know that. I remember how that feels."

"I don't want you to *remember* it," I said.

"I want you to feel exactly as I do."

"I'm twenty years older than you," she said. "It doesn't feel the same. It doesn't hurt so much. It's better. Softer." She seemed distracted, as though she was trying to recall something.

"What are you thinking about?" I asked, seeing her blush.

"When I was in Egypt, there was a man, a trader in corals, who taught me how to dive in the Red Sea. He was a friend of the Bedouins. He traded with them."

"You swam in the Red Sea with him?" I asked before I could find a way of saying it differently. She turned to look at me, her head tilted a little, and smiled.

"Yes, there were many of us, the Bedouin men and the local divers who taught us how to reach the corals. Are you jealous?"

"I don't know," I said, embarrassed. "I think I am more jealous of you — of your life — of everything you have done, the places you have been. And yes, I am jealous of that man, the Portuguese man."

"Davide, yes," she said, her face darkening. "I've been looking for him. But everyone is in hiding in Paris. Nothing is where it used to be. I was hoping Saint-Vincent might know where he is. But he doesn't."

"Silveira," I said slowly.

"Yes," she said. "Davide Silveira. The man I traveled with in Egypt. Do you listen at all? You are always daydreaming."

Silveira. This was the man Jagot called *Trompe-la-Mort*. The man who defied death. I did not like the sound of him.

"How long have you known him?" I asked.

"Since Egypt. That's seventeen years now. A long time. You know, Daniel," she said, changing the subject, "your questions are like the heads of the Hydra — cut off one and another grows in its place. You will kill me with your questions. It's a good thing I am leaving Paris."

"No, it isn't," I said. "Look, Lucienne, surely if it is a case of mistaken identity, you could go to Jagot and explain it; you could prove he has made a mistake. And then you would be free to come and go in Paris as you wish."

"Lucienne Bernard is an exile and an émigrée — there is no reparation for her."

"Other émigrés are being given reparation. Wellington is bringing in new laws."

We sat there for a long time looking down over the Jardin until she said: "There are no mistaken identities, Daniel, and there is no putting things right or being free. Not anymore. Not for me. I steal. I stole. *We* steal things . . . You understand? It's what

213

we do — Manon, Saint-Vincent, and I, and sometimes others when we need them. It's what we've done for twenty years. It has paid for everything — Saint-Vincent's botany and his expeditions, my work on corals, my book, microscopes, library, the house in Italy. After the Revolution, the émigrés paid us to take things back from the museums and libraries and galleries. We were good. We made a lot of money. But we stopped six years ago when things went wrong. We all left Paris and tried to start our lives again in different places. But Jagot, there was no stopping him. If his man hadn't died, perhaps, things might have been different."

In the silence that followed, we watched a heron fly slowly across the Jardin, disappearing into the wide branches of the cedar. Now I also understood the presence of the antique dueling pistol I had come across in the atelier only days before. It had been recently cleaned and loaded.

12

Time was suspended in Paris. Rumors circulated. Wellington was afraid, Fin said, that moving the horses would be too much for the French people, that the horses had become a symbol. But the Venetian ambassadors were still in Paris and pressing hard for their return. They said Wellington was waiting until he had enough soldiers. Everywhere — on the bridges, on the columns, in the palaces — workmen were chiseling Napoleon's initials from newly laid stone.

At ten o'clock each night the lamp carriers began to fan out across the city, hailing the fiacres, caterwauling, accompanying late-night walkers through the city to their front doors, looking for more trade. Oil lamps with their swinging circles of light were passing away, Céleste said; they belonged to the old century. So did the lamp carriers and the oil merchants and the sellers of the Artraud lamps; the engineer Philippe Lebon was already lighting his Paris house and garden with gas — he had vowed to light all of Paris this way. Soon there would be no more shadows in the city. Soon there would be no more night in Paris.

M. Lebon is in league with the enemies of France, the lamplighters, lamp carriers, and oil merchants whispered to anyone who would listen. All Paris will explode. And if they can't blow us up, they will choke us with their fumes and black smoke.

One night, as we sat on Lucienne's roof, in a gully between two gables, looking down over the city, I asked Lucienne about the embalmed animals Geoffroy had brought back from Egypt. There were rumors, I said, that Cuvier stored six of them in the cellars of his museum. It was a clear night — bright stars flecked a blue-black arch of sky and even at midnight the roof tiles were still warm from the September sun. I sat behind her, my arms around her while she smoked a cigar. I kissed her neck.

"So," she said and laughed. She blew a single smoke ring into the night air, gray on black. "Cuvier has the mummified animals now, does he? They belong to Geoffroy. They've caused a lot of trouble in the Jardin. You know, when I worked with Geoffroy in Egypt, he used to be just like you — always asking questions, one after another. Now he says very little."

"Where did they come from?"

"An Egyptian trader took us to the Well of Birds," she said, "just a few weeks after we arrived. In the middle of fields of melons and lettuces, piles of rubbish and old stones — all that's left of the ancient city of Memphis — there is an entrance to an underground temple called the Well of Birds. You climb down by rope — it's the only way in. Under the ground there are labyrinths and passageways that stretch for miles, all of them lined with thousands of mummified birds inside earthenware jars, like so many bottles of wine. They are sacred birds; each has its own priest and altars. Geoffroy bought ten of them. Then he started buying mummified cattle, cats, crocodiles, and monkeys as well, all of them at least three thousand years old. He wanted to use them to show Cuvier that species had transformed. I warned him — I told him they'd be the same. And of course, when Geoffroy did unwrap them back in Paris in front of Cuvier and all the professors and assistants here they *were* the same. There were no cats with wings or cattle with fins or fish with fur. So Cuvier won again. And of course,

Cuvier mocked Geoffroy for months. He's hardly published anything since."

"So there is some proof," I said, "that Cuvier's right? The mummies were the same then and now. So species haven't transformed." The cat sitting on the roof beside me in Paris was the same as the cat on the roof in Egypt three thousand years ago — four legs, whiskers, a long tail. It was obvious. A cat was a cat was a cat.

"Of course they haven't changed," she said, "not in three thousand years. Lamarck knew that. Animal forms take much longer to change. Three thousand years is nothing. Just a blink of the eye, Lamarck told Cuvier that, but nobody listened."

"And how do you square that with Genesis?"

"What do you mean, 'square it'?"

"Make it . . . fit, add up. Bring one thing in line with another."

"Bring one thing in line with another?" she repeated. "I don't need to. Science isn't about making things fit with the Bible. Genesis was written two thousand years ago by men who didn't know what we know. They weren't trying to explain how the world began, not scientifically. It's a creation story. A good one. But there are others. In Egypt they say air and water, darkness and eternity joined to form a blue lotus called Ra. In Syria they say —"

"So the Bible's not true. Are you saying that?" I could see the pulse beating in her neck. I watched it quicken.

"It's always a battle with the Bible." She sighed. "It shouldn't be. But Lamarck's ideas about transformism keep spreading across Europe whatever Cuvier says or does, no matter how much he insists that all species are fixed and unchanging. No matter how many times he insists there's no proof of transformism. All the students who sit at his lectures, they go back to Hungary or Brazil or Russia and they talk."

"How long have you been thinking about all of this?" I asked.

"Me? Thousands of years. It is the only interesting thing to think about. In my grandmother's library, I read Buffon. Then Aristotle and De Maillet's book *Telliamed*. . . . Later, when I came to Paris, I signed up for Lamarck's lectures. That was when he first started talking about transformism — 1802, 1803, I think. It was exciting — everyone was speculating about how life began. Everything seemed possible. When Daubenton gave his lecture and announced that the lion could no longer be called the king of beasts because there were

219

no kings in nature, the crowd cheered. You could say anything then. Think anything. Not anymore."

Professor Lamarck, now seventy-one — the anatomy students called him "the Old One," *el Viejo* — kept to himself in his house in the Jardin des Plantes, where he lived with his third wife and four of his grown children: three unmarried daughters, Rosalie, Cornélie, and Eugénie, and a deaf son, Antoine, who was also a painter. Little Aristide, Lamarck's youngest son, had been sent away to the Charenton asylum, six miles southeast of Paris. They called him "the *Aliené,*" the lost one. Other than melancholy Aristide, only two of Lamarck's children had escaped the crowded house in the Jardin: Auguste was now an important engineer in Paris; André had joined the navy during the Revolution and was stationed out in the Caribbean.

Cuvier and his protégés sneered at Lamarck; they praised his taxonomic work while ignoring or ridiculing his transformist ideas. But while Cuvier may have called Lamarck a dreamer and a poet, Lamarck had a large and loyal following among the anatomy students. He'd been awarded a medal for bravery in the Seven Years' War, he'd told Ramon, when he was a soldier back in the 1760s. He wasn't going to give up what he believed, not easily. He knew how to manage a battlefield.

"In Edinburgh no one talks about these things," I told Lucienne. "Or at least not in public. Sometimes in the student societies, when the professors are not around, someone will talk about transmutation, one of the students who has been here to study, but —"

"It will be the same again in Paris in a year or two," she said. "Geoffroy is almost blind. Lamarck is old and his eyes are beginning to fail. Cuvier is winning his battles and closing down the conversation. Now the king is back, hiding behind Wellington's soldiers. It is not a good time to be in Paris. You should have been here ten, twelve years ago. Not now."

I thought of what awaited me back home — the gray landscape, my father's disapproval, and my brother's blind faith.

"I am glad I'm here now," I said. "I only want to be here now."

Fin and Céleste teased me relentlessly about the widow Rochefide, whom they had never seen. Fin often complained that he did not see enough of me either and lamented the loss of our drinking days. He suggested that

I ask the widow to join us for dinner, and one night when the excuses I gave on her behalf had grown particularly thin, I simply shrugged and said, "There is nothing I can do. I have no control over her comings and goings. What can I say?"

"I sympathize, my friend," Fin said, looking over at Céleste with an exaggerated expression of adoration. "Do I have any control over Céleste? She is my master. I am her slave. What is to be done with these women? We will have to go back and marry British women, you know, if we are to have any control over our destiny."

"Tell me when you are ready, M. Robertson," Céleste said, "and I will buy a ticket for you and a wedding present for your new wife. Then I might find a man for my bed who does not snore . . . Perhaps Mme. Rochefide thinks she is too good for us," she added. "Perhaps she is too grand to mix with shopgirls and students."

"Don't be ridiculous," I said. "She's not like that."

They never did guess that the tall man in the green silk jacket whom they glimpsed me walking with from time to time and whom I called M. Le Vaillant, the botanist, was actually the elusive Mme. Rochefide, nor would they have believed any of the rest

of the story that I had begun to unravel —
the beguiling tale that twisted out from a
garden in Marseilles through prisons and
guillotines to the pyramids of Egypt and the
caves of the Red Sea.

In mid-September a rainstorm began out in the Atlantic and continued for several days. The HMS *Northumberland,* accompanied by a squadron of ships, was sailing away from Madeira toward the equator through the storm, taking a route calculated by the admiral to avoid the contending trade winds that were so variable at the equator itself. On board, the Emperor played cards with his generals under the supervision of his British guards. He complained of the treachery of Ney and of the stupidity of the American government; he called the king of Spain a fool, the emperor of Russia weak; he had praise only for Wellington. Wellington had had luck on his side, he said. "I should have died at Moscow," he lamented, revealing his hand, "for there my glory ended."

Despite the rain, the Emperor would not forgo his evening walk on deck. Those one-hour walks with his two generals in torrential rain meant that the famous gray greatcoat, hanging in the cabin on its coat stand, never entirely dried out. Steam from the clothes created beads of condensation on all the windows. Napoleon talked to Las Cases of September in Paris and the roses he had brought back for Josephine from all across Europe that would now be flowering in the garden at Malmaison. I would exchange one hundred days on this infernal ship for a single hour walking in Paris at dusk, he said.

In a small damp cabin at the other end of the ship, Countess Bertrand and Countess Montholon, with the help of a single nursemaid, tried to keep their four small children entertained: three-year-old Tristan Montholon and the three small Bertrand children, Henri, Hortense, and Napoleon. These wives of Napoleon's exiled generals had thought, when they had agreed to accompany their husbands into exile with the Emperor, that it would mean adjusting to life on a small estate in England. Neither had imagined a rock in the ocean, the island that Napoleon continuously referred to as the Siberian wasteland of the Atlantic.

When the British statesman had announced their destination all those weeks ago, in a letter from the British government read out in the captain's quarters of the *Bellerophon*, Mme. Bertrand had tried to throw herself overboard. Now the Emperor barely spoke to her. He had no time, he said, for complaining women.

13

On September 23, the English and French papers were full of the news of Talleyrand's resignation and its consequences. Talleyrand, the great French statesman and Napoleon's right-hand man, was a chameleon, one English journalist wrote, changing his skin, his clothes, his colors, to fit the politics of the day. He'd kept power through three regimes: under the king, then through the Revolution, then under Napoleon, and now he had even brokered the restoration of the king and the return of France to its pre-revolutionary borders. First a priest, then the king's bishop, revolutionary, exile, foreign minister, grand chamberlain, a prince under Napoleon, now king maker, Talleyrand was a man in constant transformation. But even he had to go. Some said the time of chameleons and turncoats was over. But it wasn't. Not yet.

I was with Lucienne when the bronze

horses came down three days later. Sophie had, at my request, invented a false errand that released me from the Jardin for a whole day without incurring Cuvier's disapproval. Now we were caught up in the crowd, all swarming in one direction — toward the place du Carrousel merging into a many-headed, many-limbed tide. We were jostled, pushed, elbowed, knocked about, carried forward. I reached for Lucienne's hand, afraid for her, but she wouldn't give it. "I can look after myself," she shouted in English as she disappeared into the mass of bodies, still dressed as a man, in a tailored brown velvet coat that had seen better days, white breeches, and high boots.

The crowd stopped abruptly where the street met the entrance to the square blocked by a line of standing Prussian soldiers, like a wave breaking against a harbor wall. Beyond them, a mass of men dressed in pale-blue-and-white uniforms, a thousand foot soldiers of the Austrian army, sat or lay on the stones of the square, blocking access to the Arc.

"We can't get through," Lucienne called out, catching up to me. "They're not letting anyone past. We can't see it from here."

I pushed my way through the crowd, and Lucienne followed me, until I reached the first mounted Austrian officer. As quietly as I dared, I asked permission to pass. Hearing my English voice, the officer gestured to me to join a group of foreigners gathered under a cluster of parasols.

"Why so many soldiers?" I shouted to her. "What's Wellington doing?"

"It's to keep out the Parisians. They've shut up the palace to protect the king. Look." She pointed in the direction of the palace, where all the shutters were closed. "What kind of king is too frightened to face his own people and has to be protected by the Allied army?"

In the Grand Gallery of the Louvre, people pressed up against the windows, pointing, gesticulating. Journalists from the world's newspapers also stood in front of us in the square, their artists assembled with easels. This was a political performance. Here was proof that Napoleon was not returning. Show the French people. Pull down the horses, the chariot. The Emperor Napoleon is no more.

Shielding my eyes from the sun, I could see the first of the four horses moving slightly as more ties were unfastened. The crowd, gathered around the perimeter of the square, groaned or gasped, I couldn't tell which, and began to point. The bronze horse swung into the air, high above the square. My head swam. I felt a rush of blood, the sense of flight and fall, people pressing in from every side; I watched pins of lights come on across my vision and then go out. I fainted.

When I came to, a crowd had gathered. I looked up to see heads silhouetted against a bright white sky. Lucienne had disappeared, and a man with a voice I recognized was making the crowd disperse.

"Ah, M. Connor," Jagot said. "You should be more careful in this sun. You need a hat."

"Yes," I mumbled, allowing him to help me to my feet. "The sun is hotter than I had realized."

"I am glad to see you again, M. Connor," he said, waving away the last onlookers. "It has been a long time since we last met — a month perhaps. Paris has been good to you, I think."

"Yes, it has, thank you," I said, relieved that Lucienne had gotten away.

"My men tell me you are now working in the Jardin," he said, "and that your things — the papers, the corals, and the bones — they have come back to you. It is most unusual, you see, for stolen things to come back in such a way. There is usually a story behind such things. Is there a story, M. Connor?"

"There is no story," I said quickly, wondering what else Jagot's men might have told him, what else they might have seen. "It was just a mistake," I said. "It wasn't a theft at all. My travel bag had been taken by another passenger — a man — not by the woman I described to you. He, the other passenger, tracked me down and returned my things. All of them." My hands had begun to shake. I put them in my pockets.

"Good. That is good news, monsieur. So you must come and give me the name and the address of the passenger who took your bag by mistake, the man who returned your things, because that person might be able to tell me something about the woman you described seeing on the mail coach, the savant, Lucienne Bernard. I will send a man to your lodgings to take details. Perhaps I will even come myself. Good afternoon, M. Connor. Remember, you must buy a hat for this sun. *À bientôt.*"

He slipped away into the crowd.

I walked to the Turkish café on the rue de la Victoire where Lucienne and I had agreed to meet if we became separated in the crowd. But though I waited for two hours, she didn't come. Instead I heard the clatter of wheels approaching. A number of carts flanked by Prussian cavalry and infantry made their way slowly over the cobbles. For all the world it looked as if they were coming for me. The four horses, each in a separate cart, lying on its side on a straw base, bronzed hooves pawing the air, passed alongside me, so close that I could see into their eyes — eyes that had looked down on Rome, Constantinople, and Venice, for hundreds of years. For them I was nothing, of no significance.

Now I wondered if Jagot's apparent disappearance for almost a month had been engineered to make me — us — feel complacent. The stakes were high. I thought of what Manon had said about Coignard's body being found in the Seine with no hands or feet. Jagot had been following Coignard that day in the fiacre; Manon had said that Coignard's tortured body had been thrown into the Seine as a warning to others on Jagot's list. How much more proof did I need of the danger we were all in?

Whatever I had chosen to believe, Jagot was not a man to abandon his prey. He was just taking his time. For a month I had been distracted, enraptured by Lucienne and by my work at the Jardin. But that was no justification for failing to protect her. While I had been blinded, Jagot's men had continued to watch and to file their reports. The net was closing in.

I had to get Lucienne out of Paris.

For Professor Cuvier, pacing in his studio in the museum, the hands of the clocks seemed to be moving faster than usual. A Dutch professor of medicine and chemistry and the rector of the University of Leiden, M. Sebald Justinus Brugmans, was on the road to Paris, sent on ambassadorial duties by the newly reinstated stadtholder of Holland. Somewhere on the outskirts of Belgium, Brugmans had stopped to see the battlefield of Waterloo, and in his bed in the inn on the road from Waterloo to Paris, he was reading through his notes, preparing for his meeting with Wellington.

Brugmans had been sent to Paris to reclaim the world-famous collection of the Dutch stadtholder, requisitioned by Napoleon when he captured Holland. It had been transported in 222 cases carried on 103 wagons, then shipped by barge from The Hague along the North Sea coast and down the Seine into Paris. The cases were filled with rare books, specimens, scientific instruments, rocks, and the complete skeletons of a fifteen-foot giraffe, an orangutan, and a hippopotamus.

These specimens — thousands of rare fossils, minerals, bones, shells, and crystals — now filled the shelves of the museums of the Jardin. The stadtholders' collection was now Cuvier's collection. Brugmans was coming to Paris for restitution. He was patient; as a young man he had written a dissertation on the effect of rain on plants, and he had spent long hours tapping the barometer and waiting for rain. That experience would stand him in good stead for the waiting game he was to play in Paris in 1815.

In his house in the Jardin, the Baron Cuvier, sleepless, in a purple robe, paced his studio trying to think of what terms he could offer Brugmans, trying to think of ways to persuade the Dutch professor and Wellington that those objects must stay in the Jardin. Without those thousands of objects from the stadholders' collection, the Museum of Comparative Anatomy, he would say — indeed all the museums of the Jardin — would be nothing. What he knew all too well was that without the stadtholders' collection Cuvier would be nothing.

In his house on the quai Voltaire, the director of the Louvre, Dominique-Vivant

Denon, the man they called "Napoleon's eye," the man who had personally drawn up the list of artifacts to be taken from the great museums and galleries of Europe, was overseeing his men, who in some haste were packing up a series of valuable paintings and objects. Time was running out for Denon. That day Wellington had asked him to account for a series of objects listed as stolen that were still unaccounted for — unaccounted for because Denon had made them disappear from the Louvre into his own cellar: a Caravaggio painting, Egyptian artifacts, a Titian drawing, and a sixteenth-century cabinet of curiosities called the Montserrat Cabinet. And now that Wellington was coming to the quai Voltaire, these objects needed to disappear even deeper into Paris. Completely beyond sight. But Denon had a plan.

14

"Delphine has asked to see you, M. Connor," Lucienne said the following morning, a Sunday, when I finally woke and went to find her writing at the table among the corals, in her blue silk dressing gown. "She writes to thank you for the figurine of Napoleon you sent her last week. She says it is a good likeness but a little too stout. Would you like to visit her with me? If you have time — that is, unless you would like to sleep some more."

"Of . . . of course," I stuttered. This was the day I had resolved to urge her departure. Although I had tried several times the night before, she had changed the subject, and now I was wary of telling her about the conversations I had had with Jagot — the accusations and the threats. "Yes, of course I'd like to go," I said. "But I wish you'd warned me. I was thinking about one of those little wooden boats they sell in the

Luxembourg Gardens. I was going to buy one and ask you to take it to her."

"She'd prefer some accurate news of Napoleon to one of your boats, I think," Lucienne said, pulling on her shirt and trousers. "What the nuns tell Delphine about the Emperor is always distorted by rumor. Manon took her a map and some pins so that she can trace where he is on his journey. She has that on her wall. I must remind her to pack it into her luggage."

"Lucienne," I began. "You must be especially careful. I think Jagot may be closer than you think." It was too vague, but it was a start.

"Jagot won't move yet," she said. "He can't. He's waiting. Manon is going to take Delphine back to Italy, and I will follow next week. I have my ticket. But there are a few things I have to finish in Paris first. Newspapers," she said. "Remind me to buy some newspapers so I can tell Delphine about the Emperor's journey. The ship crossed the equator, they say, two or three days ago. He's unlikely to be rescued now. But I can't tell Delphine that. She is convinced the Americans will capture the *Northumberland* and crown him Emperor of America."

Lucienne was wrapping a long, narrow object in brown paper and tying it with string. "I have an errand to run," she said. "And I want to show you a new place that won't be in your guidebook." Although I knew she had to go, I could hardly meet her eye.

A few moments later she said, "It's a week, Daniel. A whole week more. Please don't look so dejected. I have already stayed a month longer than I had planned to. Seeing Jagot yesterday, like that in the crowd. So close. That worried me."

"But shouldn't you go immediately?" I asked, relieved that I might not need to tell her about my conversations at all. "He is so close. He could find you at any moment. Look what happened to Coignard."

"A week," she said. "I need a week. Manon is already packed. I know what I'm doing."

The air was cool by the river, the trees beginning to lose their leaves after the heat of the summer months; in the wind the leaves, browned, curled, and desiccated, scurried along the pavement, hissing, scraping — the sound of winter approaching. In a strange way it reminded me of home, of the autumn landscapes of Derbyshire. The Daniel who had walked those hills with his notebook and geological hammer seemed a stranger to me now. That Daniel could never have imagined what it was to be so tangled up with love and anticipated loss.

Lucienne, dressed in a long green velvet jacket with a high collar and white cravat, sand-colored breeches, and boots, walked fast, striding as if she owned everything, as if all these streets and that great swollen river and all the boats on it were hers.

She was leading me north, away from the river at the quai de la Rapée. We twisted and turned, following side streets, weaving in and out, around construction sites and piles of rubbish, past the frames of half-made buildings. In one place an entire street had been pulled down, leaving the sides of houses shored up with wood and metal girders, like a theatrical set. Workmen were lifting up cobblestones at one end of the street, masons laying them again in another. Here and there I saw FOR SALE signs, in English. We might have been walking in London, I thought, for there were as many English voices as French ones.

A building craze had started in Paris. All the quarries were exhausted, and new ones had to be opened up on the outskirts of the city. There were new houses everywhere; whole neighborhoods grew up overnight. Anyone with any money was buying up the old buildings or investing in plans for shopping arcades or new residential districts. Paris would not stand still. No one would have known there was an economic crisis that year.

Lucienne finally stopped at a small sign on the wall of a house in the rue de Picpus. It read WOMEN OF THE SACRED HEART.

"The nuns run a school here for the children of the poor," Lucienne said. A nun appeared at the door, her eyes lowered, and recognizing Lucienne, she smiled and waved us through. Addressing Lucienne as M. Duplessis, the nun led us through dark, cool corridors to a cobbled courtyard, where she brought us glasses of lemonade and gestured to us to take a seat at the garden table.

A few minutes later, accompanied by one of the younger nuns, Delphine appeared, framed in the stone archway of the door, carrying a single white rose. She was no longer dressed in orange satin but wore the dark and simple convent uniform, her hair plaited into coils on the back of her head. As soon as her eyes adjusted to the sunlight and she saw Lucienne sitting at the other end of the path, she ran toward us; then, a few feet away, she glanced back at the nun who had accompanied her, stopped, curtseyed to Lucienne, and passed her the rose. Lucienne laughed and held out her arms.

The nun smiled to Delphine, who clambered up onto Lucienne's lap and kissed her, burying her head in the nape of her mother's neck.

Lucienne began to unpin the child's hair, uncoiling the braids, and shaking out her curls, while she spoke to her in soft Italian, and passed her the glass of lemonade. Delphine talked as if she would never stop, sometimes to me, sometimes to Lucienne, sometimes to the young nun, who also spoke Italian. I could not follow.

"She complains," Lucienne translated, "that they put her to bed too early. They have chickens here; she has given them all names. She talks about the other children. It's a great novelty to her, all these children to play with. It is good for her, I think. In Italy, she spends too much time with Manon and me and her books. She is too serious. You know, sometimes she sounds more like a woman than a child. They teach her to be a child again. That is good. She wants to stay longer, she says. And of course she wants to know about the Emperor. What do I say? I told her that soon he'll be on his new island, where they have a beautiful garden waiting for him, and chickens. That made her happier."

I fell asleep in the sun under the apple

trees watching mother and daughter playing ninepins. When I awoke, Delphine was standing over me, her face blocking the sun, dropping small leaves onto me, one by one. She laughed to see me wake and clapped her hands, spinning around and around so that her hair and her clothes billowed out until, dizzy, she fell over. For a moment I could imagine something of what it must be like to be the parent of a child — to feel that exquisite tenderness always shadowed by fear.

At a word from her mother, Delphine stood up, smoothed down her dress, and then addressed me in Italian, very properly, holding out a small white hand.

"She says she is glad to know you," Lucienne translated again, "that she hopes you will call again and that next visit you will have time to see her chickens. You see, she sounds like a little woman."

Delphine embraced her mother, picked up the ribbons and pins that had been scattered across the table, and ran back inside for her afternoon sleep, the nun following. She stood under the arch to wave at us, then disappeared into the cool passageways of the convent.

"Now that you have met Delphine, properly," Lucienne said, "I have something else to show you. Another important person. Part of my sad history. Part of the sad history of Paris too, the part no one wants to remember."

At the far end of the courtyard another gate led through into the bright sunshine of a long rectangular garden. It was a modest convent garden, nearly empty but for a few late white roses blooming between lines of yew and lime trees. No lavish displays of summer flowers. There were no arbors or follies, no fountains.

We turned through a second gateway into a plot of land that had been walled off from the rest of the garden. There were three or four new tombs and gravestones, with tended grass in between and a few trees casting shade. It was not like English graveyards, full of ivy and wildflowers, crumbling headstones covered with every color of lichen. This was austere and manicured. It was too open to the sky, I thought, too seared by the sun.

"They closed all the religious houses during the Revolution," Lucienne said. "A doctor bought this one and turned it into a private asylum. They brought the mad people here. The ones who were rich enough."

Of course. The traumatized mad. The walking dead. I imagined women in white dresses milling around us like sleepwalkers, or the bandaged walking under parasols in the garden, in the shade of trees. A man with a long gray beard rocking backward and forward in a striped deck chair. A woman singing the "Marseillaise" out of key.

"In the summer of 1794," she continued, "while the inmates watched, three workmen made a hole in the wall over there, wide enough for a cart to drive through. They also dug two deep trenches in the corner over there."

There was no sign of the trenches now. Just a few meager headstones over grass that did not seem to want to grow. A red squirrel ran along the top of the wall, stopping and starting; it jerked its head from side to side, sniffing the air, watching us.

"Orders of the Revolutionary Tribunal, Robespierre," she said. "No one told the patients what the trenches were for. The staff knew. The director knew. A few days later three men drove carts piled high with corpses straight from the guillotine in the place du Trône-Renversé. There were more than a thousand bodies. The inmates watched over a wall while the executioner's assistants undressed the bodies, stripping everything from them."

"Why?"

"That is how the assistants were paid . . . They could keep anything of value they found on the bodies. They should have burned them like they do in India."

I thought of the corpses I had read about on the battlefield of Waterloo, stripped of their valuables by English soldiers in the dark, letters taken from pockets, rings from fingers, buttons from jackets — to be sold as souvenirs or pawned in Paris.

"It was hot," she said. "June. They piled the heads on one side, the bodies on the other. The clothes, they went over there — separate piles for the different assistants. The jewels, rings, and coins went into separate baskets. Every now and again one of the assistants was sick."

"How do you know this?"

"I just know. I . . . heard," she said.

I imagined disembodied heads, Medusa and the Gorgon, Judith and Holofernes. The bloodied heads, all sinews and flaps of skin, kept resolving into marble and alabaster in my mind, growing out of size. But the bodies of the guillotined dead must have been supple and rotting. I felt the vulnerability of my own body and wondered what I might have done if, like her, I had lived through such times, seen bodies hacked to pieces in the street, carts piled high with the dead.

"It took them a long time," Lucienne continued. "More than two weeks. They must have hardened to it. The women's bodies . . ."

I imagined Venus de Milo in the monastery garden, her head missing, blood running from her missing arms.

"What are we doing here?" I said. "Can we go? I don't feel well."

Lucienne ignored me.

"They say man is the highest of animals. The smell was so bad here that the men had to build a wooden cover over the trenches with a trapdoor large enough to fit the bodies through. They used pitchforks. I wonder about those men. I wonder what they dream about now."

"The headstones are new," I said, shivering. "Someone hasn't forgotten."

"Amalie Zephyrine," she said. "Princess Amalie Zephyrine von Salm-Kyrburg of Hohenzollern-Sigmaringen. A German princess. Poor Amalie. Both her lover and her brother went to the guillotine, and their bodies were thrown into the trench. Amalie bought this plot of land to make a memorial for her brother. A few tourists come, but it's at the bottom of the tour list, after the visit to the battlefield of Waterloo, the Louvre, the place Louis IV; the catacombs are more interesting, they say, because you can actually see the bones there."

She was following the wall, moving between the new gravestones. I followed. "It's here," she said. "Saint-Vincent said it would be."

She was peering at a large stone plaque on the wall, running her fingers down the lettering. "Amalie has started to trace the names."

She began to read out the names and occupations of the dead, like a kind of incantation: "*cultivateur, domestique, tisserand, instituteur, prêtre, fabriquant d'étoffes, vicaire, contrôleur des douanes, épicier, cabaretier, soldat autrichien prisonnier de guerre, infirmier, garçon meunier . . .* The two de Sombreuils, do you think they were father and son?"

"I don't know," I said, lost in images of blood, the sound of the crowd cheering, hands tied together . . . a day like this, I thought — hot, birds singing. A few years after I was born.

Her fingers traced the carvings of a name. One of hundreds. It read: Lucienne du Luc. 23 ans. Comtesse.

"My name," she said. "That's my name.

Lucienne du Luc. I was a comtesse once. A countess in prison. An enemy of the people. There were thousands of us. They moved us from prison to prison; each building was one step closer to the guillotine. It was like Dante's circles of hell. We played cards. We played cards for hours and hours."

The sun was low now. She lay down on her back on the grass, shielding her eyes with her arm. She clenched her fist. Lucienne Bernard, the infidel-thief, had been a countess. I had easily imagined her as the child of a wealthy and reclusive grandmother, but a countess . . . She would have had servants, carriages, estates, jewels, wardrobes full of silks and satins. Yet here she was sitting on the grass in a graveyard dressed as a man, hiding from a police agent.

I sat down on a tombstone, my head spinning. The warm, sweet smell of crushed grass rose through a swarm of gnats.

"Were you . . . an enemy of the people, I mean?"

"Of course," she said. "We all were. Not just the aristocrats, the dukes and the duchesses, but also the priests and the grocers and the cabaret artists."

"I don't understand," I said. "How did your name come to be listed here?"

"A woman in the prison took my name. She stole it."

"Why would anyone do that?"

"I don't know." She sat up suddenly. "I didn't know her. I had never spoken to her. *Mon Dieu.* Perhaps she was mad. I can see her now. Her red hair all cut off. She stood up and walked toward them when they called my name — as if she was sleepwalking. I stood up too, but when I saw what was happening, I sat down again, very slowly. I've thought about it ever since. The way I sat down again. The way I let her do that."

"So she went to the guillotine and you didn't?"

"Yes. And her body was stripped and thrown into the pit — over there — with the others. Her name was Lucienne Bernard. She wasn't important to the Revolutionary Tribunal, it seems, so I was released from the prison a few months later. Paris gave me a new name. Afterward, those of us who got away . . . we were a new kind of animal." She paused, standing up, and steadied herself against the gravestone. Then she began to unwrap the parcel she had carried with her.

"A promise," she said, by way of explanation. "Another reason I had to come back to Paris one last time."

Inside the paper was a long, thin splinter of green slate on which she had engraved Lucienne Bernard's name and birth date: 1776–1794.

"At least it is *something*," she said, as she pushed the slate into the ground near the wall. "She wanted to die. I know what that feels like, for I did too. But she stood up and I sat down. I might have ended up down there with all the other bones. Instead I was given a life I didn't want. When you have wanted to die as much as I have, it makes you reckless with your life afterward," she said, then stopped. "But now there is Delphine, and I try not to be reckless. It is a resolution I have made." She smiled sadly. "I don't seem to be doing very well."

"Resolutions," I said. "I have resolved to give up resolutions myself. I'm not very good at them either." I kissed her.

"Don't look at me like that," she said. "I'm not upset. I don't need your pity. I wanted you to see this garden, that's all. I wanted you to see it with your own eyes. Everyone should see it. So that we remember just how noble the human species really is."

15

When I knocked at the locksmith's atelier two days later, answering a note she had sent, Lucienne came to the door wearing her workman's trousers, her shirt undone and her feet bare. She seemed tired and her face was swollen. When I looked more closely, I could see that it was also bruised.

"What happened?" I asked, alarmed. "Somebody did this to you, didn't they? Somebody attacked you . . . When . . . where? Was it just one man or several? I'll find them — the cowards."

"In the alleyway, down there, last night. Just one man. But for God's sake, Daniel, I told you before, I don't need rescuing. I can look after myself." She turned away coldly.

At the other end of the workroom, through the frame of the half-open door, a woman and a man sat at a table in conversation, their attention focused on the table itself, where they appeared to be playing cards.

Manon Laforge and Alain Saint-Vincent, surrounded by corals and shells and packing cases. As I stepped into the atelier, Lucienne, seeing the direction of my gaze, walked back toward that room and pulled the door closed.

"What kind of miserable coward would attack a woman in an alleyway?" I asked. "Did he rob you? Did he touch you? Was it . . . ? Was it a man, a boy, tall, short, fat, thin? Did you see his face?"

"Yes, I saw his face."

"Then you must make a report. Someone must find him."

"Make a report? Yes, of course. Go to the police, yes. Daniel, you know I can't do that. Be quiet. I need you to listen."

Through the closed door I could hear the others talking in French; I could hear fragments of speech now and again. Lucienne ran her hand through her hair and looked at me as if she was trying to frame a question. A single strand of hair stuck to her face.

"Everything is good for you again at the Jardin, yes? Cuvier trusts you. You are doing well there." I wasn't sure what frightened me more, the coldness of her manner or the menacing implications of this night attack.

"Yes," I said, lowering my voice. "What is

this, Lucienne? Somebody has attacked you and you won't tell me who or why. And now you want to talk about my work at the museum. You never tell me anything. You don't trust me. You treat me as if I am a boy, as if I am useless. What *am* I to you, Lucienne?"

She didn't answer. She seemed to be struggling with herself, walking up and down the room, about to speak and then not. I opened the front door and walked toward the top of the staircase, looking down through its curves and angles to the floor below. I couldn't do it. I couldn't just leave. I kicked the wall and then turned back.

When I came back in to the room, Lucienne was looking toward the door. I slumped into a low chair in a corner, defeated.

She shrugged. "You think such bad things of me," she said. "You think I have no feelings for you. You are a blind man."

"Yes," I said slowly. "I *am* a blind man. You have made me blind. And I can't leave you. You can't ask me to do that. Please. Whatever has happened . . . however bad things are, let me help. There must be something I can do. But I can't do anything unless you tell me what's happening . . . He might come back."

"There is trouble," she said. "Bad trouble. Like a spider's web. You will get caught in it too and it will get worse. But I can't get out of it. I asked you once to help me, and then I changed my mind. But now I need to ask you again."

She opened a drawer, took out a piece of folded paper, and passed it to me. "I should have left Paris before. I was so stupid."

I began to unfold the paper she had given me.

"It's a map of the Jardin des Plantes," she said. "An old one. It's of no use to me. It doesn't have any of the new buildings on it, the ones they've built in the last five years. I need to know where everyone in the Jardin lives, and I need a detailed map of Cuvier's museum, with all the new exits and entrances, including the cellars. I need the names of all the people who live in the buildings, from the guards to Cuvier's family. I need to know how the locking systems work. Even the feeding times in the menagerie. And I need the information soon, very soon. Three weeks or sooner. The clock is ticking. Do you think you can do that? Is it possible?"

Lucienne's face and posture were utterly impassive now.

"A man came to see me yesterday," she continued, pacing, "someone I used to know, someone I worked with before. He came with a commission — a job — for us. I said no. Saint-Vincent and Manon, they said no. I said to him, we don't do that work anymore. But this time he says we can't choose. And he won't let me leave Paris until we bring him what he wants. He's dangerous."

She gestured to the bruise on her face, the swelling and the cut. I imagined a knife. A blade flashing in the light. Her hands were grazed and cut. She had fought back. It was difficult to imagine she wouldn't. I felt an ache cut through me like a knife. I couldn't protect her and she didn't want me to. And I felt guilty. Deep down, I'd always known she'd have to pay for the time she'd stolen and the risks she'd taken. She'd stayed in Paris for me — or at least partly for me. I could have made her go.

"Yesterday?" I said. "For God's sake, why didn't you send for me?"

"I didn't need you yesterday," she said sharply. "Today I do. I haven't slept, worrying about it, about you. You have everything ahead of you. This will be a big risk. You could lose everything —"

"I don't care about any of that," I said.

"It's my fault this has happened. I persuaded you to stay in Paris. You wouldn't be here now, if —"

"No," she said. "I stayed. You didn't make me. That's not your responsibility. It's mine."

"But why you? There must be other thieves in Paris, professionals like you who can do what this man wants. You can't be the only one."

"Yes, but what he wants is in the Jardin des Plantes, it's in Cuvier's museum. And I know that museum better than any other thief in France. No one knows that building like I do. Or at least I used to. He knows that."

"What can be worth the trouble? Some old bones, a mummy or two? There's nothing there."

"A diamond. One of the biggest in the world. It belongs to Denon, the director of the Louvre. Denon and Cuvier have made a deal. Cuvier is hiding some of Denon's most valuable pieces in the cellar of the museum: a cabinet of curiosities, some paintings Denon won't part with, and some Egyptian artifacts. In return for hiding them, Denon will help Cuvier negotiate with M. Brugmans."

"Cuvier is hiding Denon's stolen collection? That's ridiculous."

"Cuvier's clever — he knows how to get what he wants. He always has. He's a politician. He'll do anything to keep that collection in his museum."

There was some kind of truth in what she said; I had seen Vivant Denon leaving Cuvier's house several times over the last several days, taking the back staircase. I had thought little of it at the time — Cuvier was always receiving some dignitary or other. The picture Lucienne painted of Cuvier's dealings unsettled me. But then I thought of my own ambitions, that relentless acquisitive curiosity; in Cuvier's position, would I have behaved any differently?

"How long do you have?" I asked, finally.

"The end of October. Denon has arranged for his collection to be taken out of the country then. So we have one month only. It's almost impossible. Cuvier knows all of us, and his guards have descriptions. There are more locks in the museum now than there are in almost any bank in the city. I need you to get me in. There's no one else who can do it." She was dressing now, tucking in her shirt, taking the waistcoat from the back of the door and doing up the buttons one by one, arranging her hair and neckerchief carefully in front of the mirror near the window. "You don't know this man, Daniel. If I could find a way out of it, I would. I promised Manon, for the sake of Delphine. I said there would be no more commissions. But this time we cannot choose."

"Delphine?" I said. "Manon was going to take her back to Italy . . ."

"It's too late," she said. "If only Manon had gone yesterday . . . She wanted to, but I'd made a promise to take Delphine to Malmaison to show her Napoleon's house. She wanted to see it before they left . . ." She paused, her eyes full of tears. "Daniel, what if he finds out about her? What if he finds out where Delphine is?"

"He won't," I said. "Not if you do what he tells you to."

I was struggling now, weighing up the risks — an illustrious future lost, perhaps even prison — against what was at stake, thinking not just of Lucienne and her accomplices but of Delphine in the convent garden.

"Just a map?" I asked. "That's all you need from me?"

"Just a map."

"I know someone," I said, thinking. "Joseph Deleuze could draw up a map. He knows the garden and the museum like no one else does. I could try."

"Will he do it quickly?" she asked, turning to look at me. "I can't do anything until I have a map. I don't even know if it's possible to get in there until I've seen it. It must be very detailed, very accurate. Then I can make a plan."

So that was it. Just a map, she said. As if the map was of little consequence. But a few minutes after we had begun to talk about the map and Deleuze, we both knew the threshold had been crossed, and the details of that crossing and what it meant would be determined later.

Why did Daniel Connor take this path rather than the one he was supposed to take, the one he thought he wanted to take, what Rev. Samuels would call the righteous path, the one that went with Cuvier, with hard work, apprenticeship, patronage, the one that would almost certainly lead to success? Why instead did he take the path that led into the muddy and shadowy labyrinths with the heretics and the thieves? You'd have to ask him that. I am no longer that Daniel Connor. That one, that boy, is many Daniels ago. Several lost skins ago.

Desire was there from the beginning. That I remember. But that's an easy explanation for why the boy on the mail coach became the boy of the labyrinths and salons and gambling houses, for how the anatomy student became a thief. A philosopher-thief took me to her bed and talked of time stretching back so far it made my head spin, talked of water moving over mountain ranges over millions and millions of years, drip on drip, small rivulets carving rock; she whispered of colonies of corals creating continents, of the minute skeletons of chalk creatures making cliffs, of seabeds heaving up and slowly pushing fossilized oyster beds to the peaks of mountains hundreds of miles up and away from the sea; she murmured of continents drifting apart and back together again; and she entwined and enraveled mind and body so you stopped knowing where one finished and the other began.

People talk about falling among thieves. I fell among thieves in the city of Paris in 1815, except that it didn't feel like a falling at all — it felt like a flight.

"My people," she said, nodding toward the closed door. "They'll be your people now. You can trust them with anything."

One of the first things that Manon said that day when Lucienne finished explaining about the map, was: "Lucienne, Alain's found Silveira."

"Davide?" Lucienne's voice was quiet and steely. She glanced at Alain, who looked away before he spoke.

"Yes. In Paris. I heard some rumors a few days ago, and had some friends look for him in the old Jewish quarter. One of them sent word this morning."

"Vraiment?"

"He's back in the rue du Pet-au-Diable," Manon added

"*Merde. Merde.* It was always like this. He's always too late. I've been looking for him for weeks, and now he just turns up in the rue du Pet-au-Diable when it's too damn late. I wonder if Jagot knows. It won't be long. If we know he's there, Jagot will know."

"My man said that Silveira has Sabalair with him," Alain said. "That makes a difference. Jagot won't move in on them until the time is right. And if they are in the rue du Pet-au-Diable, Jagot hasn't a chance — Silveira can disappear like a ghost in those streets. My man said Silveira is back in Paris looking for you, Lucienne. Word reached him that you were here."

"Well, his timing's perfect, *hein?* It is quite the reunion now."

Alain, hearing the flint in Lucienne's voice, changed the subject, veering back from the edge of something dark that had entered the room with Davide's name. "It's impossible, you know," he said. "We can't get into the museum again. They have more guards in there now and a whole set of new locks. We might as well put the chains on our wrists and ankles and go straight to Toulon."

Manon intervened. "Remember that job in the rue Saint-Pierre? You cut the glass in five seconds and cleaned out in seventeen. You said *that* was impossible. For you everything is always impossible — until you do it."

Lucienne turned to the others. "We are going to need more money. I need to rent two floors of a house overlooking the Jardin and it won't be cheap. We must have equipment and transport, and we'll need a set of false documents. That will cost more money than I have."

"Reuben?" Manon asked.

"No. Reuben's retired."

"Who then?"

Lucienne walked back to the window. "Silveira," she said.

Alain turned on her. "Are you mad?"

"We have no choice. We need him. I'm

going to see him. Tomorrow."

"Start with the pawnshop in the rue du Pet-au-Diable," said Saint-Vincent. "I asked around yesterday. He's not been back long. And take Daniel with you."

16

The rue du Pet-au-Diable runs through the Jewish quarter of the city, the name an ancient echo of derision and prejudice. An old menhir stood on that spot in the Marais, near a house that had been used as a synagogue until the Jews were expelled in the twelfth century; locals called it the Hôtel du Pet-au-Diable, the house of the devil's fart. The medieval French poet and notorious thief and murderer François Villon even wrote a ballad about it. Its name survived in the street name. The Parisian Jews who worshipped there, of course, did not survive.

Lucienne and I took a narrow street off the rue Tisserand that led into a maze of more narrow, covered passageways, unlit and, in the early evening, dark and forbidding and muddy underfoot. A child, a small boy with a dirty face and bare feet, stood pressed up against the wall in the first alley.

"Are you lost, mister? Want some help?" he said and grinned. Then he said something else, which I couldn't follow. It still surprised me that no one could tell that Lucienne was a woman in man's clothes. This boy took us both for men. He didn't question it.

"No, we know where we're going," Lucienne said, passing the boy a coin.

"Why don't we get him to take us there?"

"Have you learned nothing in Paris, Daniel? If I ask him to take us, he'll lead us into a cul-de-sac, and then he and his little friends will rob us — and then probably beat us too."

"But he's so young."

"Oh, believe me, his friends will be older."

Behind us in the darkness, I heard the boy give a sequence of whistles, some short, some long. More alleys led off to the right and to the left. When I peered down into them I could see small groups of children looking toward us, whispering to one another. Eyes bright in the darkness like wolves.

"We'd better be quick or they'll head us off," she said, urgency in her voice.

"Do you know where we're going?"

"Of course. You don't think I'd risk us getting lost down here?"

"But this M. Silveira is rich?" To either side, the ornate carved doorways of derelict hotels showed signs of richer times. Now the smell of urine and rotting meat rose from the walls and the mud beneath our feet.

"Yes. Very. He's in the diamond trade. His family ships red coral from the Mediterranean coast to Goa. They trade the coral for diamonds, ship the diamonds back to London for cutting and polishing, then sell them. They have a monopoly. A very successful one."

I imagined Silveira sitting on a golden throne in a warehouse full of red and white coral, a pile of tangled and polished branches stacked high behind him.

Suddenly the whistle was answered by another ahead. And to the side. As we reached the next junction, we were surrounded by children, boys jostling us, converging on us, pushing and talking. "Monsieur, monsieur. Are you lost? Let me show you . . . We take you . . . This way. This way. You go left here and then take the second right . . ."

"Just don't speak to them," Lucienne said. "Don't be drawn in. Keep talking to me and look straight ahead."

"What should I say?"

"Just keep talking."

"All right, all right."

A boy appeared from an alleyway slightly ahead to the right. He was older, perhaps fifteen. He stood there, legs slightly apart, blocking our path, a wooden bat in one hand. The smaller boys walked around and in front of us, pushing, babbling; I glanced behind me. Another older boy had stepped into the alley behind us. There was no way out. The boy with the bat looked at Lucienne, taking her in. Lucienne looked back at him, and touched her middle finger to the spot between her eyebrows. He said something to the younger boys that I couldn't follow. They looked up at Lucienne and then dropped back. Suddenly we were alone in the alley with only the boy ahead. He touched his finger to the point between his eyes and then disappeared too, into the darkness.

"Joaquim," she said. "He knows me. He's in charge around here."

I took a deep breath, my body still trembling. I had been prepared to fight.

"Why do the Indians buy coral?" I asked, finally, remembering our conversation as we walked on.

"Funeral rites. The more red coral you take with you on the pyre, the more important you are. They store it up ready to burn. It's an investment. Let's go."

"That's strange," I said, glancing into the darkness around us.

"They don't care for diamonds as much as we do," she said. "It's a matter of aesthetics."

"Why does he live here, then, if he's a diamond dealer?"

"He's safe here. All his networks start in this square mile, but they stretch everywhere — London, Goa, Madras, Brazil. He used to have a house in the rue du Temple. That's where I last saw him. Things must be difficult if he's back here. He is hiding."

Ahead the alleyways led through an entrance to a narrow street. We quickened our pace. As we stepped out of the maze, I could still see the children watching us in small groups from openings that might have been rabbit holes. On the narrow and cobbled rue du Pet-au-Diable, most of the shop fronts were either boarded up for the evening or permanently closed, except for a pawnshop that carried a sign saying EZRA MOSES — CURIOSITÉS ET BRIC-À-BRAC over the window. Lucienne stopped in front of it. The street was almost deserted.

"Bric-à-brac," Lucienne said, lowering her

voice. "It could mean anything. The old shops in this quarter are often fronts for something else. Jagot tried to establish an outpost down here, but he failed. Even his contacts can't get him in here. They'll tear down these old streets now; build wider ones, streets in which they can see. Streets like these hide people."

I could see our reflections framed in the window: two men, the younger one in a brown jacket, the older one in gray-green, running his hand casually over the old books that had been arranged on a small bookcase outside. Behind the glass, the window displayed suits of mail standing like ghosts, fantastic carvings, rusty weapons, shells and ornaments, figurines in china and wood and iron and ivory; tapestries and strange dreamlike furniture. A placard in one corner announced in French: "Watches and jewelry exchanged and repaired. Buttons, bullets, and teeth from the field of Waterloo."

"Bric-à-brac," I repeated, recalling my anatomy lessons and the jars of body parts I had seen in the anatomy theaters of Edinburgh.

"There are several curiosity dealers down here," Lucienne said. "They don't do much passing trade. They are more like agents.

They sell *objets* to collectors: shells, furniture, relics, horns of unicorns — that kind of thing. Waterloo relics sell best of all now they say: weapons, buttons, even stones from the battlefield. A friend of mine, English, bought a Waterloo thumb, nail and everything, from a man in the Palais Royal. He keeps it in a bottle of gin. What a strange mixture of books. Look: Homer, cheap romances, Euclid, Descartes, and this . . ." She picked up a tattered copy of a small red leather book. "A life of the Polish Jew Salomon Maimon, philosopher."

A figure in worn clothing appeared at the door and looked at us both encouragingly. "Good day, sirs," he said. His face belonged to a man of about thirty, but though he was only seven or so years older than I was, he looked much older, older even than Lucienne. He had a dark, far-off gaze.

"What is the price of this book?" Lucienne asked slowly.

The shopkeeper took the book and examined its flyleaf, saying, "There is no price, I'm afraid, sir. The shopkeeper is not in. He has gone to dinner. Will you wait?"

"M. Silveira?" Lucienne whispered.

"Qui?" The shop assistant kept his eyes on Lucienne in rather too studied a way, I thought.

"Silveira. Davide Silveira," Lucienne repeated. "We will speak in English." She too had become very still. The street children, who had slouched closer in the last few moments, began to whisper among themselves. *Trompe-la-Mort. Trompe-la-Mort.*

"What makes you think you will find him here, monsieur? This shop belongs to Ezra Moses." Then he paused and said: "Is he, perhaps, a relative of yours?"

"Will you tell M. Moses," Lucienne said, ignoring the question, "when he returns from his dinner, that M. Dufour has called and would like to see M. Silveira. Will you do that for me? We will wait in the café at the end of the street. Perhaps you will come and find us."

The shop assistant handed Lucienne the book wrapped in newspaper: "You are interested in Jewish history?"

"Yes, I am," Lucienne said quietly without smiling.

"I believe M. Moses will take fifty sous, sir," he said. "For the book."

"M. Moses will have one hundred sous for his trouble. We will be at the coffee shop. I trust we have an understanding. *Dufour.* Be sure you say that name to him."

"You had better step inside, M. Dufour. The coffee shop is not safe for . . . *les étrangers.* I will take your message to M. Moses and bring you a reply in an instant."

"As you wish."

"My name is Malachi. I am M. Moses's nephew."

Inside the shop — which smelled of dust, damp, and great age — the lamps were turned down low, casting distorted shapes against dirty purple walls. Piled high on every side were small statues, relics, silver objects, carvings in ebony, open drawers full of silver spoons, pictures in gilt frames, armor, birds' nests, and shells. A few minutes later Malachi returned, more ashen-faced than before. "You can go up," he said. "Top of the stairs. First door to the right."

Behind the red velvet curtain that hung across part of the doorway, I could see a man sitting at a long oak desk beside some expensive optical equipment and a small, carved cabinet. An Oriental pirate, some dark-aged Aladdin, unshaven and brooding. He looked directly at us, assessing us as though we were objects to be traded. He wore a long robe of a dusky wine color trimmed with silver braid over a linen shirt and dark trousers, more like a corsair from *The Arabian Nights* than a Parisian dealer in corals and diamonds.

"Silveira." Lucienne's voice established a

tone. A distance.

"Lucienne Bernard," Silveira said. He did not stand or even smile; his eyes narrowed.

Still no one moved. I stood behind Lucienne in the dark of the hallway, looking at the room through the door frame — rich golds and reds. A crimson room. A room from a painting. Hushed, private, sensuous. On the table there were several dishes of food. I could smell spices I didn't recognize. A loaf of bread, a pomegranate sliced in half in a silver dish, its seeds gleaming like jewels in the half-light. I imagined a woman on a bed in the darkness of the far corner, naked, the line of her back curved against the coiled draperies of red satins and silks. But in that dark corner there was another man, dressed in black, standing very still, his hands together. He neither spoke nor acknowledged us. He was an old man. Tall and bulky with dark skin, a high forehead, and his white hair cut very short.

"You remember Sabalair," Silveira said. "He remembers you."

"M. Sabalair," Lucienne said, nodding toward the old man.

"Who's the boy?" Silveira asked, waving a fly from the loaf of bread.

"What boy?"

"The boy behind you."

I shifted awkwardly. Lucienne turned and remembered me. "Daniel Connor," she said.

"One of yours?"

"Yes."

"Honest?"

"Absolument."

As she stepped into the room, I took several steps toward Silveira and held out my hand across the desk. He shook it without much enthusiasm.

"Enchanté, monsieur," he said. I was clearly an inconvenience. There was a lilt in his voice, and a gold tooth became visible when he smiled. He had a large gold hoop in one ear and a chain around his neck, which moved when he did, shifting across the dark skin and white hairs of his chest. He pulled the folds of his gown around him, then gestured to Lucienne to take a seat opposite him. Silveira placed two or three mint leaves in two small glasses and reached for a silver teapot, pouring hot amber liquid into one.

"Take a seat, boy, over there by the window. Here, finish off these." He got up and placed a small terra-cotta dish on the mahogany table by the window seat and passed me a fork, a napkin, and the glass of mint tea into which he had sprinkled something that looked like chopped walnuts. I did not like being called a boy.

"Quails," he said, gesturing at the dish. "They're good, but you can't buy good ginger in Paris anymore. They need more ginger. Fresh. Grated, not powdered."

"No, thank you," I said.

"Just eat," he said. "They are good."

I cut into the brown flesh of the small bird, releasing hot juices flecked with lemon seeds and slivers of ginger. Silveira waited, his back to Lucienne, watching me.

"What do you think? The ginger is not good enough, is it? I will order some from Goa, good, fresh ginger."

"I'd forgotten that," Lucienne said.

"What?"

"Your obsession with food."

"Obsession, you call it? You of all people."

Something indefinable passed between the two of them, an atmosphere, an intimacy, a presence greater than the two bodies they occupied. A history as pungent as ginger. Silveira took his seat back at the desk.

"What brings you to Paris?" Lucienne asked. "They told me you were in Goa."

"People say many things. Goa, Madras . . . yes. What happened to your face?"

"*Rien.* Nothing of consequence." Through the window on the street, I could see that the boys had found another man to plague, their dark shapes swarming around him. He stood still trying to wave them away, without success. He seemed old and tired, easy prey.

"You have a commission, Lucienne."

"How do you know that?"

"You come to find me. And you are just a little bit afraid, I think. You bring the boy to protect you. I like that."

"What?"

"That you are a little afraid. That is new."

"You have Sabalair," she said. I glanced over at the old man standing in the shadows. He didn't even look up at the sound of his name.

"Yes, I have Sabalair."

"And you think I'm afraid of you?" She smiled. "Have I ever been?"

"It is more complicated than that. I think you must have a good reason to come back to Paris. And if you have a commission, you need money. That is why you come to me. *C'est vrai?*"

"C'est vrai."

"So what is it this time?"

"The museum in the Jardin."

"*Again?* You can't go back in there."

"So people keep telling me."

"It would be easier for you to break in to the Banque nationale . . . and what could Cuvier have left in there that you could possibly want? You must have all the corals now."

"We've done it before."

"It's not a good investment."

"You haven't heard what the commission is yet. You don't know."

"Go ahead." Silveira stood to pour more mint tea and passed me some bread. "You Englishmen need to be taught how to eat. Too many meat pies and bad beer."

"What's the trade like now — diamonds, I mean?" Lucienne asked, changing the subject.

"Horrible. All the big buyers, the English dukes and earls, they want to buy pieces of old France — Sèvres porcelain, chandeliers, portraits, furniture. Collectors are everywhere. That is why I am here. Diversifying. You know, you can sell everything now in Paris. I could sell my own skin if I could do without it."

"Diversifying?"

"Exactly. They want objects with history. Not just diamonds, but diamonds with history. Do you remember that little room off the marketplace in Jaffa, Lucienne? The one with the red walls."

"I remember plague in Jaffa. I remember the leeches in the water. I don't remember the room off the marketplace."

"The sandstorm."

"No, I don't remember the sandstorm."

"I remember the sandstorm. Sabalair remembers the sandstorm. You do remember, Sabalair, don't you? The dead horse, digging her out of that tent? Once she was grateful. She owes us her life. Now she forgets. If I ask her, perhaps she will even say she has forgotten the sound of the desert fox we heard at midnight in the sands of the Wadi Rum."

Sabalair said nothing. He did not move. His face showed no expression.

"So you have become a dealer in Sèvres porcelain?" Lucienne asked. "Not like you to settle for so little. You should be buying up Napoleon's things. Someone has paid a fortune for his carriage, they say, and his wardrobe and horses, even his Dutch coachman. They will all go to England, like a traveling circus."

"Diamonds," Silveira said, "are what I know best. But in Paris everyone wants the old set diamonds. The English dukes and barons, they send their agents to me. Old diamonds, they say. We want very old diamonds. But most of them have been bought, I say to them. They are difficult to get."

"What do you know about the Satar diamond?"

Silveira laughed and tipped his head back. "Someone has told you a bad story, my friend. The Satar is a myth invented by the East India Company."

"Denon has it." I watched Lucienne with rising admiration. Her pacing was impeccable. If this was a kind of duel, Lucienne Bernard and Davide Silveira knew all the moves.

"In Paris?" he said, his voice rising.

"Yes. In the Montserrat Cabinet."

"The cabinet's in Paris? It was in Spain."

"Your informers are slipping, Silveira. The diamond's been in Paris for ten years in Denon's collection in the quai Voltaire, hidden inside a mummy in an Egyptian sarcophagus. But two weeks ago it was placed in the vaults of Cuvier's museum in the Jardin, inside the Montserrat Cabinet. Denon has asked Cuvier to hide it for him."

"*Mon Dieu.* You are being truthful with me?"

"Yes."

"Exclusive trading rights?"

"Yes," Lucienne said. "Absolutely. Do you think you might have a buyer?"

"I can set up a bidding war even before you have it; my rich Englishmen will give fortunes for it, especially when I tell them they are in competition with one another.

Excellent. Yes. This will be most interesting. I have a condition."

"Yes."

"I want to go in there with you this time. The museum."

"Out of the question. Too much of a risk," she said, firmly. "Besides, Saint-Vincent will never agree to it."

"Saint-Vincent is in Paris? But I heard he was on the exile list."

"He was. He's in hiding."

"Just make him agree. Whatever Lucienne Bernard says goes, yes? Or does it?"

"This has a history, Silveira. You know that. We can't pretend nothing happened."

"So let's get it right this time. No mistakes."

It was that day in the velveted room above the pawnshop in the rue du Pet-au-Diable that something else began to shadow the longing that I felt for her. The French call it *la jalousie.* I wouldn't have known what to call it then. As if something had passed for a second over the sun, the realization had come to me as soon as I had seen Silveira's face — that he, Silveira, not the poet-locksmith Dufour, who died in Toulon, was Delphine's father.

If the physical similarities between the

corsair and the spirited raven-haired child were striking to me, I wondered, what must they have seemed like to her, Lucienne Bernard, struggling to give nothing away as she looked into the face of the father of her child, who, I also saw, had no idea that he was a father? It would be another two weeks before either of us talked about what I had recognized in the room above the curiosity shop, as Silveira provoked her with talk of sandstorms and horses and tents and the red room off the marketplace in Jaffa. She expected me to keep that secret to myself, and I did.

One afternoon in early October, having crossed the equator and successfully navigated the vicissitudes of the trade winds, the sailors of the HMS *Northumberland* hauled aboard an enormous shark. Dragging it out of the waves was one thing; wrestling it, still alive, onto the deck of the ship was quite another. The Emperor, interrupted in dictating his memoirs below deck, hearing the shouting above, climbed up onto the poop deck, where the Bertrand children and Emmanuel, the fifteen-year-old son of Las Cases, had gathered at a safe distance to watch.

The admiral's warning cry came too late, for as Napoleon approached to examine the patterning on the creature's dorsal fin, the shark, now in its death throes and gasping for air, brought that tail across the deck in a final spasm, knocking over five sailors and the Emperor. When Las Cases, his son, and the two generals rushed to pull Napoleon out from under the tail of the now-dead shark, they were certain the impact had broken both his legs, for the Emperor's cream-colored breeches were covered in blood. It was Emmanuel Las Cases who pointed out that the blood had in fact come from the shark. The Emperor, visibly shaken but only bruised, was carried back to his cabin, where his surgeon attended him. After a glass of brandy, he sent a note to the captain requesting that the shark's bones be stripped and boiled and then sent directly to Professor Cuvier, care of the Museum of Comparative Anatomy in the Jardin des Plantes in Paris.

"Watch what you eat tonight, Bertrand," the Emperor muttered to his general over dinner, his eyes glittering. "This English cook is capable of anything. They tell us it is burgundy, but it is vinegar. They tell us it is beef, but really they feed us shark. They may be fine soldiers, but their cooks are barbarians."

17

Two days later, on the fifth of October, one of the pair of red-necked ostriches died in the Jardin menagerie. Fifty-two years old, born amid the sand and grass plains of Senegal, having survived captivity in three menageries in Holland and France, and having laid hundreds of eggs that failed to hatch in the climate of northern Europe despite the increasingly eccentric incubating skills of her keepers, Antoinette had finally died by choking on a coin thrown to her through her fence by a Prussian soldier who had ignored the entreaty on the gate not to throw objects. The ostrich had always had a passion for coins — the shinier the better. This one had proved fatal.

I had begun to set things out, piece by piece, as best I could, keeping my secrets to myself, taking calculated risks, being opportunistic. Cuvier wanted new assistants in his laboratory; there were several new animals that needed to be dissected and stuffed, including the red-necked ostrich. I had resolved to ask Fin if he wanted the work, as I thought it might help to have another pair of eyes in the Jardin. Of course, no matter how much I longed to, I had no intention of actually telling Fin about the plans to break into the museum. I did not want Fin or Céleste to become caught up in Jagot's investigation or Lucienne's planned theft.

That afternoon was brighter than most, the kind of brightness that hurts your eyes. Fin and I found Céleste drinking with her friends in the café in the Marché des enfants rouges. The market of red children. These were orphaned children who wore red cloaks and who had lived there once in a school built by Margaret of Navarre. The red children were now gone but their name lived on. All the names of these streets in Paris seemed to retain vestiges of their past. However many laborers the Bourbon government hired to remove Napoleon from the streets and his insignia — the bees and the eagles — from the buildings, the Emperor remained everywhere.

Céleste's friends laughed at us as we approached, nudging her and rearranging their hair. She led us away from the café up a metal spiral staircase to a balcony overlooking the market. Laid out below, stalls covered in white cloths were arranged in rows, as if by species, I thought: clusters of fish stalls over to the right piled with shellfish in shallow glass tanks; over to the left, flower stalls behind which women in white aprons tended vases of lilies, delphiniums, and late sunflowers; at the far end spice stalls where the Moroccan and Arabic traders drank tea at brass tables behind boxes of spices.

"It's more private here," Céleste said. "You can't hear yourself down there."

"What were your friends saying," I asked, "that was so funny?"

Céleste laughed. "You're pretty, M. Connor, with your curls and your blue eyes and your smile. They were saying what they would do with you. *Non, non, vraiment,* you don't want to know." From her basket, she produced us a bottle of absinthe, a glass, and a small cake that smelled of tamarind.

"Thank you," Fin said. "I'm hungry and my head hurts."

"You're always hungry, *chéri*. Always eating, eating. There was nothing left in my cupboard this morning. You know, M. Connor, your friend here, he ate all the bread and all the chocolate. I had to go shopping."

"I am mortified," Fin said with mock

shame. "I must have had too much wine. Let me give you . . ." He reached inside his jacket for money.

"You gave me plenty of your coins last night, *citoyen*. Enough to buy more brandy and eat a queen's breakfast. Now you're blushing. How funny you are." She laughed, placing her hand against his cheek. I looked away.

At the same time the smell of her, the perfume on her clothes, the absinthe, and the heat unsettled me. I watched her as she ran her hand up Fin's leg absentmindedly. In an old life, I might have asked for strength to conquer such desires; now the thought no longer even occurred to me. Even the language of prayer seemed false and euphemistic here in this beautiful secular city where the priests had not yet regained their foothold after their return from exile.

Daniel Connor was shedding another skin. What would be left of him?

I turned away to look down into the square beyond the market. Out there everything came and went: artists sketched, beggars begged, horses stood in shade, vendors leaned up against lemonade stalls piled high with lemons, people queued talking in the sun. A cat with one ear sat on the edge of another balcony close by, watching us. Its eyes closed slowly, then opened again.

"Stop it, Céleste," Fin said without conviction. "My friend is here . . ."

"It's hot, Fin. And I need a siesta. Perhaps I will find a friend for Daniel — for a siesta. It won't be difficult." She smiled at me. "My friends. Which one do you like?"

"No, thank you," I said, thinking of Lucienne.

"Someone must do something," Fin said, kissing her. "My friend M. Connor is losing his heart to the beautiful widow who lives with her cats and pigeons. He needs to be distracted. Quickly. I speak as a doctor of course."

"Daniel's dark lady," Céleste said, placing her back up against the wrought-iron railings of the balcony and crossing her legs. She passed me the bottle again and smiled knowingly.

"Have some more absinthe, Daniel," Fin said. "It's good for your head. Last week, Céleste, when Daniel was very drunk, he talked about the widow all through the night. He was confused — sometimes she was a woman, sometimes a man. This is serious, you see. We have to do something. Being in love is one thing, losing your mind is another. He can't even sleep properly anymore. And I hardly ever see him."

"I haven't lost my mind," I said. "I was drunk, that's all. That dreadful brandy of yours. She's in trouble," I added, the absinthe searing the back of my throat. "I've promised to try to help."

"Daniel Connor is not *losing* his heart," Céleste said, "he has already lost it. What will I tell my friends?"

"I think you are jealous, Céleste," Fin said, winking at her. "You are jealous of Daniel's woman. If I talked about a woman like Daniel talks about this one, would you be jealous? Perhaps I should be jealous of Daniel. Perhaps we should all be jealous of Daniel."

"Eh bien," Céleste said. "I'm listening. Tell me about her. *Un peu. Un petit peu."* She brought two fingers up, making a little gap between them, and peered through, squinting as if she was looking through a peephole.

"I don't want to talk about her," I said, clumsily, suddenly afraid that I would drop my guard and tell them everything. "You are both impossible. You take nothing seriously. I won't talk about her. But I do have a proposition for you, Fin."

"A proposition? How very exciting that sounds."

"An ostrich died in the Jardin yesterday.

That's three animals in the laboratory, what with the bull and the llama. Cuvier wants them to be dissected, drawn, and stuffed quickly. I put your name forward. I hope you don't mind. I thought it would be good experience. A reference from Cuvier could be valuable. M. Rousseau wants you in there tomorrow morning. What do you think?"

"Hey, Fin," Céleste said. "You can bring me ostrich meat. If it's not turned too much, of course. I don't want to be sick. We will have an ostrich dinner."

Fin agreed, of course. He agreed to give up his position at the hospital and transfer to the museum, not because of the promise of stolen ostrich meat, but because he knew, as I did, that working in Cuvier's laboratory, even as a temporary dissector, would take him several rungs up the ladder, the ladder that might end in a job that would get him out of Paris and back to a prestigious position at Saint Bartholemew's Hospital or at the Royal College of Surgeons. For me, having Fin in the laboratory had to be of use — some use — in the impossible task I had agreed to.

The absinthe and the lack of sleep had made me delirious. *Everything is upside down,* I wanted to tell Céleste, *and I don't know how to get it back the right way up. And no, I can't sleep for thinking of the map and Lucienne's swollen face, for thinking about him, the nameless man in the shadows who is making her work for him, and now this other man, the coral trader who is the father of her child.*

"You've had too much of that absinthe, *citoyen*," Céleste said as Fin headed off to buy coffee for us all. "It will make you ill. You're not used to it. Did your mother never tell you about the dangers of strong drink?" She began to lean toward me.

"You're Fin's girl," I said.

"I am not Fin's girl. I don't belong to anyone," she said, her chin tilted upward. "We are in France, monsieur. Here you can own things, but you can't own people. I own myself. I can kiss who I like. I can do what I want. Fin knows that. He is not like other men."

"I think he is," I said. "I think we are all the same."

Céleste's eyes were remarkable. They were blue-green, but when the sun brightened, her pupils narrowed into small black dots and a ring of gold appeared around them like the sun rising behind a storm cloud. I was suddenly mesmerized watching that gold ring appear like a fugue around the black.

"Someone should warn your dark lady," she said. "That Daniel Connor is in love with her."

Love. That was startling. Bald. Uncompromising. Céleste watched me closely. Whatever this thing was that had lodged in my flesh, it did not feel like love any longer. I had been in love before, I wanted to say to Céleste, with a pretty girl, a cousin who was demure, accomplished, and well groomed. I had loved her. Or at least that's what I had told myself. But this was now something else. Something dark, something with feathers and claws.

18

October brought an Indian summer. Everything dried up. The leaves on the trees, curled up, brown, and scratchy, seemed to be suspended, waiting to drop. The first week of October circled into the second week as I waited for Deleuze to bring me the final drawing of the map.

A couple of weeks before, I had said to old man Deleuze in the coffeehouse in the Jardin: "You know this place better than anyone. You really ought to write a history of it." When he didn't answer, I began to flatter him: "I'd say no one knows more about the Jardin and its history than you do. And the baron's not going to live forever, is he? What will happen then? The world will want to know the truth about Cuvier."

"The truth?" asked Deleuze.

"I hear there are many stories about Cuvier they tell in Paris."

"What kind of stories?"

"Well, some say he's a tyrant and a bully and that he won't countenance new ideas. Who will be there to contradict them in the future?"

"Lies. All lies," Deleuze said, scratching the back of his hand, where the chemicals he worked with had raised a rash the color of raw meat. "The baron hates speculation, that's true. He is a man of fact. But all those tales about him being a bully and a tyrant, they're all lies."

"I know that of course. But how will other people know? Unless someone tells them otherwise? Now, a book, a history, written by the right person, would make the world see that the Jardin des Plantes is the greatest scientific institution in the world. Such a book might describe every detail of the work in the museum, the people who work here, the animals in the menagerie. All the facts. A list of all of France's greatest men of science. Imagine — your name would be there listed next to Cuvier's. Joseph Deleuze, assistant botanist. Entered Jardin in 1795. Translator of Erasmus Darwin's *Loves of the Plants . . .*"

I remember hesitating, ashamed by how easy it was to reel in old man Deleuze, holding up a mirror to his future glory and walking slowly away from him so that he would follow me, because he would want, above all, to keep that mirror in his sight, holding his reflection a little longer. I surprised myself at the ease with which I had taken to this deception. I could hear myself flattering and cajoling but then I reminded myself what was at stake.

"Of course." I said. "It would be a monument. It would be read in libraries in hundreds of years by students of science who will ask: How did they do that? How did those French men of science build one of the greatest museums in the world? You could call the book *Utopia's Garden*."

"I think," Deleuze said, scratching his chin, "I'd go for something a little less poetic. Something like *The Jardin des Plantes: A History*." As he spoke he swept his hand through the air as if seeing his book in some shop window in a busy Parisian square.

"Why don't you start by drawing a map of the whole Jardin?" I suggested. "With a list of the people who work here, where they live what they do. Once you've got that in place, the rest will follow. You could draw all the buildings and number them and have a key with names of all the lodgings, the menagerie, the amphitheater, and the glasshouses."

"But that would take a long time. You can't just draw a map any old way. You have to do it accurately, with measurements. I would have to get permission. It would have to go through committees."

"You can do all of that later. Once you've shown Cuvier a decent map and drawn up the list, then you can tell him about your plans. I'd keep it a secret for now. You wouldn't want anyone *else* deciding to write the same book. Like M. Rousseau. He's been here a long time too."

"You're right. A secret. Yes, I like that," he said.

"I might even be able to help you get it translated into English. I have connections."

"You do?"

A week later Deleuze had inky fingers and rings of darkness under his eyes. For a week he walked continuously around the perimeters of buildings in the Jardin, counting his paces and noting down the numbers; he carried notebooks and devices for measuring angles; he walked from the corner of one building to another corner, counting, and then he turned and walked back, counting again, just to check.

"You need to be more discreet," I said to Deleuze, but his eyes were blank. "You don't want anyone else to know what you're doing yet."

He had given up writing his animal-magnetism book to make this map. Everything had stopped for this, except the Jardin itself. Every day the Jardin seemed to mutate a little more; you could always hear the sound of banging and sawing — new enclosures, new glasshouses, bricks and mortar, earth, wood, plaster, cabinets, cupboards, alterations, new buildings, and demolitions.

Deleuze showed me his first sketch, frustratingly incomplete, on the tenth of October. It was hard to read. He had begun to trace out the rectangles and right angles of the botanical borders and the curves of the walks through the menagerie and its pens and cages, the blocks that represented the houses of the professors and their assistants and their assistants' assistants, complete with little dots that were supposed to look like trees from above. It was good but it wasn't finished. It took him another week, and in the meantime I waited. We all waited. Everything was in limbo.

In Cuvier's library, at my desk, alongside the other scribes and aides, I continued to copy out page after page of his manuscript of volume 4 of *The Animal Kingdom,* mapping every corner of the avian world, minute descriptions of the curves of claws, or the patterns of plumage, or the precise colors of an egg, or the geographical distribution of bird after bird, noting them all down exactly as Cuvier liked them to be copied, checking all the accents, every last semicolon and hyphen just as he instructed.

The bird volume was almost half completed, but there was a growing sense of urgency in the library that occasionally bordered on panic. Since Sophie Duvaucel, under Cuvier's orders, had announced that we were now to increase the rate of bird cataloguing from one bird per week to two, we were now all working ten-hour days to keep up. There were no extra assistants appointed. There were none to be had.

Most of the birds we drew were illustrations of stuffed specimens displayed behind glass either in the Natural History Museum or in Cuvier's Museum of Comparative Anatomy; some came from storerooms wrapped in paper. Those that belonged to the stadtholder's collection were now brought out and lined up along the shelves of the library in order of priority, birds in waiting, birds in glass-fronted boxes, or folded in paper inside closed boxes. All were labeled. I had a list of the birds that I was to draw, and all through October a procession of birds of different colors, shapes, and sizes passed across my desk, so many that my dreams were feathered and whatever I touched, I could feel plumage perpetually against my fingers. I remember the English names of the birds better than the Latin ones I was supposed to use. That October I painted the supercilious Widowbird, the Magellanic Stare, the Esculent Swallow, the Dwarf Warbler, the Sumatra Bee-eater, and the Purple Gallinule.

In the laboratory, a few buildings away, Fin and several other young men, including Cuvier's stepson Alfred Duvaucel and his friend Pierre-Medard Diard, working in overalls at dissection tables under the direction of M. Dufresne, senior taxidermist, stripped, flayed, dissected, and studied under microscopes the feathers, bones, feet, and beaks of another series of birds, looking for common structures and patterns. Fin had already mapped the nervous system of the dead female ostrich from the menagerie, a nervous system until now inadequately understood; now he was mapping its digestive system. Once that was complete the flayed ostrich would be placed in the bath of acid at the back of the laboratory to strip it back to bleached bones, and then the skeleton would be stitched back together with wires, mounted, and sent over to Cuvier's museum, where a space had already been made for it in Room 2.

I was glad of the precision and concentration the work required, though Lucienne's words twisted like smoke through everything I wrote. *I need you to get me in.* What was the attraction in those words that excited and aroused me, that brushed across my skin? *I need you to get me in.*

"M. Connor," Cuvier said one evening, stopping abruptly as he swept by the desk where I was working late to finish the description of the Black-crested Tern. Accompanied by his stepdaughter, Sophie Duvaucel, he was on his way to his Thursday-evening salon. He cleared his throat before continuing, "M. Connor, you have set a pace for the completion of this volume that is to be commended. You have an attitude to your work that is to be commended. Mlle. Duvaucel says you are to be depended upon in all things. You are discreet, trustworthy. These are important qualities. I commend you, sir. I do indeed. I have been asked to recommend three or four young men for a position at the University of Leiden. I would like to put your name forward, M. Connor. It is a prestigious post.

Once you have finished here, of course, with the bird volume. In perhaps two or three years' time. You understand?"

"Thank you, Baron," I said, trying not to show my excitement. "I am grateful to be of use."

"What he means, M. Sycophant," Sophie said a few minutes later when Cuvier had left the room, "is that you must not refuse the Leiden job if it is offered to you. He also has plans to send you and my brother to Sumatra, plans that will involve considerable *discretion*. You will need to think about that, if you want to be *of use*, of course." She smiled. "Are you discreet, M. Connor? Yes, I think you are. Discreet, charming, and completely unfathomable. That's a fine combination. There will be important rewards, of course, for such work. Positions of consequence. Now, you must excuse me. The baron does not like to be kept waiting."

I had heard of positions such as these — such men were Cuvier's eyes and ears, planted in the universities and laboratories and courts of Europe, or in the colonial outposts of Asia, employed not only as important collectors and field assistants, but also as assistants to his rivals, other natural philosophers in the British or Dutch colonies who were putting together collections to rival Cuvier's. Parts of such collections, they said, would occasionally go missing en route from one country to another. Important and rare skeletons sometimes disappeared. There were always explanations — a ship that had run aground off a rocky coast, a cart that had lost a wheel in the jungles of India, an attack by natives on the border of Tibet. An entire boatload of hundreds of stuffed exotic birds had once disappeared on the Madeira River somewhere between Pôrto Velho and Abuná. It was never found.

These assistants of his were always well rewarded, their names listed in footnote after footnote of Cuvier's published works, their reputations accelerated, their work in the universities of Europe guaranteed. "It is a case of keeping up, staying ahead of the game," Sophie said, "for the reputation and honor of France, of course." *Yes,* I wanted to say. *This is exactly what I have always dreamed of.* But there was something in her tone that suggested such a post might be a mixed blessing. It was always difficult to read Mlle. Duvaucel. Sometimes she seemed to mean exactly the opposite of what she said. Only a few days before I had found her staring out the library window and when she had asked me about work, I had turned to her and said: "But you, mademoiselle, are you happy here? Does the work not burden you?"

"What a strange question," she said, smiling. "You know, no one has asked me that before. M. Connor, since it is you who ask, I consider myself to be one of the most privileged women in France. Here in the Jardin I do a hundred things every day that no other woman can do anywhere in the world. You see what I do. You see how busy I am. I read scientific papers and books. I don't have to wait for my brothers to finish with them — the baron sees that they come straight to me. I read to the baron; I translate for him, edit for him. I have his confidence and I argue with his conclusions. I mount specimens. I draw; I classify. I host the baron's salons, where I meet some of the most interesting men in Europe. In a few years, I will travel to England with the baron. Look at what I might have been — what my convent friends have become. Married. Bored. With nothing to do. No, M. Connor, the work here at the Jardin does not burden me. You think like a man."

Brugmans was now in Paris, staying at the Hôtel Royal; he also was waiting, biding his time. He was a good ambassador and he knew how to apply pressure. There was going to be no rushing into the Jardin with soldiers for him. He wanted to make Cuvier sweat. He knew how it was going to be: First Cuvier would offer replicas of the specimens; Brugmans would refuse. Cuvier would try again. He would refuse again. A dance. Repetition with variation. Eventually the Dutch ambassador would agree to take replicas in exchange for a thick portfolio of political concessions, treaties, and trade agreements. Stalling was essential. The choreography must be slow if he was to return with all the trade agreements he had been entrusted to negotiate.

In the library each day I watched Cuvier. Tormented by this waiting for Brugmans to act, he became increasingly irascible. He found fault with everything. He walked up and down, moving from one desk to another, never stopping for long. None of the assistants dared mention Brugmans's name. Under the pressure of waiting, tired from the long hours on the book, and preoccupied by what I knew was being planned in the locksmith's atelier, I was often distracted, weighed down by a vague sense of guilt and dread. I had begun to avoid sharing lunch with Achille and Joseph, even Fin,

using my work as an excuse to stay in the
museum. Sophie Duvaucel quietly hovered
over all of us, checking our drawings, collecting manuscripts, returning books to
their place on the shelves, fetching specimens from other museums or books from
other libraries. She was always calm, always
ahead of the game.

19

In the second week of October torrents of rain made the roads almost impassable. It was dark all day long and gusts of wind rattled the panes of glass in the windows.

Since our descent into the rue du Pet-au-Diable I had barely seen Lucienne or heard from her. I had called at the atelier several times, but there was no one at home. I struggled with jealousy; there were so many questions I had no answers to. It had been impossible to gauge, that day in the darkened room above the curiosity shop, what Lucienne felt for Silveira now. I could no longer think of her without thinking of the Portuguese diamond dealer. I saw them in room after room, limbs intertwined: in the red room off the marketplace in Jaffa, in a white tent with wind-billowed walls, in the room in the atelier among the cats and the corals, in the bed where I had been.

At night, sleepless, I walked through the

streets of the city peering down into the workings of cellars and alleyways that opened up everywhere in the streets or picking my way through the rubble of the changing cityscape.

"She'll be back," Fin said, guessing the cause of my return to the rooms on the rue de l'École and the reason for my midnight wanderings. "You'll see. Just give it a few days. Just give it time."

She had sent me a note on the morning of October 8 to tell me that she was leaving Paris for a few days but that I was not to be concerned; she had preparations to make and would be back in Paris on the fourteenth. She hoped, she wrote, that the map might be ready by then. Her tone was cool. She offered no explanation or apology.

On the afternoon of October 14, Lucienne called a meeting. I slipped away from the unfinished illustration of the Dwarf Warbler and the pile of notes that accompanied it, notes that I had yet to turn into a full natural history of the bird. It was easy to claim illness. I had lost weight and I was pale and hollow-eyed. Sophie kept urging me to take better care of myself.

The address was a building on the rue de Seine, which ran down the east side of the

Jardin. Silveira had rented an old warehouse that faced the high wall of the Jardin, not quite directly opposite Cuvier's museum but almost. The house agent, who had been paid more generously than he had expected by a man whose business card read "Abraham Fuerguerer, Trader in Diamonds," asked no questions. The building and the three or four on either side had been bought up by speculators, so the rent was cheap. They would be demolished six months later to make way for new apartment blocks and a wider street.

When I arrived that morning in the rain, carrying a copy of Deleuze's finished map, someone had placed a painted sign on the iron railing outside the house that read AT-TENTION. RESTAURATION EN COURS. DÉFENSE D'ENTRER. There were bags of plaster and a few bricks arranged on the steps and an old wheelbarrow was turned upside down among some flowerpots.

It was Manon Laforge who met me at the door that opened off an alleyway down the side of the building. She was wearing the white dress again, a very simple white cotton dress, muddied now along the hem. She showed me through the ground floor and up a steep and very narrow staircase to a long dusty room on the third floor. Oak rafters and beams black with age lined the ceiling, and the floor was littered with boxes and piles of books with a few bookshelves along one of the walls.

The six long windows facing the Jardin were covered by pages from old books that Manon had glued across each pane of glass. There were a few gaps so that it was possible to see out and across to the Jardin without being seen by anyone in the street. Daylight illuminated print running in all directions, casting the words of Molière or Racine or Rousseau onto the opposite wall, upside down, right side up, inverted.

A long polished worktable scattered with papers, books, maps, and drawings occupied the center of the room, surrounded by a few chairs of different shapes and sizes. A fire burned in the hearth.

"You look ill," Manon said once I had slumped into a chair near the fire and pulled off my wet boots. "Is there something wrong with you?"

"She's back?" I said, glancing toward the door.

I wondered later whether if I hadn't looked quite so dejected and broken, she would have said anything to me that day. For if Manon hadn't been struck with compassion for me then, a compassion that disarmed both of us, it's difficult to imagine where things might have ended up.

"Yes, yes. She's back. Everything is all right. You have nothing to worry about. Really. She's angry with everyone else, not you."

Her sympathy, that look of understanding she had for the hollow-eyed signs of my distress, undid me. The questions that had kept me walking through long nights all spilled out at once.

"Was he with her? When she went away? Did he go too? Silveira?"

"Of course. She had to talk to him about something."

"She's told him? That he's Delphine's father? Why does he need to know?"

"You know, then? *D'accord.* We disagreed about whether Silveira should know. We quarreled about it. She didn't want him to know but I did. Delphine was beginning to ask questions, and, well, I said it would be wrong not to tell her who her father was, and if *she* knew, so should he. I had strong feelings about that. Well, I would, wouldn't I, Lucienne said. I had so little to lose. She did, of course, have something to lose. That's why she came to Paris. There were other things too — the corals, other people she wanted to find, but it was Silveira she

310

came for. We have stayed in Paris too long looking for him, and see what has happened. I don't like Silveira. He's impetuous and unreliable, and he's been nothing but trouble in the past, but I still think he had to know. And now, we won't be able to get out of Paris again without his help."

"What does Lucienne have to lose?"

"Her liberty — the way she lives. You don't know Silveira."

"Has he seen Delphine?" That scene — the father and the daughter — I could hardly bear to imagine that.

"No one can see Delphine, Daniel. Lucienne should have told you. I told her she should tell you. Jagot has Delphine under guard at the convent at Picpus. She blames me. Well, she blames everyone, mostly herself. And she does not sleep. She makes herself ill."

"Jagot?" I said. "Why Jagot?" I was so tired I was afraid I was caught somewhere between my dreams about Jagot and this room on the rue de Seine.

"Jagot is the man who attacked Lucienne, Daniel. Jagot is the man who commissioned us to do this job. He will keep Delphine under guard until Lucienne brings him the diamond. No visits are permitted. The nuns do what they can, but it's dangerous for them too. Lucienne always said Jagot would find her. I underestimated him."

"Jagot commissioned this? What does he want? The diamond or Silveira?" I was sick with dread, seeing piece by piece the part I had almost certainly played in bringing Jagot not only to Lucienne's atelier but also to the door of the convent. All Jagot had had to do was to follow me and set a series of traps in my wake.

"He wants both," Manon said. "And he'll get both. He's clever. Silveira will be a big prize for Jagot. Once he has Silveira in Toulon, the Society of Ten Thousand will fall and Jagot's power in France will be beyond question. He will have as many men as he asks for. And there's a reward for Silveira. But if the diamond goes missing, which it will of course — that's part of Jagot's plan — then no one will suspect him of being the thief, even if Denon accuses him of it directly. Denon is going down; Jagot is going up."

I had been blind, just as Lucienne had said. Completely blind. *It's the little things that matter,* Jagot had said. *Nothing is insignificant. Eventually all the little things start to add up.*

All thieves have an Achilles' heel, Jagot had said to me in the fiacre that day. *You just have to find it.* In this case the Achilles' heel was the five-year-old daughter of Lucienne Bernard and Davide Silveira, a child that Jagot had traced to a convent on the rue de Picpus.

"It's barbaric," I said. "Jagot is a monster to use a child in that way."

"He's only doing what everyone else in Paris is doing — scavenging, picking over the remains of Napoleon's treasures. He is a vulture like the rest. He uses Lucienne because she is one of the best thieves in Paris, and because through her he can reach Silveira."

"One thief to catch another," I said. It might have been one of Jagot's mantras. "So Jagot is going to make Lucienne betray Silveira to save Delphine?"

"That's what he wants her to do, yes."

"And will she?"

"Never. She will never betray Silveira. She will think of some other way. But it will be very dangerous. I want to tell you to leave Paris, Daniel Connor," Manon said, taking a seat next to me by the fire, her fine features softened by the flames. "I say to Lucienne that it is bad luck, the boy being involved — he is young and unpredictable. How else can we do it, Manon? she says. How else can we get in? And then she tells me about the guards and the window locks and the security checks. And she asks me, and my trouble is that I too can see no other way. I don't like it. I don't like the plan. I don't think it will work. So I say to you, M. Connor, if anything goes wrong . . . if you are responsible for anything that goes bad . . ."

"I know," I said, "I know. Don't you think I feel responsible enough already?"

"We are all responsible, monsieur —"

She didn't finish. Saint-Vincent had arrived with a bottle of port and some pastries from the Café des Mille Colonnes carried in a white box tied with a pink ribbon.

"*Sacré Dieu* . . . Saint-Vincent," Manon exclaimed, putting her hand to her heart. "I thought you were a ghost. Don't do that to me. I'm not so young."

"I'm sorry." He grinned, nodding at me. "I have my own key. This looks cozy. What have you two been talking about?"

"I was showing M. Connor around," she said. "I was telling him about the book dealer who rented this place. I've used some of the old books M. Monsard left to cover up the windows so that we can't be seen from the Jardin. We are lucky. Another four or five months and this whole building will be gone. There are beds upstairs and an old printing press on the floor below."

I stood up and went over to the window to look through one of the gaps in the printed pages. I could see the high brick wall of the Jardin and a building beyond that.

How might a man feel, I wondered, after six years of silence, to be told that a woman he had loved and lost and searched for had borne his child but had not told him? What might he feel if that child was now in mortal danger, only a few streets away, yet beyond his reach?

"Well, M. Mapman," Saint-Vincent said. "What can you see over there, over the wall?"

I described everything I could see, trying to impose my memorized aerial view — Deleuze's map of the Jardin — onto the few buildings and trees we could now see rising from behind the walls. As I did so, I tried to shake off the effect of Manon's revelations and that phrase of hers — *if anything goes wrong.*

Down in the street, fiacres scattered muddy water from their wheels. A fine haze hung in the air now that the rain had eased. Students came and went with umbrellas, dodging the fiacres and the puddles.

The east wall of the Jardin des Plantes

stretched to the right and left in front of me, old brick, in different shades of red, orange, and pink, joining up the gaps between houses. Plants grew in the cracks. A wall and a terrace of houses broken only by the small arched entrance to the gardens, where five security guards sat in a guard-house playing cards, taking it in turns to question and search each person as they went in or out.

I pointed out the red roof of the black-smith's directly opposite us, and Cuvier's museum, which was the largest building on this side of the wall, its windows boarded up and grilles fitted. Then Cuvier's house next door, then his laboratory. Geoffroy's house was farther down, all the curtains closed. Then Thouin's house and beyond that the trees that marked the site of the experimental garden.

"Look," I said as church bells struck six o'clock. "The third window on the left of Cuvier's house. There's light. Right on time. He's just walked back through the top floor of the museum and into the side entrance to his bedroom. He's dressing for dinner. He is very punctual."

Down there in the street, through the rain making deltas on the window, I watched another fiacre make its way down the street.

A fiacre pulled by a horse I recognized. Jagot's fiacre. *You are blind, Daniel Connor,* Lucienne had said to me repeatedly, and the extent of my blindness astonished and silenced me now. Here was the man pulling the strings.

20

Lucienne and Silveira arrived together a few minutes later, stooping through the low doorway with wet umbrellas. She looked tired. She wore Silveira's robe, the long robe I had seen him wear in the room in the rue du Pet-au-Diable, fleece-lined with the silver embroidery, the robe that smelled of ginger and garlic, the desert, and the sea. I didn't like seeing her in his clothes.

Both were quiet and serious. Silveira nodded to Saint-Vincent and Manon, his bow slightly mannered, his hand on his heart in, I supposed, an Arab greeting. *"Citoyens,"* he said, nodding to each of us in turn.

"Silveira," Saint-Vincent answered, shaking his hand.

"Sabalair is not with you?" Manon said.

"But of course. He is downstairs, watching the street."

"You weren't followed?"

"No," Lucienne said. "We came by boat

and then through the underpass."

"Half of Paris is looking for you, Silveira," Saint-Vincent said. "You have put us all at risk coming here."

"The other half of Paris is looking for you, M. Saint-Vincent," he said. "All of Paris is looking for all of us, I believe. We could offer ourselves up for ransom. We would be rich."

"You are already rich, *citoyen.* Do you need more?"

"That, my friend, is not your business."

"Enough, now," Lucienne said, glancing at me with a look of burdened weariness. "Stop. We have work to do. Daniel, do you have the map?"

I nodded. I could not speak.

Silveira's clothes were dusty. He wore large gold rings on his fingers. Byron might have looked like this, I thought, after a night on the road. He wore no waistcoat, only a crumpled white cotton shirt. His face was deeply lined; it was the face not of a diamond trader but of a man who had spent most of his waking hours on board ship, where wind and rain had weathered him. He smelled of leather and brandy. He had shaved his neck and trimmed his beard since I had seen him in the rue du Pet-au-

Diable, and I noticed a small cut on his neck.

In Lucienne, dressed today in a simple brown-and-gray-striped silk waistcoat under Silveira's coat, I looked to see where the man became the woman, the woman the man, and failed to find the border.

"Daniel, I have the books and papers I promised you," she said, passing me a parcel wrapped in brown paper. "I found them in an old trunk, when I was packing yesterday. There's a copy of Lamarck's *Philosophie zoologique.* You can keep it. I have two. And Erasmus Darwin's *Zoonomia.* It's heavy. And there's a copy of Peysonnel's paper on corals too."

"Lucienne Bernard is a savant still," Silveira said. "She thinks she will find the key to everything with her books and her microscopes. Soon she will tell us the reason for everything and why this bone fits into this socket and why ducks' feet are webbed, and why corals have found three different ways to reproduce themselves, and why animals have no roots, and why plants don't feel. Apparently there is an answer, you see, M. Connor, and Lucienne is going to find it. Nothing else matters, eh, Lucienne?"

"Perhaps. Perhaps not," she said, meeting

my eye. "There are other things that matter to me."

Silveira interrupted. "Now she looks casual, even, how do you say, nonchalant? Perhaps, she says. *Peut-être.* And then she shrugs her shoulders. In truth, M. Connor, she thinks no one will find the answers to the fossils or to the origin of the earth until all the priests have gone. I say to her these beginnings of time will never be known, so why try. Let the philosophers argue. I tell her the priests will never go. I tell her we need the priests. I tell her she should give up her obsession with beginnings and think about the present and the future."

"*Tais-toi,* Silveira," Manon said. "You are being quarrelsome. Enough."

How might a man feel to learn that he is the father of a daughter he has never met? Angry, it seemed. This interminable duel of theirs, fought in deserts and on mountains, on the shore of the Dead Sea and in the marketplaces of Egypt and now in a warehouse overlooking the Jardin des Plantes — I wondered how it might have begun. Perhaps they no longer remembered.

Lucienne stood at the window peeling off pieces of paper to make a larger square in the glass. The rain had stopped during the night, but the trees had taken a battering from the storm so the chestnut tree outside looked as if it was holding on to its last leaves only by an act of absolute concentration; now and again four or five large yellow and brown leaves slipped away into midair, hovering for a moment before a gust caught them up.

"It took me a long time to glue up that paper," Manon said. "Don't take it off again."

"It makes me feel hemmed in," Lucienne said. "There's no light in here."

"Now, Citizen Connor," Silveira went on, "Lucienne Bernard will tell you, of course, that it is important to be free. She will tell you that freedom is important above all things. To be free to think, to ask questions, free from the kings and the priests and men like Cuvier. She is a fighter for freedom, M. Connor."

Lucienne turned back to face him, her black eyes flashing.

"Freedom to think, yes, that matters. Freedom to ask questions, that matters too. Clever students like Daniel come to Paris believing every thought is possible here. It isn't. It was, but it isn't anymore. The priests, kings, aristocrats, they are coming back, and what freedom we had — it will go. And yes, I do believe that freedom matters. Because for a short time we had it."

They both seemed entirely oblivious to the rest of us.

"Freedom to think?" Silveira said. "That is nothing. What about rights? They gave us Jews equal rights during the Revolution. They made us equal to everyone else in France — in law. Already, in just five years, those rights have gone. Already it is hard to be a Jew in this city. My people are leaving again. Yes, we can think, but now Davide Silveira must hide in rooms above a curiosity shop in the rue du Pet-au-Diable."

"At least you *had* rights, even if they took them away again," Lucienne hissed. "For all the noble rhetoric of the Revolution, did anyone suggest giving women rights? What did the Revolution do for us? *Égalité?* It is all empty rhetoric. We are still slaves to the laws and petty tyrannies of men. If we have the right to go to the guillotine, to fight alongside our brothers at the barricades, why do women not have the right to mount the platform of government? That matters. I care about that."

"The price of bread is rising again. That matters. Five thousand babies are left at the Foundling Hospital every year. That matters."

"You are not hiding because you are a Jew,

Silveira," Manon interrupted. "You are hiding because Jagot has you on his list, because of crimes."

"That is a family matter," he said. "Jagot has a long memory."

"Everything is a family matter for you, Silveira," Lucienne said. *"L'honneur de la famille. Sacristi.* You will get us all killed for your family honor. The map?" she said, turning abruptly to me. "Daniel?"

I unfolded my copy of Deleuze's map of the Jardin and spread it across the table, securing its edges with pots and books, grateful to have something to do to escape the cross fire of accusation and counteraccusation. The others took seats around the table. Saint-Vincent lit the lamp and poured coffee from the pot on the fire.

The map was a long, vertical oblong. To the north the wide ribbon of the river ran horizontally across the thick grainy paper, crisscrossed by quais and bridges. Inside the oblong of the walled garden there were two distinct halves. To the right, a series of boxes marked out in right angles the various borders and buildings around the edges. To the left, the menagerie grounds were all curves and twists, a series of winding paths and circles. And down in the bottom left-hand corner were the spiraling paths of the labyrinth where I had sat with Lucienne. Each section on the map was marked with a number.

"There's a key," I said. "Deleuze has numbered everything. I've copied it out in English and French."

Over the top of the map I placed another piece of paper — a list. It had forty-seven numbers corresponding to locations on the map: the beehives, the labyrinth, the cedar of Lebanon, a dairy, the park and hut for the zebra, the garden for experiments, borders for aquatic plants, flowers for ornament, greenhouses, hot frames, seed gardens. It was like a poem, I thought.

"It's good," she said. "Very good. I hope M. Deleuze is getting some sleep now. Show me, Daniel," she said softly. "Show me everything that is important, everything new. We must make a plan. We must make the very best plan."

As I described what they had in front of them — the four entrances to the Jardin, heavily guarded, the number of guards, the locking systems, the gates checked night and day, the keys checked in and out, the windows locked, grated, barred, checked, and double-checked — the impossibility of the task became increasingly evident.

I put another map on top of the first, the rectangular floor plan of a two-story building with four sides built around a courtyard: Cuvier's museum. I had devised the map from a prose description written by Joseph Deleuze. Each new map took us farther in, farther down, farther into the heart of things, and closer to the diamond.

"The Comparative Anatomy Museum," I said, smoothing out the folds in the paper. "It used to have an entrance directly onto the rue de Seine on the east side of the gardens, but that door was bricked up last year. The main entrance to the museum is therefore from the Jardin, through this door here."

I ran my finger around the perimeter, showed them the long side of the building that housed the museum. I told them that Cuvier had fitted iron grilles to all of the windows at street level and had designated the rest of the building, the other three sides, as lodgings for his assistants. It was never empty.

"Impressive," Lucienne said. "Cuvier has made the museum into a fortress. It's impenetrable. And the vault? How do we get in?"

I described the entrance to the cellars

through Room 2 of the museum, an entrance that had once been a trapdoor in a flour warehouse, and before that in a coach house. It was two doors, opening onto a staircase, that were now hidden by a plinth on a sliding mechanism that carried a full-sized rhino skeleton from Java. Room 2, I told them, was now the centerpiece of Cuvier's museum, and was almost impossible to get into. Cuvier had ordered a refurbishment of the entire room and there was always someone in there, assembling or dismantling the bones for cleaning, rehanging them, repainting the signs, dusting the shelves, or polishing the floor.

"We will go in on the night of Brugmans's visit," she said. "The night that Cuvier gives a party in his honor. Those are our orders. The twenty-ninth of October. That's fifteen days."

"We break in during a *party?* You are joking," Saint-Vincent said. "That's suicide. So, we're supposed to get into the Jardin past the armed guards here, who will be checking the papers of everyone who goes in and out, into the museum to the private party, where we will be stopped again at the door here. During this party we get down into the cellars by moving a plinth with a skeleton of a rhino on it, find the cabinet, wherever it is, and the diamond, and get it and ourselves out again, all of this while there's a party going on and the place is full of royalty, princes, and diplomats? Does Jagot think we're magicians? Or just fools? It would be easier to rescue the Emperor from Saint Helena than to get that diamond from Cuvier's museum."

"The Emperor arrives on the prison island today, the papers say," Manon said. "No one will rescue him now. No one can. He must know that. It is a bad end for him."

"We've done more difficult jobs than this," Lucienne said, sensing our spirits falling. "But we have to know what is what. One of us must watch the Jardin day and night from this room for at least a week. We will take turns watching and making notes. I want to know when the guards change, when the feeding times happen. We have to know every single routine and schedule."

Silveira grinned broadly. "Lucienne is a magician," he said. "She would rescue the Emperor from his prison island, if they asked her, if they gave her a ship and a map."

"Manon is right," Lucienne said. "You would need an army to rescue him now. There is no way back to Paris for him."

"Or for us," Saint-Vincent said gloomily. "There will be no way back for us either."

On the evening of October 14, under cover of darkness, a small crew of red-coated British soldiers rowed the Emperor Napoleon ashore from the fleet of man-of-war ships anchored off the coast of Saint Helena. Jamestown itself was nothing but a cluster of houses in a wide ravine at the south end of the island, a valley in a vast expanse of gray rock. To the Emperor's eyes it was just a series of flickering lights clustered around the shore.

Despite the darkness, the entire population of the island had turned out, pushing and jostling for position, disappointed to be able to catch only the occasional flash of a diamond star pinned onto the Emperor's dark overcoat as he moved among his entourage, straining their eyes for a glimpse of that small cockaded hat. The sentries in their red coats had to use their bayonets to clear a route through the crowd. They stare as if I am a circus animal, the Emperor muttered to his generals, *une bête feroce.*

Napoleon had arrived. No one, his jailors told him with pride, had ever escaped from Saint Helena.

21

Lucienne came to the empty warehouse that night and found me struggling to stay awake in the leather chair placed at the window in the dark of the room, drinking brandy, watching the lights from the watchman's lamps moving about in the Jardin, taking notes. Her mouth close to my ear: *Are you awake?* The smell of perfume, wood smoke, and brandy. I remember the heat of the brandy on my tongue; the mattress we found in the attic and pulled down in front of the fire. Naked amid dust and insects in the firelight, we watched the goings-on of the street through the moonlit night: the lights, the prostitutes, the watchmen checking doors and windows.

"What do you see?" Lucienne asked, her fingers on my back, sometime between two and three o'clock in the morning, as I leaned up against the window, peering out between the sheets of paper.

"You and your life," I said. "And all the people in it."

Draped in the gold-and-green brocaded curtains we had found in a box in a downstairs room, she began to describe how she and Manon and Delphine had lived for almost six years in an Italian village she wouldn't name, a house by the sea, buried in long grass, with no road, a house that was falling to dust, that had grass growing through some of the floorboards in the pantry, a house where you had to check your shoes and your sheets for the tiny scorpions that climbed in there, a house on the top of a hill with a path winding down to the cove, and a porch that looked out toward the sea.

The books were the biggest problem, she said. They swelled in the rain. They were the only valuable things in the house, the only things they worried about, but it always cost a little more than they had to move them into town for the winter. They always moved back into town for the winter. Things were easier. There are women who come and work for us, in the town, she said. They sweep and polish, cook and clean, make the fires and blacken the hearth. In town they had parties, dinners, conversations, and guests. "There are always guests, savants and philosophers passing through the house. Some stay all winter," she said. "And then sometimes, when the mood takes me, when I get restless, I go, sometimes with Delphine, sometimes not, to Florence or Pisa."

But even in town, she said, she missed Paris. Manon complained that she was always talking about Paris: the Jardin, the latest microscopes, the museums, the arguments you could have only there. There were things she wanted in Paris, she said; they weren't the normal things that women want, like hats or gloves or lace; she missed the curiosity shops and the collectors, the museums and the people.

"I always knew we would have to come back," Lucienne said. "Once Delphine was old enough. And I think I always knew something like this would happen. You can't keep running away."

La marche. Lucienne's life, her *marche.* It made me think of Ramon's arm — stretched out among the wine bottles in our salon, his finger sweeping down from his shoulder and stopping at the fingernail — that night when he had told me about all the time there was on earth before man arrived. *Here is where human history begins,* he had said, *here at the fingernail. See how small we are and how late we have come.*

Hearing about Lucienne's life, putting it together piece by piece, made me feel small — and late. For there were others behind me, others who had lain with her. Lucienne's story stretched back into a history before I was born, a past that, like wind, snow, rain, and ice, had carved out the landscape she had come to be. This was a past that kept her on the run, not just from the consequences of her crimes, but from the cuts and blows of her memory.

"I wish I could erase all your histories," I said. "I wish there was nothing before me. That the world and all the planets turned around this bed, that everything began and ended here, with just you and me. I wish you were entirely mine. And I know that's selfish and stupid. And I know, before you say it, that Lucienne Bernard doesn't belong to anyone."

"Silveira? You speak of him?"

"Did you love him?" I needed to know, even if I didn't like the answer, I thought.

"Yes. With a kind of madness — for years. I would have done anything for him. It was the same for him. But it is always a fight. We might have killed each other, I think, if we'd been left alone. It all came to an end in Montmartre when Silveira killed Jagot's man. If he hadn't killed Jagot's man, Jagot's man would have killed me. So you see, I owe him many things. He taught me many things. I was pregnant then, when Silveira killed Jagot's man, but I didn't know it. By the time I knew, we were hundreds of miles away from each other."

"You must sleep," I said, alarmed by the pallor of her skin and unable to bear any more talk of Silveira. "You will make yourself ill. Let me do this watch. You can take over in the morning."

"I don't want to sleep," she said, her eyes brimming. "I have bad dreams. Everything ends in bad things. You know, yes? You know about Jagot? Manon told you, didn't she? When I saw you today, when you looked at me like that, I said to myself, *someone has told Daniel.* He looks at me like that because he knows that Jagot has Delphine . . ."

"Yes," I said, relieved not to have to keep her secret. "It's terrible. You must be . . . What will you do? There must be something we can do . . . the convent . . . Silveira must have men. There's Sabalair, there must be others."

"Silveira knows too. He wants to take men into the convent. I made him promise not to. I tell him Jagot's men have guns. If there are guns in the convent, think what might happen."

"But you must do something. Jagot's not going to let you go back to Italy once he has the diamond. It's a trap. He won't honor whatever promises he made you. He is hard and unscrupulous."

"I'm going to do everything that Jagot tells me. I'm not risking anything — not this time."

She was broken that night, and I knew I was part of that brokenness, responsible at least in part. And I knew that if Lucienne did not rally, if someone didn't do something, they were already in Toulon — all of them, and they would die there. Jagot would see to that. *Je suis un homme mort,* Alain had said.

"Now that I have the map, Daniel," she said, "you must not come back here or to the atelier. You must pretend you don't know us. You must behave as if we have thrown you off."

"It's too late," I said, thinking of the expedition to Sumatra that Cuvier had planned for me that would no longer be possible. "You can't rescue me. Jagot knows I'm caught up in this. But it doesn't matter. You have to find a way out of Jagot's trap, for your own sake and Delphine's and the others. Unless you take a risk, Lucienne, unless you can think of another way, you will all be in Toulon by the end of the month and Delphine will be in a Paris orphanage. Have you thought about that? There's no going back to Italy unless you *stop* doing exactly what Jagot tells you. Unless you make another plan."

"Will none of you leave me alone?" she said, pulling on her clothes and her boots. "You, Silveira, Manon. You're like flies in my head. I can't think. I can't sleep. All the time, you say, Lucienne, you must do something. Lucienne, you must think of something. She's my child and I can do nothing. There is no way out. There is no other plan. I am not a magician."

And then she was gone, disappearing behind a series of slammed doors into the night. When I awoke the next morning, stiff and hunched over the windowsill from watching, I found her on the mattress beside the fire, curled up like a child inside the covers, her hands bruised and bleeding, with Deleuze's map laid out on the floor next to her.

There's a certain kind of hunger that can't be sated. You can never get enough. The more you have, the more you want. In Paris in 1815 I never had enough of her, of the thief, the coral collector, the card player, the woman who knew, or thought she knew, how time began. I could never have had enough. I would have risked everything to save her.

Moving between the museum library and the warehouse on the rue de Seine, between Cuvier and the thieves, between order and disorder, taxonomies and mutability, I knew nothing for certain anymore. I was lost in clouds and dark waters among questions I couldn't shape and didn't understand. I still hoped I might come to know how time began. I thought about what it was that makes the birds nest and corals spawn and birds migrate and eels head for the sea. Until then, until Lucienne and the heretics, until Paris and the quarries and the mammoths and the corals, there had always been a god behind the scenes, pulling the levers, pressing the buttons, marking time, keeping order. You don't stop believing in God just like that. It's a way of seeing, a voice inside, a structure. But the picture of the beginning of time was getting crowded with different stories and explanations. I was still certain that it was about to be discovered in one of the rooms of the Jardin des Plantes.

Silveira was climbing the stairs as I left the warehouse that morning for the Jardin, leaving Lucienne sleeping on the mattress by the fire. He took the steps two at a time, his umbrella leaving a trail of raindrops behind him. He carried a basket of food. I could hear the sound of china jangling against glass; I could smell garlic and spices.

"Il pleut dehors," he said as he reached me on the staircase. "There is so much rain that soon we will grow fins." He gestured at his basket. "There is a new *traiteur* in the Marais run by a Jew from Santiago de Compostela. The food is magnificent. I brought some for her, for breakfast. She is too thin. Peppers marinated in oil. Lamb in quince. And some late peaches from the Loire I found at the market. She must eat."

"Don't wake her yet," I said. "She's finally asleep."

He paused, then tipped his head to one side so the thick curls of his hair fell in ringlets that made me think of ropes. Silveira was all sea-carved wood, the figure head of some great ship washed up on an empty beach. Out of water, never at home.

"Are you lovers?" he said, putting the basket down on a stair so that I could not pass.

I did not have time to compose myself.

"You can't ask me that," I said.

"Why not? You have blushed, monsieur.

You think I will be angry with you? You think Silveira will be jealous, is that it? You are afraid of me."

"No," I said, pulling myself up to my full height, which was still short of his. "I am not afraid of you."

"I have offended you, monsieur. I am not used to city manners and sensibilities. I say what I think. I will not say sorry for that." He took a step to me and reached for my chin, turning my head toward the light. "You have a good profile," he said.

"I have to go," I muttered. "I am already very late."

He leaned back against the flaking plaster of the wall and lifted his polished boot onto the balustrade. He was not going to let me pass.

"Monsieur, I have one more question for you, before you go. Do you think, have you ever thought, for a moment at least, that she might be a little mad? *Aliénée?*"

"No," I said. "I think she is the cleverest woman — person — I have ever met."

"Yes, she says something like that about you, M. Connor. She thinks you are very clever. You must use your cleverness to make her let me go into the convent with my men, M. Connor. You must try. This other way is impossible. We will walk straight into Jagot's net. I tell her the child will not come back that way."

"I know," I said. "I think she is beginning to see that too."

"You've seen her — the child? No one will talk to me about her. Lucienne has no likeness, nothing to show me. What does she look like?"

"You," I said, remembering. "She looks just like you. She is clever and spirited."

"Of course."

"She is like no child I have ever met. Her mother called her a dragon slayer when I first met her. She said she had seen Delphine lift an elephant and its rider with one hand."

"Good. I like that. An elephant you say . . . Does she like sailing boats? She must be taught to sail and to fence."

"Yes," I said. "Delphine would be good with a sword, I think, perhaps when she's a little older. She is only five, monsieur." I motioned to indicate Delphine's height. He laughed and stood to one side to let me pass.

"Yes, perhaps she is a little young yet. *Merci, monsieur. Vous êtes gentil.* We are all relying on your cleverness, M. Connor," he called down as I reached the front door. "Talk to her."

On October 18, 1815, in the garden of a house on Saint Helena called the Briars because of its profusion of white roses, the Emperor Napoleon, newly arrived on the island, sat in the shade talking to the thirteen-year-old daughter of the house, Betsy Balcombe, who, unlike her brothers, spoke good French. Admiral Cockburn had given permission for the Emperor to stay with the English family who lived here until his prison house was completed.

Having always imagined him to be the man of English myth, half-human, half-animal, a Gorgon with a single eye in the middle of his forehead, Betsy Balcombe was charmed by the Emperor's conversation and by the set of Sèvres china he unpacked to show her — a set that had been presented to him by the people of Paris, each piece hand-painted with scenes from his great battles and victories. He showed Betsy the painted ibis on the plate that memorialized his Egyptian campaign and warned her never to go to Egypt, for she might catch ophthalmia and ruin her pretty eyes. And, yes, it is true that I practiced Mohammedanism there, he said. Fighting is a soldier's religion. And what is wrong with that? he said when she raised one eyebrow a little. Religion is an affair for women and priests. *Quant à moi,* I always adopt the religion of the country I am in. It is much simpler that way.

The garden they sat in had myrtle groves and orange trees; it was a paradise. Locals gossiped that Betsy's father, William Balcombe, a disgraced naval officer who had been pensioned off as the naval agent and purveyor to the East India Company, was the illegitimate son of royalty. He was certainly a man in exile. His wife felt this especially keenly, and she promised her children that sooner or later they would find a way back to the mainland and civilization.

This was an island populated by exiles. Napoleon sometimes talked with the Balcombes' slave, Toby, a gardener, originally Malay but abducted and sold to Saint Helena by the crew of an English ship. "It was an infamous act," Napoleon declared to Las Cases, "bringing him here to die in slavery." But when Las Cases made a comparison with

the Emperor's situation, Napoleon was enraged. "My dear man" he declared, "there can
be no comparison here . . . We are the
martyrs of an immortal cause."

22

Lucienne Bernard slept for two days. Manon sent me a note late on the first day to say she was ill, that she wouldn't wake up, that I was to come immediately and bring my medicine bag. In the warehouse, Silveira, Manon, and Saint-Vincent waited in an adjoining room.

The scene I found when I arrived moved me. Silveira had lit candles in every corner of the room where she slept and had brought flowers from the market — late sunflowers and roses — that spilled out of vases on every surface. There were bowls of figs and grapes and the air was sweet with the smell of scented oils warmed over lanterns. Where two days before there had been not only dissent but open conflict between Manon, Saint-Vincent, Lucienne, and Silveira, now there was silence, the silence of a darkened room that smelled of oil of myrrh.

An empty blue-glass bottle stood by her bed — Manon had found it among Lucienne's discarded clothes. Silveira identified the bottle as one he had given her only days before, a bottle that had contained a strong opiate tincture given to him by an apothecary in a village on the coast near Goa. He had given it to her to help her sleep. It contained perhaps eight or ten doses, he said. In a moment of desperation, sometime after she had left the warehouse that night, she had drunk the entire bottle. She had not woken or stirred since, Manon said — and her pulse was weak. I said what there was to be said, that there was nothing that would wake her until the effects of the sleeping draft had worn off.

"She's done it before," Silveira said. "Three times. Damned woman. I should have known. Once, in the desert, when we were camped in the remains of a Roman city, she stole a sleeping draft from me and slept for a week — just to spite me, I swear. When she woke she didn't know that any time at all had passed. She had been dreaming of the sea, she said, while I worried and paced about day and night. The Bedouin women gave me myrrh oil to burn. They say it is good for sleepers."

■ ■ ■ ■

I sat with Alain and Manon through the first night. Silveira would not stay — he and Sabalair had work to do, he said. For the first hour, I sat at the window and they talked, as only Saint-Vincent and Manon could talk, one story opening up inside another, shared memories and disagreements about dates and the order and origins of things.

"There are many things I don't know about her," Saint-Vincent said, turning to me and taking a knife to slice the top off one of the eggs he had boiled in the pan over the fire. "She comes and goes. She's in Paris; but then she's gone. She's running and then she's not." He paused. "We are all running, I think. She was sixteen when I first saw her — she was living with her grandmother and Manon in Marseilles."

"My mother was the housekeeper there," Manon said, glancing in my direction. "The old marquise adopted me when she died. You know, Alain, Lucienne fell in love with you when you first came to dinner, that very first night when you talked to her about the structure of algae."

"Algae? Hardly the stuff of romance," he said.

"It was to her. She was in your bed by the end of the summer."

"She seduced me . . ."

"She was sixteen. You were her tutor."

"And I was eighteen," he said, looking at me with a glint in his eye, "and I was hardly in a position to refuse or know better. It was a fine summer. But that was before the Revolution."

"In the old times," she said. "Before Daniel was born."

"Don't start on that," I said.

"It was 1793 before I saw her again. The same year that the revolutionary commission renamed all the months and years and started the new calendar from year one," Saint-Vincent said. "It took me an eternity to remember that Thermidor was half of July and half of June and Brumaire was half of September and half of October. I'd been to university and on an expedition to Africa by then. I was working in the Jardin, in the glasshouses, attending the botany lectures when I could. It was October — Brumaire — a thunderous, wild day, just three weeks after they had taken the queen to the guillotine in the place de la Révolution, the beginning of the fifteen months of the Terror, and only a short while after they had renamed the Jardin du Roi the Jardin des

Plantes and appointed all the professors. No one knew quite what they were supposed to do or who was in charge of what but there was a great sense of expectation. Lucienne turned up the same week Marchini brought the leopard to the Jardin."

"Your memory fails you, Saint-Vincent," Manon said. "It was November. I remember very clearly. It was just after she left the prison. I had given her up for dead until the letter came. And by the time I found her she might as well have been dead. She looked like a walking corpse."

I thought of the red-haired woman Lucienne had described, the woman who had stood up in the prison, who had taken Lucienne's name, the woman who disappeared into another prison and would take Lucienne's place on the guillotine the following summer. I remembered Lucienne's guilt at having sat down again. Lucienne de Luc had become Lucienne Bernard, and the red-haired woman's bones and skull were thrown into the trench in the convent garden.

"The leopard," I said. "You said it was the day they brought the leopard to the Jardin."

"*Oui. C'est vrai.* The revolutionary committee had just issued a decree," Saint-Vincent said, "outlawing the exhibition of wild animals on the streets of Paris because they were a threat to public safety. That's funny, eh? A threat to public safety. The guillotine was released onto the streets just as the wild animals were cleared off them."

"Where did it come from?" I said, imagining a leopard stalking through the streets of Paris, its reflection caught in the glint of shop fronts and coffeehouses.

"A man called Marchini," Saint-Vincent said, "owned an exotic-animal shop near the place de la Révolution. The police arrested him and brought the last four animals in his shop to the Jardin: a polar bear, a leopard, a civet, and a monkey. Once word got out that we'd taken Marchini's animals, everyone began bringing their animals to the Jardin — you could see them all coming over the bridge, or sailing down the Seine in barges. There was a queue along the quai, and chaos — monkeys, bears, even an alligator. Dubenton was in a panic. There was nowhere to put them, and people were asking ridiculous prices. They closed the gates of the Jardin and put some of the botany students at the front gate to try to stop people from pushing and shouting. That's when I saw Manon in the crowd with Lucienne, who was holding a parrot. Lucienne was dressed as a laborer; you'd never have known she was a woman. She was thin and hollowed-out, as if her clothes were holding her together."

"They were," Manon said. "There was nothing left of her, and she wouldn't let go of the damned parrot. She'd found him in the street. He was crawling with lice and so was she. None of the doctors I found would even look at her. They said there were too many mad people in Paris, it wasn't worth the time or the trouble. They were past mending, unless I had thousands of francs, of course, which I didn't. *Mon Dieu,* I was pleased to see you that day, Saint-Vincent. I had no idea what I was going to do with her."

"She terrified me," he said. "I'd never seen anyone like that before. I couldn't look at her, poor thing. I took the parrot and gave it to the people in the Jardin. Then I took her and Manon to the convent in the rue de Picpus, where a doctor I knew was looking after a few of the *aliénés.*"

"The mad people," Manon added. "It was the only thing we could do to help her. I left Paris. I had to. It wasn't safe in the streets that winter. I went back to Marseilles, where I had family."

"And I went to my house in Bordeaux," Saint-Vincent said. "I should have taken

Lucienne with me, but what would I have said to my wife? When I returned the following autumn, I went to find her. The convent was closed and the windows had all been boarded up. There was no one there. It took me weeks to find her — she was begging on the streets outside the Palais Royal. I wrote to Manon and moved Lucienne into a room in a house in the rue Royale. Charlotte Holbach, who was my mistress at the time, gave them lodgings for the winter."

"We were in good company in that house," Manon said. "There were scores of heretics and migrants living there — people who had escaped the guillotine, atheists, libertines, philosophers, artists, and writers. Everyone in that house was either mad or sleepwalking."

"Lucienne was gambling all the time at the Palais Royal," Saint-Vincent said. "Night and day. When she played, she seemed to be in a trance. She was winning more than was natural. They kept throwing her out. She kept going back. We'd lock the door to keep her in, but she'd always find a way out."

"What was wrong with her?" I asked Manon.

"She said she could see absolutely clearly in her own head what had happened all across Paris: the dying, the rotting bodies lying in the streets, the eyes of the child she saw cut away from his mother's body in the rue du Bac, the bodies they had thrown into the trenches in the convent. She couldn't get away from it. It was a constant noise, a roar inside her head. She could go to the other side of the earth and it would follow her, she said. She wanted to die."

"She was completely unmanageable," Saint-Vincent said. "She started to break into buildings to steal things in the middle of the night. I spent half my nights out looking for her. Stealing was like gambling; it excited her. It made her feel she might still be alive. She came back to the house on the rue Royale one morning with five pieces of coral from the museum. They were from her grandmother's collection, she told us. And they might have been, for all I know. She believed she had a right to them. Who knows how she did it. Reparation, she called it."

"What's the collective noun for *thieves* in French?" I'd asked Lucienne one morning as we lay listening to the sounds of the street.

"*Un repaire de brigands.* A hole, no, a den, of thieves," she said.

Den. *Répaire.* Reparation.

A reparation of thieves.

"Then she found Léon Dufour, the poet," Saint-Vincent continued, weaving Lucienne's story out of strands of the ribboned night. "She met him in the Palais Royal, and once he'd taught her to pick locks and copy and make keys, and had taken her into his bed, she started to disappear for weeks rather than days. One night she broke into an old convent and brought back some of Charlotte Holbach's paintings, which had been requisitioned by Vivant Denon and were destined for the walls of the Louvre. She was elated."

"That was it for me," Manon said. "I'd had enough. I went back to Marseilles. I wanted a quiet life. When I came back a year later, everything was different. *She* was completely different. She dressed expensively — and as a man."

"She was using a tailor on the rue Vivienne," Saint-Vincent said.

"She and Dufour and Saint-Vincent, they were organized. She had regained half of her grandmother's collection and had savings in the bank."

"I brought her books and papers on corals and zoophytes from the library in the Jardin," Saint-Vincent said, opening a bottle of brandy. "We were making a great deal of money. We had our first commissions from émigrés that winter: the Louvre, the museums in the Jardin, a monastery or two, five private houses: sixteen paintings, four necklaces, and a collection of curiosities. We charged more and more. We could because we were good."

"And Egypt," I said, meaning Silveira. "How did that happen?"

"Once the police started looking for us seriously — and who could blame them, we were a thorn in their side — I arranged for her to go to Egypt with Geoffroy," Saint-Vincent said. "She met Silveira there. They disappeared into the desert, and when she came back to Paris, years later, she had changed again. The same, but different. She started her book on the corals out there, based on conversations she'd had with Geoffroy and with Silveira and the coral traders and coral divers who worked with him."

"It was 1803 or 1804 — a long time — before she came back to Paris," Manon continued. "By then I had a job drawing botanical and animal illustrations in the Jardin."

"And I was working for Lamarck," Saint-Vincent said. "Lucienne signed up for the lectures Lamarck gave that summer in the amphitheater. It was a remarkable time — it was the summer that Lamarck first began to talk about transformism. The priests were gone; the menagerie in the Jardin was getting bigger all the time; Napoleon was sending us animals from palaces all across Europe: lions, camels, ostriches, and gazelles. And then a zebra arrived from South Africa —"

"And Lucienne?" I interrupted, afraid that we were about to disappear into the menagerie and never find our way out.

"I was stationed at Dunkirk in 1805," Saint-Vincent said, "and then in Austria, and I fought at Austerlitz, so once again we lost contact. I was wounded there. They don't give you honors or medals for being wounded, you know. And she was in Paris, back with Dufour. Sometimes she would summon me — if she had a new commission, if she needed me — but mostly she didn't. I was in Prussia and Poland in 1807, busy bayoneting Cossacks, but I missed the Battle of Eylau because I was ill . . ."

Hearing those stories about Lucienne was like turning the pages of a book, but I couldn't fit them together into anything that looked like a life with a trajectory, an arc, a beginning, a middle, and an end. I imagined her in the desert in white robes and then again in a derelict house among books, or with a parrot, standing in a queue at the gates of the Jardin.

"I hope Napoleon remembered to take my map," Saint-Vincent said as he began to fall asleep. "I expect you didn't know that I drew the very first map of Saint Helena. Yes. It's true. *Absolument.*"

"No, I didn't know that."

"My crew docked there en route back from Mauritius thirteen years ago. I collected butterflies too so I presented Napoleon with my map and the best butterfly in my collection when I got back to Paris."

"What was it like?" I saw a bare rock rising out of endless ocean.

"The butterfly? Spectacular. Blue and white with piebald markings —"

"The island."

"Oh. The island. Forty-seven square miles of paradise: samphire, tea plants, gumwoods, redwoods, she-cabbage trees, and some of the most beautiful ferns I've ever seen up on the ridges. Not such a bad place to be imprisoned."

In October 1815, the Emperor's captors provided lodgings for him in a marquee adjoining the Balcombes' ballroom. Soon Betsy Balcombe was bringing tea to the Emperor every morning in the shady grove of vines where he liked to work. He would only stay at the Briars for three months, until the paint had dried on the walls of his new prison, Longwood.

In the Briars' garden the Emperor continued to assemble the story of his life, dictating each account of battle or victory to each member of his household in turn, producing the great flow of words that would make him a legend. The Emperor was surprised by the poignancy of some of his memories. A dog came to embody all his feelings about war. "In the deep solitude of a moonlit night," he told Las Cases, "that dog came out from underneath the clothes of a dead soldier. It rushed at us and then returned to its shelter, howling with pain. It licked its master's face and then rushed at us in turn. It was asking for help and seeking revenge at the same time. Nothing," he said, "has ever made such an impression on me on any of my battlefields."

Betsy, who would leave Saint Helena for England with her mother a few years later in the wake of allegations that her father had been smuggling Napoleon's letters off the island, spent the rest of her life talking about her conversations with the Emperor of France, until she could no longer remember where the edges of dream and reality began.

The garden at the Briars, then full of white roses and oranges, would not last another ten years. The East India Company, which owned the house, bought it when the Balcombes left the island. They planted mulberry trees there and tried to cultivate silkworms. The enterprise failed, and the garden, where an Emperor had once unwrapped a Sèvres bowl to show a child a hand-painted ibis, reverted to wilderness.

23

Early on the morning of October 18, only a few hours after she had risen from her bed and asked for coffee, fried fish, and a loaf of bread before pulling on the plaster-splashed clothes of a laborer retrieved from the back of a cupboard, Lucienne took me back to the Jardin des Plantes.

"I have an idea," she said. "I want to see what you think before I tell the others. And don't tell me I'm not well enough. I am perfectly well. We have twelve days. Twelve days is not long."

"You're not still planning on going in?" I said. "That's madness. I told you —"

"Doucement," she said. "Silveira says they've doubled the guard at the convent. They're expecting trouble. They are not going to get it. We play the game, Jagot's game. Right until the end."

We were early so we had to wait for the gates of the Jardin to open. Lucienne sat on the edge of the stone parapet on the quai, kicking her boots against the stone impatiently. The clothes were too big for her and made her look thin, but she had color in her cheeks and had walked so quickly I had hardly been able to keep up with her. I thought of the broken woman with the parrot standing outside the gates of the Jardin in 1793 among the keepers and cages and wondered if Lucienne remembered her too.

The embankment was now empty. It began to rain a little, light autumn rain. The drops made intersecting circles on the water which streaked and stirred the rainbow colors of the oiled surface. A few barges began to make their way downriver; an oarsman or two took coins from a few early passengers. It made me tired to watch these moving things. It was cold.

"Before Napoleon, all of this was just mud," she said, "open land. On a day like today there'd be only swamp between here and the river, a little quai over there and timber yards and piles all along here and gardens farther down. People walked across the swamp on planks. Everything sank into the mud. Now look at it."

She was staring out across the water, lost in thought. Both banks of the Seine were clustered with washing women, casting great sails of white into the water, scrubbing fabrics of every kind against the wooden sides of washing boats or against the wide shelves of the wooden structures that jutted out into the water. Fabric, hung on lines to drip and billow in the wind, made white squares and rectangles against the green-brown of the moving water and the ragged platforms of wood. I had tried to draw them, these women with their white scarves tied across their chests and their black dresses and white bonnets, but they moved too fast.

"You were right," she said. *"Je suis désolée."*

"About what?" I said.

"About everything. Well, almost everything. Jagot. You were right about Jagot. You are still wrong about species. *Stupide,* if you don't mind me saying so. Daniel Connor is still blind about species."

"So you say," I said, and smiled. "Pigheaded, crow-headed, fish-headed. Whatever you say."

We looked down over the thin stretch of mud at the platforms on the river where bargemen stacked wood or hauled coal, and where all that wood, nailed and bolted against the water's movement, made a

fragile, splintered existence, a kind of shan-
tytown.

I thought of the huts I had seen spring up
alongside the canals that were being built
across the north of England — temporary
shacks, like something that had been expelled from some hellish region underground. At night you could see them across
the moors, lit up, smoky, loud with drinking
and shouting. As a boy I had been fascinated
by them, watching from the hill above as
the figures of men dug deep into the earth;
from time to time they used explosives to
blast their way through a rocky hillside.
There were fatalities. I had seen men,
bloodied and half-alive, carried from the
moors into the town. Some had later been
buried in the local churchyard.

Here, even in Paris, I thought, in this most
stony and solid of cities, ichthyosaurs and
plesiosaurs had once swum. Even now min-
ers were digging out their bones from the
quarries of Montmartre and the canal workings of Derbyshire. In the Jardin, where
rows of plants made neat squares in the
manicured lawns, here too there had been a
seabed populated by trilobites and sea
squirts and other creatures that I could
conjure an image for but not name. El-
ephantine creatures would have lumbered

their way up the hill of Montmartre, where windmills now turned against the skyline.

"You've changed the way I see things," I said. "Everything, the whole world, looks different now. Older. Even more of a miracle than before. I see mammoths everywhere."

"You must join an expedition," she said, "like Saint-Vincent did. Get a job as a ship's naturalist, and then you can sail around the world collecting specimens and taking trips inland, up into the mountains. Then you will start to understand how it all fits together. Go to countries you've never even dreamed of: South America, Chile, Australia . . ."

"Where would you go, if you could go anywhere?" I asked, thinking of Cuvier's plans to send me to Sumatra, which seemed to me a land full of exotic princes and palaces buried deep in monsoon-drenched jungles. I couldn't tell her about Cuvier's promise. I didn't want her to know how much I was risking.

"The Keeling Islands," she said, "halfway between New South Wales and Ceylon. Silveira's been there. He says there are coral reefs there that are the largest he has ever seen. And New Zealand. And Tahiti and Peru . . . or to the fossil coral beds on the mountains of Timor."

Beyond the wooden platforms, the Seine, swelling, rising, and falling, had left the imprints of its own movement on the mud printed like the annotations of music or the marks of wind on sand. There were the prints and scratchings of men and river birds and animals — horses' hooves and the paw marks of dogs. A boy, in the water up to his waist, appeared to be looking for treasure, filtering river water and mud through an old sieve. He had already amassed a neat pile of driftwood. Later he would tie the wood into bundles and sell them as firewood at the market.

"What do you see?" I asked.

"Lamarck calls it *la marche,*" she said. "He calls it progress. He assumes everything is moving forward, progressing, improving. That process is still a straight line though — even for Lamarck. I don't see straight lines. I see a net. Nature is a great tangle, like the coral reefs. Like a garden in which everything lives on everything else, some things changing, others staying almost the same. Everything — animals, trees, rocks — made of the same materials."

"And if the Bible . . ." I couldn't finish the sentence. My questions were breaking up; I didn't know how to frame them. "And if?" I repeated and stopped.

"Look at this rock," she said, running her finger along the pink-white stone of the embankment wall. "See the madrepores, the circles here and here, and these sea creatures here, mixed in among the shale. Their bodies made the continents, over millions and millions of years. Not God in one sudden sweep of his hand. Napoleon may have built the wall, but sea creatures made the stone."

"There is no god?"

"That's not what I said. Who am I to say? Who are any of us to say?"

"Saint-Vincent thinks there is no god. He is a heretic."

"He might think it; he would not say it. He has principles. He keeps these things to himself."

"And Manon?"

"Manon? She *would* say it. Out loud. *Oui.* She would shout it. Her mother was a Catholic. She died in torment, terrified of damnation. Manon watched that and it was enough for her. She *is* a heretic."

"And Silveira?"

"He goes to synagogue. He reads the Torah. He keeps the Sabbath."

"He believes?"

"No. Silveira has no god. He says it's a Christian obsession, this insistence on God, on belief, on talking about it all the time.

For him, it's the rituals, his people, *l'histoire,* that matters. It is his anchor. The root of everything. Yes, I think that's what he would say."

"There it is," she said once we'd made our way through the Jardin. "That building, with the green roof." She gestured at a hut in the middle of a small enclosure just outside the Botany Gallery, where a few students waited in the rain. "I didn't see it on the map until the other night, after I'd drunk the sleeping draft. It's listed as number nine on the map. I tried to stay awake but . . . On the key you've labeled it as the entrance to the quarries. Is that what it is?"

"Yes. Inside the hut there's a set of stone steps that lead down to the quarries."

"Just as I had hoped. How did it get there?"

"You mean who built it? Men with spades and pickaxes and wheelbarrows, I expect. It goes a long way down."

"*Mais, non. Why* is it there?"

"Cuvier and Brongniart had it built a few years ago, when they were writing the joint paper on the rock strata of the Paris basin, I think. They wanted to see the rock layers as far down under the city as it was possible to go. Cuvier uses the quarries for teaching occasionally, when he's doing his lectures on fossil bones, but mostly the entrance is unused."

"And the steps go all the way down to the main quarry system?"

"Straight down, yes."

"Can you get me the key to the hut?"

"I've no idea where it's kept. But I can probably find out. I'll try," I said, seeing her frustration. "If it's important. But why?"

"*Alors.* Jagot's orders are that we leave the Jardin by the gate at the river entrance on the night of the party. He will wait for us there. That is where we're supposed to hand over the diamond. And although he says he won't, that is where he will arrest us. Instead we will change things a little. We will leave the Jardin a different way — we will go down Cuvier's staircase, through the main quarry system, and then back up into the streets of Paris. We will do things my way."

"That's brilliant," I said. "Jagot will never know how you got out. It will be as if you've disappeared completely."

"Except that Jagot will still have Delphine. You forget that. Now, Daniel, listen to me. I want you to tell Jagot that we're going out through the quarries. I want you to warn him that we will break the deal. Find a way to make sure he is waiting for us, exactly in the passage de Saint-Claire, and make sure he brings Delphine."

"Why would you want me to do that? He'll arrest you down there. You'll lose your advantage. It's madness."

"Daniel, you must trust me. I have a new plan. I think I can see a way to rescue Delphine, take ourselves off Jagot's list, and make sure you keep Cuvier's patronage and your position at the Jardin. I want you to go to Jagot tomorrow and convince him that we have had a quarrel and you want revenge."

"He won't believe that."

"Tell him you've been betrayed. Convince him you're full of revenge. Ask him for a reward. Then he'll know he can trust you. Jagot understands greed. Tell him you've overheard me talking to Silveira about a theft in the Jardin and an escape through the quarries. Give him the details. Tell him we plan to meet in the passage de Saint-Claire at seven o'clock the morning after the party."

"But he will be there waiting for you."

"*Exactement.* In the quarries I know my way and he does not. Down there we will be running the show. There are nearly two hundred miles to disappear into. It's time we took ourselves off Jagot's list."

"And how do we do that?"

"We will be magicians after all. We'll put on a little show of our own, in our subterranean theater. You don't understand. You don't see, do you?" I shook my head. "Jagot must have his revenge. We can't change that. So we let him have his revenge. We make him think he has won. To do that, we must stage some deaths."

24

In the coral room of the locksmith's atelier
the stuffed crocodile had disappeared; the
corals were almost gone; the shelves were
bare. The room had a new echo to it.
Wrapped in strips of purple silk torn from a
dress abandoned by an émigrée who may or
may not have survived the Terror, each piece
of coral had been folded into the brittle
darkness of the dried and shredded seaweed
that filled the packing cases.

Lucienne's flight back to safety in Italy,
now postponed until after an audacious
theft that might still take her in another
direction, to Toulon, was now prepared for.
Packing cases had been nailed down, labels
glued to wood. Her departure was inevi-
table, I knew, but the waiting was almost
intolerable. Alone for a few minutes one
afternoon, I found a label pasted onto the
corner of one box written in a hand I did
not recognize: *Ufficio Postale, La Spezia, Ita-*

lia. La Spezia. I couldn't even remember where that was — somewhere to the north, perhaps, up near Turin. Only one cabinet remained, the long table, and the map. Soon she too would disappear — they all would, taking flight again like the swallows that gathered along the Paris rooftops.

All that autumn there had been rumors that Napoleon was already back in Paris, hiding in the quarries and planning to retake the city, rumors carried by lantern men, fiacre drivers, and street sweepers passed on to anyone who would listen. Some wine smugglers even claimed that they had seen the Emperor down there; he had an army, they said, that might come up through the ventilation shafts at any time, night or day.

The stone quarries ran like a rabbit warren for hundreds of miles beneath the Parisian streets. They had been mined for thousands of years, it was said, rock carved out and hauled up to provide the stone with which to build the city.

When gases from the shallow and overcrowded graves in the Les Innocents cemetery asphyxiated a family living in a basement nearby in the rue de la Lingérie in the last years of the eighteenth century, police lieutenant general Alexandre Lenoir proposed closing all the Paris graveyards, disinterring the bones, and building an ossuary in one section of the abandoned quarries. Grave diggers worked at night, then carried the bones on covered carts through the streets; laborers carried the bones down into the quarries in sacks. The great leveling had begun even before the Revolution, people said, when the bones of murderers and nobles, priests, mistresses, and maids became mixed up belowground without headstone or marking.

Twenty years later, in 1809, the emperor Napoleon appointed an ex-viscount turned mining engineer called Louis-Étienne Héricart de Thury to oversee the quarries and the catacombs, to map them and make them safe. Héricart, now inspector general of underground works, walked the streets aboveground and below, directed the decorative rearrangement of the bones in the area that housed the catacombs, named and inscribed large sections of the tunnels to ensure that no one would get lost down there or starve to death, and counted and mapped sixty-three shafts or wells — *puits* — all over the city, a catalogue of holes, some with steps, some just holes. Some were ventilation shafts, some abandoned wells. In 1815 there were sixty-three entrances to the quarries and catacombs, sixty-three holes into the underground of Paris, and one of them began in the Jardin des Plantes.

"Why do you tell me all of this now, M. Connor?" Jagot had asked, sitting in the pews of the church of San-Roche, where I had asked him to meet me. The church smelled of mold; high arches swept in every direction, rhythmic curves of light against the darkness.

"I am grateful, of course," he said, peeling an orange. The juice fell in thick drops onto the brown wool of his trousers. "But it is a little unusual, *n'est-ce pas?* You and Lucienne Bernard are friends, no? That is what is in my files. It is unusual for friends to betray each other. Now you come to see me, I think: What is happening here?"

"She has someone else," I said. "There was a fight."

"M. Silveira?" Jagot said slowly, putting a segment of orange into his mouth. "Silveira is back in Lucienne Bernard's bed and now you come to me to betray them? You are jealous, *oui?* You want revenge?"

"Monsieur," I said, "you told me to watch. You told me to listen. That's what I have been doing. Watching and listening."

I was glad of the shadows in the church;

the less Jagot could see me and read my expression, the better. Jagot, it seemed, had taken the bait. As far as he was concerned, I was a new opportunity. He had laid his elaborate trap for Lucienne and Silveira, and now here was Lucienne's jilted lover, the jealous boy Daniel Connor, offering to help — in exchange, of course, for some reward. He might have tried to maintain a stony exterior, but Jagot's delight was palpable.

"And the man who commissioned this robbery," Jagot said, his head tipped to one side as he watched my reactions closely, testing me to see how much I knew. "Do you have a name for him?"

I was nervous.

All you have to do is get Jagot to bring Delphine down to the quarries, Daniel, she had said. *I don't care what you do or say to make that happen, but everything depends on Jagot bringing Delphine down there.*

"No, monsieur," I lied, returning his gaze. "I don't know the name of the man behind this. That is something I can't discover, although I have tried. They never use his name."

"And you say their rendezvous is in the passage de Saint-Claire — the morning after the theft? So all I have to do is to wait for them to come out — like rats from a sewer. Yes, that is good. So where will they come out, M. Connor? Where will I wait to catch my thieves?"

"They will separate and go in different directions," I said. "At least that's the plan. They will all come up through different shafts. There are many entrances to the quarries, I think."

"*Merde.* That means we'll have to go down ourselves," Jagot said. "We'll have to wait for them in the passage de Saint-Claire. That is where we must put out our nets."

"They know the quarries well," I said. "Perhaps you need bait. Something to make sure you keep them there, to stop them from slipping through your fingers."

"Good idea, M. Connor." He paused for a moment, calculating. "*Bien sûr.* The child. Perhaps when you have finished working for the baron, you will come and work for me. You have a mind that works like chess. I will need you to keep listening, of course. Tell Madame Bernard that all is forgiven. Convince her. Keep a notebook. Write down everything — even the little things. You must go with them into the museum that night — to make sure you bring them to me."

"I can't do that," I said, taking a deep breath — this was the most difficult part of my dissemblance. Jagot must make me his inside man, but I must not agree to his plan too easily. It would make him suspicious. "You can't ask me to do that," I said. "It's much too risky. What if they find out that I had told you? Silveira is dangerous. He might . . . I don't know what he might do. And what about Cuvier?"

"I will straighten everything out with Professor Cuvier afterward. You are valuable, monsieur. Already you are the senior *aide-naturaliste* in Cuvier's museum, after — what is it? — three months. My men tell me that Baron Cuvier has plans for you. Your future is secure. Now, if you will help me to bring in these people who are also the enemies of Cuvier, you will see how your value increases even more for the baron."

And of course, I agreed.

"You are an ambitious man, M. Connor," Jagot said. "You are a credit to the baron."

He knew the quarries from before, he told me that day, from the days when every criminal in Paris knew them; he had often hidden there. Now every police agent must get to know the quarry tunnels, he insisted, their nodes and intersections, the places where they had been shored up to prevent the roof caving in, the places where the walls formed long passages as wide and high as streets or arcades, or where the tunnels lead to caves as large as churches.

And he talked of Silveira. When Jagot talked of Silveira it was always with admiration. "Silveira has many women," the police agent said that afternoon, "but it is always Paris and Dufour's mistress Bernard that he returns to. So, when we watched Bernard, we also watched *Trompe-la-Mort*. He was always somewhere close by. Now they have come back to Paris. And I will catch them all in the same net. He returns to Mme. Bernard one time too many. And now there is a child. She brings the child to Paris, puts her in the convent in the rue de Picpus, and goes to find Silveira. And then I find her. Every thief has an Achilles' heel, M. Connor."

"Yes, monsieur," I say, "I remember."

At Longwood, the Emperor was under constant surveillance. A guard of the Fifty-third Regiment, a park of artillery, and a company of the Sixty-sixth were permanently encamped at his gate, the soldiers' spyglasses focused on the windows of the house. Between Longwood and the town a further post of twenty men encircled the entire headland and enclosure. At night the chain of sentries almost touched one another. Out to sea, two men-of-war patrolled the island and two frigates watched over the only two landing points.

Longwood belongs to the termites, Las Cases complained, pointing out to General Marchand the corner of the billiard-room floor in Napoleon's prison house that was riddled with holes. The termites — exiles too, shipwrecked, washed ashore on a Brazilian slave ship — now lived in the walls and floors of all the houses on the island, chewing wood into the pulp with which they built their own vast and dusty nests.

Termites thrived in the damp of Longwood. Las Cases ordered logs to be burned in every fireplace, but the heat only turned the prison house into a hothouse and the mildew extended its silky threads still farther. The paper swelled. The doors stuck. The windows fogged up.

As Napoleon, in his last six years, shored up paragraph after paragraph of his memoirs, spreading maps and diagrams of battles over the green baize of the billiard table, storing words that would themselves be rewritten and expanded by others, swelling into scores and then hundreds of books on the life and battles of the first French Emperor, the termites were eating their way through walls, floors, tables, and chairs. You could almost hear them. One day there would be nothing left of the Emperor's prison house, not a single plank of original wood, window frame or floor. Dust to dust. And ashes to ashes. It was this reflection that kept the Emperor laboring at his memoirs until the end.

25

The twenty-ninth of October, the day of the party, arrived. At seven o'clock, at the gatehouse on the rue de Seine, while three uniformed guards checked identity papers and letters of invitation, I glimpsed the tiny shape of Jagot's fiacre, curtains drawn, parked down where the street met the quai. I passed over my papers to the guards without looking back.

"Can't get the damned smell out," Fin said when he met me by the corner of the amphitheater, where the shadows stretched across the clipped oval of grass. "I've washed and changed my clothes, but it's in my skin — that smell . . . Wine spirits and arsenic soap. I've probably absorbed so much now that I'm as well preserved as those two-headed calves in Cuvier's museum. Can you smell it? How bad is it?"

I leaned toward him and sniffed. "You can smell it," I said, "but it's not too bad."

"I'm too tired to be sycophantic to Cuvier tonight," he said. "I could sleep for a month at least. I'm only here because he wants a full turnout for Brugmans. Why can't people get jobs just because they're good? What was the bloody Revolution for, eh? Now everything depends on being nice to the baron and smelling good and having clean fingernails and a good reference to take back to the surgeons in England. I don't want to be nice to the baron and my fingernails are filthy. I need a large glass of wine."

Inside the mirrored hall, among vases of orange and red-striped canna lilies, Cuvier's wife and daughter, the melancholy Clémentine, dressed in black, received their guests. Liveried footmen took our coats. Upstairs in the parlor the baron stood robed in state among a group of fawning foreigners. Baron Georges Léopold Chrétien Frédéric Dagobert Cuvier, member of the Institute of France, professor and administrator of the Museum of Natural History, member of the Academy of Sciences and of the Royal Society, et cetera. He was a pillar of the academy and a bastion of the French establishment. I counted ten footmen.

"It must take over an hour to get his clothes off," Fin said. "It's practically a suit of armor. Do you think he wears a corset?

One of Mme. Cuvier's perhaps?" Fin had already had too much wine. He'd been drinking at the tavern after work with the taxidermists. Cuvier was in his purple robes that night, robes he had designed himself for official occasions, embroidered in gold and encrusted with medals.

"Lamarck's here," I said. Over in the corner a tall, thin man with white hair leaned against a wall, sipping from a glass and talking to a small woman dressed in black. "That's his daughter, Cornélie. She does all his writing for him now, to save his eyes. And that's Geoffroy over there, talking to Sophie Duvaucel. And that's Brongniart, the professor of mineralogy, and Desfontaines, professor of botany. Christ, they're all here. Seven, no eight of the professors. It's a united French front. The negotiations have begun."

"Cuvier looks like he'd be entirely at home in Versailles," Fin said. "And there he is — the villain, Brugmans, well, villain at least as far as they're concerned. Tonight he has all the power."

From where I was standing, Brugmans's face was impassive, wide and full, but his eyes showed absolutely no expression at all. He was going through the motions, it seemed, as if he was a marionette. If he was enjoying the power of his position, I thought, he certainly wasn't prepared to show it.

As rector of the University of Leiden, Brugmans was familiar with the politics and machinations of men of science. He was a tireless negotiator: Joseph Banks had summoned him to London ten years before to negotiate a price for the 3,461 sheets of mounted dried flowers and plants that made up the herbarium of the dead George Clifford. It had been a delicate business.

"M. Connor." A woman's voice. I turned to face Sophie Duvaucel, who had walked over to talk to us.

"Mlle. Duvaucel, may I introduce my friend M. Robertson?"

"*Enchanté, mademoiselle,*" Fin said a little stiffly, taking her hand.

"I do believe," she said in English, "that I overheard you two men speaking in English a few minutes ago. You know, I don't believe anyone is supposed to be speaking in English this evening. I think the baron expects—"

"Are we being chided, Mlle. Duvaucel?" I said.

"No, quite the contrary. I was hoping that I might join you in your little act of rebellion. My English is weak, you see, and I think if we keep our voices down, we might take a few turns in English without being overheard. It will add some danger to an evening that promises to be especially dull." She smiled.

"I think we could manage a little English," Fin said grinning. "If you command it, I mean; we are not in a position to refuse."

"Oh, yes, I insist," she said. "Would you oblige me by going through all these formalities of conversation in English?"

"Mlle. Duvaucel," Fin began, "we have not met before. I work for your father. I have recently joined the laboratory. I work alongside your brother M. Duvaucel, under the authority of M. Dufresne."

"I envy you, monsieur, all that skin." Fin did not blink, nor — and I admired him for this — did he glance in my direction for support. Sophie, it seemed, was in high spirits. With the pressure of Brugmans's imminent arrival, I had not seen much of her of late.

"It's messy, mademoiselle," Fin said. "Not as good as it seems."

"No. There is not much in this world that is as good as it seems, *n'est-ce pas?*"

"It depends," I said. "On your expectations. Whether they are low or high."

"Oh, my expectations are, I believe, un-usually high."

"Well, then, many things will not be as good as they seem."

"Bravo, how wise you are, M. Connor. Now I think it's time to try a different subject. Now I will ask you about how you have been enjoying Paris. I hope you have been along to M. Reaux's circus on the rue Saint-Honoré to see the Hottentot woman dance. M. Reaux has a rhinoceros on display there too. They call her the Hottentot Venus — the woman, that is, not the rhinoceros."

"No, mademoiselle. I have not."

"Then you must be quick, M. Connor. They say she is dying. All the men in Paris want to see the Hottentot woman dance, while there is still time."

"Yes," Fin said, a little embarrassed. "I've been there."

"And are they as people say?" she said. "Her parts, I mean. They say they protrude like a man's. Is it interesting?"

"Well, it's rather distasteful really. She dances a little. Then reveals herself, part by part . . ."

"It is alluring, seductive?"

"No, it's a freak show. A circus. She wears a mask. But yes, her body is remarkable. From the scientific point of view, I mean."

"And you, M. Connor? Does the body of the Hottentot woman interest you?"

"No," I said. "No. I don't think I would want to see that."

"She fell down on the stage last night, they say. Drunk."

"Why do you take an interest in this woman, mademoiselle?" I asked.

"My stepfather bought her a few weeks ago when he was sure that she was dying, of course. I hear daily reports about her health, like weather reports. She is coming here, to the museum — as soon as she is dead. She's in the last stages of syphilis, you see, although she is still young."

"Surely you can't buy people in Europe," I said. "She's not a slave." The conversation was making me angry, an emotion I could not afford that evening.

"Oh, you can buy dead people, monsieur, in Paris. My stepfather buys dead bodies — for the purposes of enlightenment, of course. He's going to dissect the Hottentot Venus in the laboratory where you work, M. Robertson. Then he'll make a series of casts. She's to go in the main hall in the museum between the orangutan and the male African. A prize exhibit. She'll be more famous here than she is onstage. She is to be promoted from the freak show to the museum."

"That's grotesque," I said. "There's something very degrading in that."

"Yes, M. Connor," she said suddenly, her voice at a whisper. "There is something very degrading in that. It sickens me. There are sometimes things here in this house and in this museum that sicken me."

"Sophie?" Clémentine Cuvier had approached us, dressed in her old-fashioned dress with ruffs at the neck. Her hair was pinned rather too tightly to her head, giving her a pinched expression.

"M. Robertson, may I introduce my sister, Mlle. Clémentine Cuvier. Clémentine, M. Robertson. You know M. Connor, of course."

I glanced over to Cuvier. In the corner near Brugmans, he seemed to be struggling. A little pale, a little sweaty, he had lowered himself into a chair. His secretary, Charles Laurillard, passed him a glass of water. I couldn't imagine Cuvier out in the forests of India collecting wild animals. No, he sent his protégés to do that. Some of them would die collecting for him.

"Will you excuse me, messieurs," Sophie said. "We have duties."

■ ■ ■ ■

At the same moment, on the night of October 29, 1815, while Cuvier performed for the Dutch ambassador, in another part of Paris on an unlit road in a region called Picpus, a fiacre followed a woman in a black fur-lined coat who was walking toward the convent carrying a child's soldier's uniform wrapped in dark blue tissue paper and tied with gold ribbon.

Manon Laforge knew she was being followed, of course, but it didn't stop her from feeling anxious. It was meant to be this way. All was as it should be. It was all part of the plan she had gone over and over again with Lucienne. This was the most difficult part of the plan to choreograph.

"It's the only way," Lucienne had explained to me. "If Jagot knows we're going to break the deal and escape through the quarries, he will take Delphine from the convent and bring her as a hostage in exchange for the diamond. Which is exactly what I want him to do. Once Delphine is down there in the quarries, I can reach her. We will be on my ground. But Delphine must not be alone with Jagot's men. She will be afraid. She must have someone who can protect her if anything goes wrong. I can't go; it must be Manon."

So this part of the plan had depended on the staged and slow exchange of secrets between me and Jagot over the course of the previous week. *Manon Laforge will try to rescue the child from the convent on the night of the robbery,* I wrote. *Nine o'clock. When your men change shifts. She will come to the side door dressed in a black fur-lined coat. She will carry a parcel — a red soldier's uniform for the child. A disguise.*

Excellent. A second hostage will only strengthen my hand, Jagot replied by return.

Manon looked around. There was no one else in the street, just the fiacre moving toward her. She was anxious, despite the carefully orchestrated plan. She knew there were risks on every side. She walked faster. The blinds of the fiacre were drawn. It moved very slowly, following her through the night as she passed the dark ponds and the clearing, as she headed toward the darkest end of the street, to the side door of the convent, where a nun took the parcel from her and a few moments later passed out a small child dressed in a red soldier's uniform.

Manon told Delphine that she was going for a midnight walk in her new costume.

Stranger things had happened. The child talked incessantly about chickens, snails, about her new friends. She was excited. She brandished her soldier's sword.

"Whatever happens now, Delphine, you do exactly as I say, you understand?" Manon whispered. Delphine nodded.

Manon recognized the voice of Jagot as he stepped out of the fiacre and called to her sharply: "Madame Laforge," he said, "there is nowhere to run. For the safety of the child . . ."

She ran anyway, taking Delphine's hand. Her fur-lined coat, bought from the second-hand clothes shop on the alleyway that ran off the rue Vivienne, a coat that had once belonged to a countess who had lost her head, her house, and her name, slipped off her shoulders as she fell.

Delphine, disoriented by the night and imagining herself to be fighting against the English on the side of Napoleon at Auster-litz, brandished her sword to defend herself and her fallen compatriot against the sweaty and unshaven police agent. Jagot and his two men soon disarmed her but she left several tooth marks on the back of Jagot's hand.

Manon Laforge and Delphine Bernard were now the hostages of Henri Jagot. They were about to spend a few hours under guard in an inn called the Black Cat, on the corner of a street near the Jardin des Plantes, where Manon would order Delphine madeleines and tell her again about Napoleon's battle positions at the siege of Toulon.

26

In Cuvier's drawing room the butler rang a bell for silence. Because the guests were now deep in conversation and reluctant to stop talking, he rang it a second time.

Cuvier stepped into the center of the room, speaking in perfect clipped French, which was simultaneously translated by his secretary, Charles Laurillard: *"Mesdames et messieurs,"* he began.

"Ladies and gentlemen," Laurillard followed.

"In honor of our guest, M. Brugmans," Cuvier went on, "we will now take a tour of the fifteen rooms of the Museum of Comparative Anatomy, before we adjourn here for further entertainment. Please. If you would gather in the hall downstairs, we will enter the museum through the main entrance."

Fin emptied his glass of wine. So did I. I shouldn't really be drinking, I thought, but

I wasn't going to impose any rules on myself just yet. It was going to be a long night.

The thirty or forty guests and Jardin attendants followed Cuvier out onto the landing and down the curved staircase into the hall, where the canna lilies glimmered in the light of velvet-shaded lamps. The butler took his position at the front door; Cuvier took his position on the staircase above us. He waited until the crowd had fallen silent, then began to speak slowly, turning from time to time to address M. Brugmans; a corpulent man, expensively dressed, from his necktie to his medaled dark blue frock coat, to the jewels of his shoes, he puffed himself up like a courting bird.

"Gentlemen, ladies. Please take your time in the museum entrance hall. There is much of interest to see."

Cuvier descended the staircase to take up his next position at the door; the professors of the Jardin lined up behind him on either side of Brugmans. When Laurillard opened the door, a string of paper lanterns strung from trees marked a path from Cuvier's house around to the museum entrance. A cloud unveiled the moon, illuminating a fringe of flattened trees. The night air was cold and damp, full of the smell of leaf mold and abandoned bonfires; a lion roared or yawned somewhere in the menagerie and out on the clipped lawn a small band of musicians played chamber music under a blue canopy.

Spots of light punctured the dark bushes and enclosures of the menagerie to the left, where I could hear the muffled sound of peacocks and the cries or grunts of creatures I could not recognize. It was the evening feed. I looked at my pocket watch. "They're early again," I said aloud, thinking of the feeding schedules I had watched and recorded through long nights in the warehouse.

"What's early?" Sophie Duvaucel had dropped back to accompany me the few yards through the garden.

"The birds," I said, quickly. "They're early to migrate this year. That usually means a harsh winter. It's cold, don't you think? For October, I mean." I offered her my arm.

The guests gathered outside the front door of the museum while Cuvier stood on the threshold. His next stage. The servants brought the lights closer to him. They had practiced this before, I thought.

"M. Brugmans, honored guests," he said, Laurillard still bravely translating. "Welcome to the Museum of Comparative Anatomy. Everything inside this building, all the many thousands of specimens gathered from around the world, have been arranged in sequence; it is nature's ordered sequence. There is no other collection like it in the world."

Inside, as if on cue, two blue-liveried servants pulled open the enormous doors; liquid light poured into the darkness, onto the assembled crowd. The hall in front of us was full of human skeletons, some casts, some actual bones, arranged as if they were standing there in the flesh, all facing the door, a salon of bone people, pinned and wired together in the hallway of what had once been a coach house. At the base of a great staircase, a skeleton stood with arm outstretched, as if gesturing in midsentence; beside it another stood limply, arms hanging low like an ape.

A theater of bones. Cuvier had arranged the skeletons into a single line to illustrate his theory on the hierarchy of races. At one end the bones were pinioned into figures in upright postures of conversation or address, at the other end of the line, they stooped, looking vacant, arms dangling; white races at one end of the line, black races at the other. I remembered what Sophie had told me and located the space at the far end of the row, where the skeleton of the Hottentot Venus would go.

In a different line altogether were the skeleton curiosities: the thirty-seven-inch skeleton of Nicolas Ferry, a dwarf from the court of Stanislaus, king of Poland, one of three dwarfs born to French peasants, who had made good money from the sale of their tiny children. There was an ancient Egyptian skeleton, bones disinterred from a tomb, and the twisted and distorted remains of the famous Mme. Supiot, who died from a disease that made her bones so soft that her legs could be twisted around the back of her neck and who, in the course of her last miserable five years — during which she bore three children — shrank in height from five feet six inches to twenty-three inches.

Several guests gasped as the smoky light fell down through the bones, giving the effect of elongation, as if the bone people were stepping or sliding toward the door. A woman pulled her shawl more closely around herself.

Skulls, ears, legs . . . I tried to remember the order of the fifteen rooms I knew so well that led off from the hall and from the landing upstairs.

Men in black frock coats and women in satins and silks now wandered among the bone people. Cuvier now stood next to a skeleton that was pinned into a tableau of horror and pain, head tilted toward the sky, mouth open in a silent scream, a stake running through the now-invisible flesh. He waited, patiently for the guests to turn their attention to him. He beckoned to Brugmans.

"May I introduce you to M. Suleiman of Aleppo, M. Brugmans," Cuvier intoned. "Please, you must shake his hand. It is a tradition here in the Museum of Comparative Anatomy for honored guests to shake the hand of M. Suleiman."

Brugmans stepped forward, bowed, and took the charred bones of the skeletal hand in his own. The crowd clapped.

"He models his lecturing style on the French actor Talma, you know," Sophie whispered. "He's good. Knows his timing. He has been practicing a good deal lately."

Cuvier began to speak again, gesturing toward M. Suleiman: "This young Syrian assassinated the French general Kléber in Cairo fifteen years ago," he said. "A French court sentenced him to death and impaled him in the main square of Cairo, where it took him four hours to die. His right hand was cut off and burned in front of him — an example to the enemies of France. We have restored his hand for our display. But if you will look closer at his skull, just here, a little closer, you will see an unusual shape . . . It is the swelling of crime and fanaticism, yes, visible on the bone, just here."

Cuvier's men eased us into Room 2, the home of the carnivore skeletons. Here, in the absence of a chandelier, the servants carried lamps that swung from side to side so that, as we walked the length of the room, between the skeletons of rhinos and whales, the lamps cast ovals of light onto rows of eye sockets and nasal cavities and jaws. Here rows of bird skulls, there rows of antelope skulls, next fish heads of every conceivable shape: heads with beaks, antlers, tusks, elongated noses, foreshortened jaws, each species arranged in sections, in shelves and rows and boxes, all staring out, visible for a moment in the swaying circles of light, then gone.

Cuvier stopped in front of a glass display cabinet and beckoned to a pair of servants to bring the lamps closer. Another servant unlocked the cabinet and passed a pair of skulls to Cuvier. Fin eased his way to the front as the servants arranged their lamps on the table in front of Cuvier. I would have moved up closer too, responding to the magnetism of our puppet master, but there was another place I needed to find. I moved slowly to the back of the crowd.

"Two elephant skulls," Cuvier began. "This one an Indian elephant from Ceylon" — he lifted it high into the air, pausing for effect — "this one African, from the Cape of Good Hope. Both elephants, yes. But are they the same species? This question of species is a puzzle that has challenged naturalists for many years."

Cuvier looked up to find the face of Brugmans in the crowd. Securing the ambassador's gaze, he continued, "M. Brugmans will know that these two elephant skulls once belonged in the cabinet of the stadtholder, the father of the present king of the Netherlands. It was one of the greatest natural-history collections the world has ever seen. M. Brugmans will know that when the French and the Dutch made peace at the Treaty of The Hague in 1796, the great stadtholder conferred these beautiful and important objects upon the French people for the enlightenment of the world." Cuvier stopped again, seeking Brugmans's acknowledgment. But the ambassador was giving nothing away. No nod of the head or slight bow. In this ambassadorial minuet, Brugmans was refusing to dance.

Cuvier, undoubtedly irritated, flushed. He was not used to such resistance. He raised himself to his full height, pointedly moved his gaze away from Brugmans, and went on — his speech a rhetorical series of carefully honed phrases and well-chosen words. *Confer. Gift. Alliance.* I could hear where Cuvier was taking this and I admired the audacity of it. This was not a competition, he was implying, not a battle for ownership; it was an alliance. Enlightenment must transcend national borders. It was all so beautifully understated.

"Until the stadtholder's cabinet came to Paris," he continued, "the world had been of the opinion that the African and Asian elephants were of different species, one wild, the other domesticated. They *looked* different; they *behaved* differently. But it was the arrival of these two skulls from the Dutch collection that changed everything. Here in the Museum of Comparative Anatomy we knew that only the bones would give us the answer. We studied the teeth. Look at the teeth — see."

Two *aide-naturalistes* held aloft large and intricate drawings of the patterns on the teeth of the two elephant skulls.

"The markings on the Indian elephant teeth here," Cuvier said, taking a stick to point at the drawings, "are like festooned ribbons. The African elephant's teeth here have diamond-shaped markings. There are absolute differences.

"Until now naturalists looked only at the *outside* of animals, at their skin, behavior and shape. Instead we anatomists look *inside* the animals to the structures beneath the skin; we use our eyes, our microscopes, and the skill of the scalpel; we look at the shapes of bones and teeth. And now, at last, after thousands of years, nature is yielding up her secrets."

There was a murmur of approval from the crowd and more applause. "She tells us that these *are* indeed different species."

"Now look at this." A servant placed a third skull on the table. Cuvier reached for it and held it up high for the crowd. The gesture, repeated for a second time, brought to mind images of the Terror — the men of the guillotine lifting severed heads to whip up the crowd.

"Large numbers of these strange skulls," he continued, "have been dug out of the ground in the far northern parts of the Old World and the New World. If you found this skull in a mine in Siberia or Germany or Canada, you might think it an elephant skull. But how can elephants live in the cold, in the Siberian wastelands, you may ask? Yes, it is a riddle. Another of nature's riddles. Ignorant people tell fantastic stories about these creatures. In Siberia people say these animals were elephants that lived underground like moles; others say that the bones were swept there by great tidal waves. But here in France, we do not tell fantastic stories. We are not speculators or poets or storytellers. We are men of science. We look at facts. We perform experiments. We learn to read the bones."

An *aide-naturaliste* held up two new drawings into the air.

"Yes, the bones have the answer, ladies and gentlemen. If we look closely at the teeth and the jaw under a microscope, we can see that this animal wasn't an elephant at all. See — the shape of the jaw here is curved. The jaw of these two latter-day elephants is not. This creature is completely different from the elephant. It is not the ancestor of our modern elephant, so we can put away our childish stories and our superstitions, our castles in the air. We can say, without hesitation, that nature makes no leaps. There is no bridge" — he lifted the two skulls again — "no bridge between this creature and this, between the past and the present.

"M. Brugmans, how are we to understand our future if we do not know our past? We need important collections of specimens for the anatomists to decipher; they are our libraries; they are books to be read. Students travel to Paris from all over the world; we teach them to read the language of bones. Here in this museum we have the Alexandria of natural history. It must not be broken up. The world will lose out. We will all lose out.

"With the combined wealth of this collection, made as a gift from Holland to France, and the genius of French bone readers, we have a science that is creating a new world. Together the Dutch and the French are making a new highway into knowledge. Who will dare follow them?"

As the crowd applauded, I maneuvered myself back toward the door frame, checking that the servants were in front of me, checking where the lights were. I stepped through the doorway and headed down the staircase lined with shelves displaying the skulls of horses, stags, and dolphins, then into the hall, where I slipped a few drops of Silveira's strong opiate from a blue perfume bottle into each of the decanters of expensive Madeira that had been arranged on the

405

table for the guests to drink after the speeches. Then I found the door to the cupboard under the staircase — unlocked, as I knew it would be — and stepped inside.

27

Crouched in the cupboard I could now see everything. Through a chink in the door, I watched guests passing through the hall, heard their feet upon the staircase above me and their muffled voices. I saw the museum porter talking to Cuvier, taking instruction, rubbing his eyes; I saw old man Deleuze exchange a remark or two with Fin, who was biting his fingernails, yawning, and looking around for me.

An hour later, once the last glimpses of light had disappeared, and the voices had gone silent, I pushed open the door of my cupboard and stepped into a lighter shade of dark. I walked through the bones across the hallway, feeling for the bottom of the balustrade, and followed it up the staircase so that I could stand for a moment at the top and survey the territory below. The glass from the chandelier seemed to have collected whatever last moments of light there were. In that setting, it looked like a great sea creature suspended like the whales and the dolphins, a great skeleton of glass, dangling its tentacles into a coal-dark sea.

Then I walked down into the room of carnivores, where a little light falling through the windows to my left cast faint shadows of entangled bones onto the cabinets. I waited.

A hand appeared at the fourth window from the right. I glimpsed three shapes up against the glass. A hand pushed the glass from the other side without a sound. A rope was thrown, and I caught it. Still there was no sound.

First one, then two, then three hunched figures, balanced for a moment on the threshold of the window, then springing silently into the room like monkeys at the *cirque du singe.* Lucienne was closest, breathing a little fast. She reached out to touch me, her fingers brushing against my lips. She wore black trousers and a black shirt tied with a thick belt at her waist. She also had a piece of dark fabric wrapped around her head — they all did — and her face was blacked out.

"The last guests left around twenty minutes ago," I told her as she locked and bolted the window from the inside. "Cuvier and Laurillard had several glasses of Madeira together once Brugmans had gone. The opiate worked. Cuvier announced he was exhausted and disappeared off to his rooms. Mme. Cuvier and her daughters retired soon afterward. The servants will have helped themselves to the last of the wine in those decanters — they always do — and there's no movement up there at all. From what I can tell, they're all asleep."

Four thieves worked in the dark. We could do this with our eyes closed; we had rehearsed it endlessly in the warehouse across the street. Figures in black moving among the gleam of white skeletons. Four figures crouched around the wooden platform on which the rhino from the cape was mounted and slid the skeleton three feet to the side. Its head rocked slightly on its frame, teeth grinning inanely. On the floor I could see the dark outline of a trapdoor. Silveira pulled it open. The wooden steps, which were scarcely visible in the low light, disappeared below.

It was dank and musty at the bottom of the steps. At first, I couldn't see anything. Then I began to make out the edges of boxes and crates and rolled-up canvases stacked on top of one another. Once Lucienne had pulled the trapdoor closed, I lit the lamp. Four figures, three in black and me in a frock coat dressed for Cuvier's party, stood staring at one another, dazed, letting our eyes adjust.

"What is all this stuff?" Silveira asked. "I didn't expect all this."

"Cuvier has hidden the choicest pieces from the stadtholder's cabinet down here too, by the looks of things," Lucienne said. "We were right — it appears he is about to smuggle them out of Paris. Don't be distracted by anything. We must concentrate. The crate we're looking for has a label with a phoenix on it. It's in the fourth room on the right off this corridor." Jagot's men, Lucienne had told me, had gotten to the Jardin porter, who had originally helped to carry the crates into the cellar. They had broken the bones in his right hand before he'd given them the information they wanted.

"You won't take anything?" Silveira said to Lucienne, grabbing her arm as we counted down the doors. "Only what we agreed on?"

"No, of course not. The diamond's the only piece we can sell, and the lock of Napoleon's hair will do everything we need it to do. Trust me."

"That was what you said the last time, my friend."

Once we were in the fourth room on the right, and the crate with the phoenix — the largest of all the crates in the room — had been found, Lucienne turned to the rest of us. "We will take two objects only, remember. Nothing else. The lock of Napoleon's hair from Vivant Denon's private collection will be our calling card. Once we are out of Paris, I will send it to Denon, to show him where we have been. It will bring down Cuvier's little kingdom for a while."

Alain began to unwrap a series of metal tools and levers.

"Remember, no marks on the crate, Alain," she said. "No one must know we've been in here. At least, not yet. Check everything before you touch it. That crate has to go back exactly as it was. No mistakes."

"I know, I know," Saint-Vincent said, his face tight. "We've done this before."

The first pieces of wood came away easily. Alain leaned them up against the wall, making small colored dots and dashes on the inside with a pencil.

"Thirty minutes past midnight," he said, checking his pocket watch. "That gives us

411

three hours at most."

As Manon and Alain lifted the first plank of wood off the top of the crate, I climbed onto some boxes in order to see down into the gap at the top.

"My God," I said.

"What can you see?" Lucienne asked.

"Shells, bits of red coral."

"Good," she said. "That's the ugly little grotto on the top of the cabinet. Johannes Lencher's work. There should be a cup mounted on silver in the middle of the corals and shells. Lined with silver with a little silver boy riding a dolphin."

"Yes. I see it." I leaned forward and slipped my hand through the hole toward the silver child riding the dolphin.

"Don't touch it," Silveira warned. "Don't touch anything till Lucienne tells you."

"Touch the boy," Lucienne said, "and you'll almost certainly trigger a secondary locking mechanism inside. It will make my job much more difficult. So please don't."

"The cup is made of coco-de-mer," Silveira said. "Worth half a million in itself to the right person."

"No, Davide," she said. "We agreed. Nothing but the diamond. You have the replica?"

"Bien sûr." He lifted the diamond replica

from his pocket; it hung in the air like a fish glinting on a line in dark waters. "It will buy us a little time, if we need it."

Saint-Vincent and Silveira continued pulling away the layers of crate they had unscrewed and levered open, lifting the planks to one side, undressing the cabinet. I swung the lamp around, onto its inlaid surfaces. Six feet tall, it was a work of art — a fantasy, made of wood and amber, in every color imaginable.

"Ferdinand of Tyrol had it built for his collection nearly two hundred years ago," Lucienne whispered, running her fingers across the inlay. "Denon's reliquary will be in the center somewhere, and the drawers will contain the rest of the collection. The diamond is in one of the inner cabinets. I don't know how long it will take me to find it. All twenty-five drawers have separate locking mechanisms."

"You don't have much time," Saint-Vincent said. "We can't be sure how long the opiate will last. It will have different effects on people."

"It's a more complicated locking system than I had expected. I want Daniel in here with me. Both of you listen out at the bottom of the stairs. Tell me if you can hear anything moving up there."

Lucienne produced a roll of midnight-blue velvet and silk from her bag. "Tools," she said. "Arrange them from left to right exactly as I hand them to you. Pull over that box there. I need a table. Now take off your jacket and put that across the top. Yes, like that. Now the tools. Be quick. Concentrate."

I placed the tools in order across the dark wool of my frock coat: blades and scalpels; keys, master keys, wax, needles, and wires. These were the tools of the locksmith and the tools of the thief.

I passed Lucienne the master key. She slipped it into the lock opening. With a single turn to the right, the panel doors swung open to reveal a series of boxes, even more intricately inlaid than the outer ones. I shuddered. Outside somewhere, up there in the distance of the garden, I heard the faint echo of a buffalo bellowing into the night air. A long way from home, I thought, running my eyes over the elaborate mosaic of ambers and ebonies, geometric designs, squares inside circles, rectangles, triangles, repeating in endless succession in the illusory corridor made by the mirrors on the inside of the doors.

Twenty-five drawers were arranged around a central arched display case, fitted out like a stage. A tiny metal ring was attached to each drawer, and each was decorated with the silhouette of an eagle, wings outstretched.

"Don't touch," Lucienne said quickly as I reached out my hand toward one of the drawers. "You have to do it in the right sequence. Touch one randomly and the others will deadlock against you. Then we'll never get in."

"There are no keyholes," I said.

"The birds are the keys."

"The eagles?"

"They're not eagles. They're phoenixes. The sequence is hidden in the birds in some way, in the pattern of their wings and heads. Hold the lamp back over in the corner for a moment. It's too bright."

I did as she said, casting her back into semidarkness.

"What are you doing?" I asked.

"Feeling the wings for a number and sequence pattern. Keep the light still and talk to me." Lucienne's delicate fingers played over the edge of the bird on the top right-hand drawer.

"Where did you learn to do all of this?"

"Dufour. He was the best locksmith in France. He taught me."

Lucienne was going through the drawers now, pulling them out one by one. She passed me a hard, polished object. "What do you think that is?"

"No idea," I said, placing the object close to the lamp.

"It's the horn of a gazelle. Just the tip. Coated in gold and sold as a unicorn's horn." She picked out a branch of highly polished red coral and passed it to me. I ran my fingers over its twists and turns. She slipped something or some things — I didn't see clearly enough — into her waist-coat pocket.

"Now that the drawers are open, the central cupboard should be easy. Here," she said, "come closer. *Regard.* I would guess that no more than a few dozen people have ever seen inside. Now it's your turn. Put the lamp on the table there. Now, here." She took my hand. "Put your finger just here on this mechanism. Pull it a little toward you, and then turn it sharply to the right."

I did. Nothing happened.

"Too heavy-handed. Try again. Do it with your eyes closed. Feel it. Toward you, and then a flick to the right."

I did. It slid away suddenly, yielding itself. The door behind the mirror opened. Inside there was only one object, about a foot high — something like a cross between a silver goblet, a lamp, and a miniature cathedral, complete with a fish-scaled spire and flying buttresses.

"Bravo," she said, and when she kissed me, my knees buckled so that I had to steady myself against the wall. All of this — the darkness, the smell of her, the boxes and the levers and the locks, aroused me.

"Denon's reliquary," she said, lifting it out carefully and placing it among the tools scattered across the wool. She reached for the lamp. "Now, if anyone needed proof of the madness of the director of the Louvre, here it is. He has adapted a rare medieval reliquary to hold the smallest objects in his collection. See, the drawers in the middle section are all labeled. They hold the powdered bones of people who have become legends: El Cid, the Castilian knight who conquered Valencia; Ximines, the medieval Spanish theologian and philosopher; Inês de Castro, the murdered queen of Portugal; and Agnès Sorel, the mistress of Charles VII, who was poisoned with mercury."

"It could be anyone's bones," I said.

"Oh, they are all authenticated," she said, her eyes shining in the darkness. "They have to be. There's a lot of money in relics. There will be signed documents. Certificates."

"Signed by whom?"

"Authenticators. People who authenticate."

"Take me with you," I said suddenly, "to Italy."

"And what would you do there, in Italy, M. Daniel Connor? You have work to do, places to go, questions to find the answers to." She pulled out some objects from the drawers of the reliquary: "Molière, La Fontaine, Voltaire — that's a tooth, one of Voltaire's teeth — and a lock of Desaix's hair. I've seen more than a hundred of Voltaire's teeth," she said. "All of them authenticated."

She was still leaning over the reliquary. I stepped toward her, and placed my hand on the back of her neck, caressing her there where skin met hair, full of longing.

"*Non, non,* Daniel, we'll make mistakes," she said, pushing me away. "We can't make mistakes."

I examined the reliquary, its filigree and arches and colored glass and ornamental leaves and handles, delicate under my fingers. Denon had given over the third side of the reliquary to his new Napoleon relic collection. There were six drawers, only two of them filled: one with the lock of hair given to Denon in Egypt, another with a signature torn from a letter.

"Look," I said, lifting a jewel from an unlabeled drawer between two others, one labeled EL CID and the other NAPOLEON. "Is this it?" I asked, passing her both the lock of hair and the diamond.

"The Satar diamond. One diamond," she said, clapping her hands together. "And one lock of an Emperor's hair to topple another."

28

If Deleuze hadn't drawn the map, if Napoleon hadn't lost at Waterloo . . . if the Dutch ambassador hadn't been in Paris . . . if I hadn't been on that mail coach . . . Like Jagot's systems of surveillance and reports, like the corals on the seabed, all the little things, all the crossings and collisions, had added up to something unexpected and of consequence.

Doors and drawers were closed, cogs slid and turned into locking mechanisms. Each phoenix was eased back into place. The black velvet cover slipped back over the polished wood corners of the cabinet again.

They positioned the pieces of crate around the cabinet and then hammered them back into place. The boy riding on the dolphin disappeared into the dark blue-black, tangled sea.

Not a shred of cloth or splinter of wood

remained behind that night on the floor of the vault around the crate; not a single fingerprint remained on a wall or glass cabinet. We took every last piece of dust with us back through the hole.

After Lucienne gave the order to put out the light, we climbed the staircase into the carnivore room by touch alone, closed the trapdoor, slid the rhinoceros skeleton back into place, listening for the catch, and made our way in single file through the dark into the hall of skeletons. We climbed the sweeping staircase, walked through the upper gallery of skulls into Cuvier's house, where a household still slept, limbs heavy, dreams dense. We unlocked, opened, closed, and relocked intersecting doors, slipped through the study rooms flanked by empty desks, down the narrow corridor past the row of bedrooms, down the main staircase, down the servants' staircase, into the servants' hall, where four servants had fallen asleep at the kitchen table. Then we were out through the window in the scullery into a garden, where a moon was just slipping out from behind a cloud.

Lucienne Bernard wanted to disappear, to be erased from Jagot's records and from Jagot's memory. She wanted that for all of them. But first, in order to make that happen, she had said we must stage some deaths. And that's exactly what we did.

Silveira, Saint-Vincent, Lucienne, and I climbed over the gate into the buffalo paddock; our feet sank deep into the dark mud. The buffalos stood looking on, eyes large and wide, their breath frosted in the night air.

"I'll catch up with you," she said to Silveira and Saint-Vincent, who were already heading toward the entrance to the quarries. "Don't wait. Leave a trail for us. I need a few minutes to catch my breath."

As the two men disappeared into the bushes, she turned to me, her eyes full of tears: "You must go back now. We agreed. It's time. Remember what to tell the guards — that you fell asleep in the museum; you woke up and stumbled on the thieves; they were armed so you followed them out into the gardens. You tried to stop them, but they overpowered you."

Somewhere over to the right we heard the sound of Jagot's dogs.

"It's too late," I said, relieved at least temporarily from the pain of saying goodbye. "I can't go back now. And anyway, Jagot expects me to bring you to him."

"Can you run?" she asked.

We ran. It was a kind of instinct. We ran from the sound of the dogs through the trees. Lights started to appear in the houses to our left. I thought of Cuvier and his household rising, as if out of a hundred-year sleep, confused and in disarray — no fires lit, clothing scattered on floors, no servants awake or alert enough to tend or tidy.

We ran past the lake with the water birds where a single flamingo raised its head and looked toward us, past the paddock with the sheep and goats and alpaca and the small ruminating animals, through the gates of the menagerie where behind us we heard the elephants bellow in reply to the sounds of the dogs.

"We have to get to the other side of that house," she said, pointing, "without being seen. It's where the professors of mineralogy and agriculture live. Stick to this side of the shrubs. We haven't got long. This place will be crawling with guards and gardeners any moment."

We reached the hut in the center of a field; Silveira and Saint-Vincent, who had gone ahead, had left the door open. Inside, we closed and locked the door behind us, shutting out the sound of the dogs.

"Cuvier's entrance to the quarries," she said, nodding at the steps that spiraled down like an ammonite or a nautilus in the center of the stone floor. We picked up the lamp Silveira and Saint-Vincent had left us. "Number nine on Deleuze's map. This staircase connects with hundreds of miles of quarry passageways; they stretch from here all the way over to Grenelle and Montrouge."

"It will swallow you up," I said. "You said that, that night on the mail coach. 'Paris will swallow you up.' It's going to swallow us both."

"Just concentrate," she said, taking the first steps down. "Watch where you put your feet. These steps are wet."

Bits of earth or mortar, displaced by our footsteps, tumbled down from stone to stone with a dull echo. I kept my shoulder to the wall, soiling my coat and cuffs with chalky dirt.

"Forty-nine steps," she said. "Héricart's book says there are forty-nine steps. It's nine meters deep."

Here and there on the walls, I could see marks in red chalk where someone, possibly Cuvier himself, had circled the imprint of a small fossil in the rock, and here and there, too, were lines where he had marked out the shift from one level of strata to another. This was another of Cuvier's theatrical stages: Cuvier, or Brongniart perhaps, had pasted various drawings and diagrams to the walls — one in particular represented a cross section of strata — labeled *étages*. *Étage* — stage, story of a building, strata. All three at once.

At the bottom of the forty-nine steps we stood at the entrance to the quarries. I hadn't expected the ceiling to be so flat, or the walls to be so white; even here in the darkness the walls hewn from white stone gleamed under the light from the lamp. The ceiling, low enough to touch, was cracked and split in places.

"Silveira's left us a mark," she said holding up the lamp to show me a black ink mark signed underneath with two letters, *DS* — Davide Silveira — and a circle with a single dot inside. "All we have to do is follow Silveira's trail through to the passage de Saint-Claire. That's what we agreed, if we got separated. We've used the quarries before."

"You know them? You can get us out? Without a map?"

"You can't *know* the quarries. They're like a dark polyp with a thousand tentacles that spread out underneath the streets. You have to respect them. We've had to hide down here several times. We have about an hour left of the lamp."

The numerous passages that forked off to the right and the left were all exactly the same as the one we were following — long, low, white. The light from the lamp illuminated only a few feet ahead of us; who knew what was beyond? I could imagine all sorts of horrors down there in the darkness: things with feathers, fur, claws, creatures of nightmare — or soldiers' limbs severed and festering. Bones. I could imagine anything.

We followed the circles with the dot at the center.

"Be careful where you step," she said. "There have been collapses — houses falling down, streets folding in."

"So why don't they close them? Seal up all the entrances and refill the tunnels? Make them safe."

"There are hundreds of miles of tunnels, Daniel. What would you fill them with? They're so big you could hide the whole population of Paris down here. The revolutionaries used the tunnels for hiding and for getting around the city. Before that, smugglers. But all sorts of people use them now. Some of these passageways open up into caverns with high roofs. I've seen printing presses down here, and near the Marais there's an illegal mint under the moneylender's house."

"A mint, underground?"

"We only saw it through a crack in an adjoining wall. It was a cavern full of tools and furnaces, crucibles, chemicals, and blocks of metal, and in the middle there was a minting machine, operated by five or six workmen. People say there's a Knights Templar temple down here somewhere."

We reached a crossing point where passageways met and where the ceiling stretched far up above us. It was supported by pillars, five or six roughly hewn blocks of stone placed on top of one another without mortar or cement. Some were deeply cracked. Between the pillars there were heaps of debris and broken stone that appeared to be the result of some recent catastrophe. The silence was so deep here that I could almost imagine being able to hear a spider spinning its web twenty feet across to the other side of the cavern. I could hear water dripping at regular intervals.

"It's much noisier at the other end, under Montmartre or Saint-Germain," she said. "You can hear carriages on the cobbles above, sometimes, dogs barking."

"We're still underneath the Jardin, I suppose," I said. "Not much to hear."

"And we're lower than usual," she said, looking around the wall to find the next of Silveira's marks that would indicate which of the seven or eight passageways we should take.

She held up a silver compass.

"I'm not going to get lost down here, not after last time."

She'd located a mark on the entrance to another passageway; we plunged into its darkness, picking our way around roof falls, piles of rock, and pools of water. I kept my hand on the walls, feeling the changes in texture and the cold, rubbing the powdery limestone with my fingers, remembering that it was made up of the remains of thousands of sea creatures that had died on some seabed millions of years beyond my own rememberings.

"Look at these pillars," Lucienne said. "One good strike with a mallet, and you could knock one of these stones out. Then the whole ceiling would come in. They closed off the area under the Luxembourg Palace a few years ago after some lunatic claimed to have blown up all the pillars in the quarries directly underneath it."

I reminded myself, with relief, that a great

river ran between me and the bones lying stacked up in the catacombs on the other side. You could become very superstitious down here, I thought.

"I don't want to die here," she said suddenly, her nerve failing her. "I don't want Delphine to die here. It's too dark."

"We're safe," I said. "All we have to do is find the passage de Saint-Claire. It can't be far."

"I have a bad feeling," she said. "Something's gone wrong."

We stopped to listen. We could just hear the barking of dogs somewhere behind us.

"Are they loose?" I asked.

"No, they keep them on ropes. They can't go fast. But they will be listening for us, sniffing us out. Put the lamp out," she said. "Listen. They're too close. If we are going to rescue Delphine we have to get to the passage de Saint-Claire before they catch us. At this rate they'll reach us first."

Now I could hear voices ahead as well as behind.

"Damn. They've surrounded us. Put out the light."

"But we won't be able to see anything," I said, doing as she asked.

I'm afraid of the dark, I thought, very afraid.

■ ■ ■ ■

A shot.

Someone had shot a gun; the detonation echoed around in the vault. Stones fell into the pool of water at our feet. The ball from the carbine had struck the ceiling just a few feet from the arch above my head. I waited for the ceiling to fall in. It didn't.

"You fool," a voice said. "You'll bring the whole city down on top of us. Put down the gun."

"Say nothing," she whispered, one hand feeling for my face in the darkness. Her fingertips traced the edges of my mouth. I felt for hers, pulling her to me in the moment in which I thought we were both about to die. Was I aroused by her or by the thought of my own death? Both were on my skin now.

"Say nothing," she said. I kissed her hand, smelling the scent of mud and something like animal pelt.

"Jagot's men are on both sides," she said. "Our only chance of reaching the others in the passage is to take a side tunnel, but we must be absolutely silent. *Totalement silencieux.*"

"No sudden moves," Jagot shouted from

somewhere close by. "No one move. Put the gun down."

"He thinks we have a gun," I whispered.

"We do," she said. I could hear her easing something from the folds of her clothing.

"Mme. Bernard?" It was Jagot's voice. Lucienne didn't answer.

"We have your friend, Manon Laforge. And the child. Such an interesting child. A credit to you, madame. You can help me, Mme. Bernard."

Still she did not answer.

He continued: "I hear you ask: How can I help you, M. Jagot? Well, Mme. Bernard, I am glad you asked. It is a good sign. You can help me by giving me the diamond and the boy. You must not harm the boy. Cuvier wants him. Now I hear you ask: 'And what will you do for me, M. Jagot?' And I say to you: I will let you slip away, Mme. Bernard, with your child. It is Silveira I want, and the boy. And the diamond, *naturellement*."

"It's not true," I whispered. "Don't make any deals with him. He won't let you get away."

"Put down the gun, Mme. Bernard," Jagot called out, "or we will all die."

"Madre." Delphine's voice echoed in the tunnels. Then resolute, dragon-slaying Delphine called out quickly in Italian: *"Madre, i*

431

ragazzi sono qui. Li ho appena visti. C'è anche l'uomo con il dente d'oro. Non abbiate paura." Her voice went silent, muffled quickly by an unseen hand.

"She says Silveira's here," Lucienne whispered. "She's seen him."

"All you have to do," Jagot called out, "is give the boy the diamond and then send him toward me. Slowly. M. Connor?"

"Answer him," she whispered. "He still thinks you're his. One-word answers only. When I squeeze your arm, stop."

"Yes," I called out.

"Can you see me if I lift up my lamp?"

"Yes."

I could see a group of black forms and the glimmer of a lamp at the end of the tunnel making a ruddy circle in the vault. We drew in close to the side of the wall as the circle of lamplight rose and widened.

"Mme. Bernard," Jagot continued. "You have no choice. You run. We run. We have light. You have none. There are six of us. Two of you. You're not stupid. All you have to do is give the boy the diamond and send him to us."

"I'm not going back," I whispered. "I'm coming with you."

There was a low whistle from where the gunshot sound had come. Almost inaudible.

Two long, low whistles and one short. I had last heard that sound in the rue du Pet-au-Diable.

"What's that?" I asked.

"Joaquim and the other boys. Silveira must have realized we were going to be cut off by Jagot's men before we reached the passage, so he sent for them. Look, now Jagot's men are closing in on us from the other end."

The air had been thick but now I could feel a slight movement around us, not quite a breeze. She felt it too. I looked up. Above us, where the ball had hit the pillar, a deep crack had opened up in the stone. Dust was falling around us. A sudden flash lit up the cavern, and in that moment I saw boys — the boys from the rue du Pet-au-Diable, their faces blackened, like night creatures, their eyes bright and wide. There were seven or eight of them. There was a scuffle, more dust, the gasp and cry of a child.

Something had happened. I could hear several voices shouting and above them Jagot, speaking in French, panicked, the lights from the lanterns scattering in different directions. "Where is she?" he shouted. "Where is the child? Find the damned child."

Then came Manon's voice. "Delphine's

433

safe, Lucienne," she called. "Joaquim and his boys have her." Then a groan — the sound of a punch or a blow. Manon had been silenced again.

"Daniel," Lucienne said quietly, "you have to go with them. Call out. Tell him I have a gun to your head. Buy me some time. We have to get Manon out."

I didn't hesitate. "She has a gun. She says she's going to kill me."

"Mme. Bernard, put the gun down."

"Daniel," she whispered. "It's time. Take this. I'm putting it in your pocket. The diamond. Tell Jagot you have it. Tell him I've put the diamond in your pocket."

"I have the diamond," I said. "I have the diamond."

"Now walk toward him," she said. "Walk toward the light down there." Then suddenly she pulled me back to her. She put her hands on my shoulders and brushed down my suit, smoothing out its folds. "This suit has seen better days," she said, kissing me so the darkness turned to blue and gold. "Now walk. Walk, damn you, or I will shoot you myself."

As I staggered forward, there was another explosion; rock falling; noise, dust, a blow to the head. I swear I saw feathers as I fell, great wings beating down there in the dark-

ness. That's one way landscapes change —
with a catastrophe, a rockfall, violence, and
revolution, theatrical and spectacular. I
heard only the dust falling and the clock
ticking.

29

Where did the gunshot come from? I was lucky, they said, very lucky. Lucienne's gun had gone off accidentally, they told me, just as she released me and pushed me toward Jagot. Her gun had fired a shot upward into the ceiling and had dislodged one of the stone pillars, already weakened by the first shot. This had brought down the ceiling. Lucienne Bernard, Davide Silveira, and their child, Delphine Bernard, Manon Laforge, and Alain Saint-Vincent had all been buried under the rockfall.

Or at least Jagot thought so. Cuvier did too. And exactly how many people died down there in the darkness of the quarries that night, M. Jagot? Two gunshots. Four thieves and a child caught in the wrong place.

But who knows for sure? The quarries do. I do. Or at least I came to know. Not by sudden revelation — an encounter on a train; a face recognized in a crowd. No, I watched and I listened for news of them. I read newspapers and I asked questions; I waited and, piece by piece, I put fragments together. One of them was a newspaper report about the giraffe that walked to Paris.

In 1826, the pasha of Egypt sent a giraffe to the king of France as a token of his esteem. Her keeper walked with her from Marseilles through sleepy villages, mile by mile, down the same roads the bronze Venetian horses had taken, and into the Jardin des Plantes. Crowds lined the streets. Bands played.

In May of that year, the giraffe's keeper walked her from the elephant rotunda, out of the menagerie in the Jardin des Plantes, past the ticket booth, under the cedar of Lebanon, and up to the top of the labyrinth and the bronze pavilion. All of this had happened, the newspaper reporters wrote, because an inmate in the debtor's prison who called himself Simon-Vincent, who was a botanist and had once fought in the Battle of Austerlitz, had asked to see the animal. Concessions were made. Though the botanist was not allowed to leave the prison, the warden had allowed him to climb onto the roof, accompanied of course by a guard, for a period of thirty minutes. A giraffe, the prisoner had said, was not to be missed. He had seen butterflies in Saint Helena, reptiles in the caves of Maastricht, the wings of great birds in the quarries of Paris; he would not miss the sight of the first giraffe in the Jardin des Plantes. How very French, the reporter from *The Times* wrote. How very French.

I had other glimpses too — in a new encyclopedia published in Paris and all the rage in London in the 1830s. There were entries by people whose names I half remembered, including one on corals and time. I recognized the voice. It made the hairs on the back of my neck stand up. There was no signature to the entry, just the initials LB. A thief, a heretic, and a philosopher who is buried now, I'd guess, in Italy somewhere near Florence, in a grave near to that of a diamond dealer called Silveira. Who knows what names are inscribed there.

In 1818, *The Times* carried a report of a diamond that sold for a considerable sum in Madras, India. A trading agent acting on behalf of an English duke had bought it from a Portuguese jeweler's agent called Sabalair in the back streets of the city. The agent had since vanished from Madras. A jeweler in London subsequently identified the duke's diamond as the famous Satar diamond, which had disappeared without a trace from Spain ten years earlier and was once said to be in a private collection that had been owned illegally in Paris by Vivant Denon, artist, antiquary, and friend of Napoleon Bonaparte. The provenance of the diamond was difficult to trace, the journalist explained. It had, some said, been stolen during a robbery in the Jardin des Plantes. What *The Times* journalist didn't report, but what was common knowledge among the thieves in Paris, was that a diamond had been recovered from that robbery, but that it had subsequently turned out to be a paste replica made, it was believed, in a Portuguese jewelry shop in the rue du Pet-au-Diable. The police agent leading the inquiry, M. Henri Jagot, had of course been furious at the discovery of the forgery but was said to be even more enraged by the thought that the real diamond had disappeared in the roof fall that had killed the thieves he had been pursuing.

Lamarck's bones are scattered in the catacombs under Paris. Burdened with debt, his devoted daughters buried him in a pauper's grave in the Montparnasse cemetery in 1829. Later, when they closed down that cemetery under new public-health laws, his bones were dug up and scattered into the miles of patterned bones in the catacombs. It's poignant, when you think about how many bones and shells Lamarck catalogued and labeled so carefully when his sight was good, that at the end no one wrote a label or carved a tombstone for him.

In 1832, Cuvier was buried in a marble tomb in the cemetery at Père Lachaise, a tomb he shared with his daughter Clémentine, who had died four years earlier from tuberculosis at the age of twenty-two, on the eve of her wedding. That same day Sophie Duvaucel, devastated at the toll her sister's death had taken on her stepfather's health, broke off her engagement to the young English lawyer Sutton Sharpe, in order to assist her stepfather with the fish volume of *Le Règne animal.* She had few regrets about those years, she told her husband when she finally married a widower, Admiral Ducrest de Villeneuve, in 1834, adopting his three children. My work at the Jardin des Plantes, she said, was the making of me.

Napoleon died from a stomach tumor on Saint Helena in 1821. There had been escape plots, but it was said that the Emperor had refused to be a part of any of them. He knew there was no way off the island, and even if there had been, beyond it, even in America, there was nowhere to hide. He was buried in the valley of the willows in an unmarked tomb.

And me? Well, things could never have stayed the same. I had taken a step into the undergrowth, where branchings and forkings chanced along a different axis, and I had begun to see the sublime contingency that is at the root of all things. I had found a set of different answers there.

I stayed in Paris through the rest of the winter of 1815, working alongside Sophie Duvaucel as a much valued and depended-upon secretary to the baron. I ran errands, translated books, wrote letters, took dictation, mounted and arranged specimens, and I began a new notebook. Sophie said I had changed. She always said it was the accident in the quarries, the shock of it. But I knew that it was the disappearance of the heretics from Paris; they disappeared with the shadows as the gaslights lit up more and more streets, leaving an emptiness there. By the end of the winter, the Jardin des Plantes had become the Jardin du Roi again, and once Cuvier had written his obituary for Lamarck, publicly mocking him, calling him a poet, a builder of castles in the air, a romancer, there was not much left in the

Jardin that Lucienne Bernard might have fought for, except Geoffroy, who emerged from his darkened rooms in 1818 with a book called *Philosophical Anatomy,* which caused a stir. When Fin, who had married Céleste and was making a good living for himself in London as a trainee surgeon, sent me notice of a position at Saint Bartholomew's Hospital, I took it. I was ready to leave Paris.

The London I returned to, the London of West Smithfield, and the anatomy students and young doctors of Saint Barts, was full of radical materialist ideas because so many of the students I worked alongside had also studied in Paris just as I had. Those men understood transmutation, and like Ramon and Evangelista and Céleste, they translated it into reformist politics. In the taverns and the back rooms of student lodgings around Smithfield and in the pages of the new radical medical journals, they called for the appropriation of church property, for working-class suffrage, universal education, the abolition of the House of Lords, and the end of privilege. It was a dangerous time. Young London doctors talked of Geoffroy and Lamarck not as heretics but as revolutionaries, as prophets of democracy and political enlightenment.

If I turned away from philosophical and political questions, it was not because they stopped being important to me but because I wanted to practice medicine. I wanted to contribute to the great reforms that were coming. And for the last forty years that is what I have done; through the reform bills and the revolutions in Europe, the coming of the gaslights and the railways and the camera and the Great Expedition, I have done my part to challenge the old orthodoxies buried deep in the parlors and church halls of provincial England. These have been small incremental changes, I tell myself, none of them significant in themselves, but they might add up to something meaningful.

I have a daughter — her name is Beatrice — who would have made a fine doctor. But it is hard to be a woman now. Even more difficult, I remind myself, than it was to be a woman in Paris after the Revolution. Some things improve; others degenerate. Sometimes time goes backward. Women, Beatrice reminds me, have no rights and few opportunities to be of use in the world or to use their natural talents. They are allowed to attend the lectures at the Royal Society but only as the guests of men. I know what Lucienne Bernard would have said about that.

I still think of her. I imagine that we meet by chance on a railway platform or a crowded street. It is always by chance, and it is always under pressure of time because one of us has to catch a train or because there is a vague sense of danger. Sometimes in these imagined encounters, she asks me if I have found love again. I say yes. Just that. I don't describe the women I have loved — the actress in London whom I followed to Rome, the heiress, the nurse, the young widow — and I certainly don't tell her about the brilliant and dark-eyed woman I married who, on first meeting at her father's house in Derbyshire, offered me the use of her library and showed me the volumes of Cuvier's *La Règne animal,* which had just arrived from Paris. She would read them in French, she said. French natural history was so much more interesting.

I don't tell my imagined Lucienne about Celia because I don't think she wants to hear about her. And I don't tell Celia about Lucienne because it has always seemed too difficult to explain how the first woman I loved was wanted by the French police and disappeared in a roof fall in the Paris quarries. So Lucienne Bernard came to be the secret that the child in the big house always seemed to be searching for. There is some peace in that.

I still wonder if there will come a day when we will know absolutely, without question, how time began or what happened in those first few seconds. I still think about the direction of time and whether we are right to imagine it as a train moving from one side of a landscape to another. I couldn't even have imagined trains back then in Paris, or omnibuses. But I did sometimes wonder if time might move in other directions — vertically, for instance, or even backward down that railway track, or along multiple branches of possibility.

Silveira told Lucienne she should leave philosophical questions alone. Some things were simply unknowable, he said; angels on a pinhead. But Silveira, I want to say to the Portuguese coral trader — if it were possible to speak to him now across the span of fifty years from this study in Derbyshire, if it were possible to cross the geographical gap that separates this house near the slanted church in which I write, to where he is, if he is still alive, which he almost certainly isn't, in India or Florence or Brazil, prison, warehouse, jeweler's shop, grave — there's a book, Silveira, I want to say, that everyone is talking about all across

Europe. You can buy it in the shops and on station platforms.

The author, an English squire, son of a respectable family, works on coral atolls; like Lucienne, he reads corals as if they were books or clocks. He thinks *like she did.* This book, well, people don't like it — or at least the bishops don't like it, but people are reading it everywhere. The author, Charles Darwin, grandson of Erasmus Darwin, builds his argument with the ordinary things, just as she did: not with corals, but with bees and pigeons and earthworms. *There is grandeur in this view of things,* he writes, reaching for the sublime through the commonplace. She would say that too. She did, didn't she? I'm sure she did.

Someone else will get there, she'd said. It's not about the Napoleons or the Cuviers. The answer lies in the one-eighth of an inch rise of seabed. Knowledge is slow, the slowness of polyps and imperceptibilities, things we can't see in the dark. The grand dramas, the bizarre, the ordinary, the fantastic, and the commonplace are all tangled together. And time isn't always a straight line; sometimes it makes a web or a net or a branching tree.

She had seen Red Sea coral spawn, she said. When the sea reaches the right temperature, when they are ripe, when the moon reaches a certain point, just once a year, down there on the coral reefs, the dark waters explode into white smoke clouds. It's like fireworks or seed heads opening, thousands and millions of them, released into the water all at once. And when the coral spawn, all the other sea organisms follow. It's like a trigger. The fishermen say it's the moon that makes them spawn, she had said, and I said: How can they see the moon? They have no eyes. Perhaps they have other ways of seeing and knowing, she had said. Perhaps we all do. There's a grandeur in that.

AUTHOR'S NOTE

This is a novel grounded in fact. Thousands of young men like Daniel traveled to Paris at the end of the Napoleonic Wars. Many of them wrote detailed descriptions of their travels and of their adventures in what was to them an exotic, occupied city. Many of them were transformed. I have invented fictional characters — Daniel Connor, Fin Robertson, Lucienne Bernard, and the thieves — and put them into a real historical situation, a community of scientists and a city that is as accurately rendered as the historical scholarship, journals, prints, drawings, maps, and other historical sources allowed. Likewise, I described the historical characters of Cuvier, Lamarck, Geoffroy, and the men and women of the Jardin des Plantes as faithfully as I was able. Henri Jagot is modeled on François-Eugène Vidocq, a notorious criminal who was appointed to run the Brigade de la Sûreté in

1811 and was one of the first private investigators in Europe. The Jardin des Plantes is still where it always was and is largely unchanged, but the streets of Paris that I describe were replaced in the 1850s by the wider streets designed and built by Georges-Eugène Haussmann for Napoleon III.

The quarries of Paris continue to be used for subversive activities. In 2004 the Paris police found a thirty-seat cinema in the quarries that had been built by a group called the Perforating Mexicans. It was connected illegally to the state power company's cables, and pipes drew water from the Trocadero gardens above. When Commander Luc Rougerie, the police chief in charge of underground Paris, was asked how many quarry entrances exist today, he replied, "There are those I know and those I don't."

Evolution was not discovered by Charles Darwin in 1859. Though Darwin brilliantly codiscovered the mechanism of evolution, natural selection, in 1859, evolution — the belief that all living things have evolved in some way from other living organisms and that nature is in flux, not fixed — is an idea that had been around in some form or other since Aristotle. Darwin knew this and paid homage to his intellectual predecessors in *On the Origin of Species by Natural Selec-*

tion. Those predecessors — scattered across the world, some isolated, others in touch with like-minded natural philosophers — believed that species were mutable, that man had evolved from earlier, simpler, aquatic filaments, and that Nature was on the move. They were bold thinkers, prepared to challenge the intellectual and religious orthodoxies of their age, and they were often ostracized as heretics and infidels. Many were also migrants perpetually traveling from one university to another in search of other freethinkers, museum collections, and libraries, and answers to the natural philosophical questions that bore upon them. *The Coral Thief* pays homage to those heretics.

ACKNOWLEDGMENTS

Thanks go first to my readers — my son, Jacob Morrish, and daughters Hannah Morrish and Kezia Morrish, Susan Sellers, Ricciarda Barbieri, Jan Michael, Giles Foden, and Richard Cook; to the magicians who have edited with such intricate skill: Kirsty Dunseath and Cindy Spiegel; to my agent, Faith Evans, for her kindness, vision, and patience, and to Emma Sweeney, my U.S. agent. To fellow writers and friends, Anna Whitelock, Patricia Fara, and Sara Crangle. To friends Judith Boddy and Richard Ashrowan. To Ed Holberton and Rich Katz, with whom I made a journey that made all the horizons bigger — through Jordan, along the Dead Sea, and into the red sands of the Wadi Rum. To the librarians of Cambridge University Library and to the British Academy who helped to fund some of the research. To Sara Perren and Geoff Wall, who gave me a Paris comparable to

Daniel Connor's Paris in their home in York in 1984, where I came of age in the shadow of Freud, Balzac, and Flaubert; thanks to Jonathon Burt for a museum of locks in Paris and a man-moth; to Steffie Muller for the trapdoor in the Paris street and what came out of it. I am immensely grateful for the distinguished scholarship of the historians of science: Mary Orr, Toby Appel, Ludmilla Jordanova, Martin Rudwick, Emma Spary, Devinda Outram, and Pietro Corsi. Any historical inaccuracies or reinterpretations I have made are entirely my own. Finally, I thank my late father, Roger Stott — his editing skills, enthusiasm, and literary brilliance were sadly missed this time.

FURTHER READING

Fiction
Victor Hugo, *Les Misérables* (1862)
Honoré de Balzac, *Le Père Goriot* (1835)
Louis Aragon, *Holy Week* (1961)
Stendhal, *The Red and the Black* (1830)

Nonfiction
Nina Burleigh, *Mirage: Napoleon's Scientists and the Unveiling of Egypt.* Harper, 2007.
Vincent Cronin, *Napoleon.* HarperCollins, 1990.
Andrew Hussey, *Paris: The Secret History.* Penguin, 2007.
Ludmilla Jordanova, *Lamarck.* Oxford University Press, 1984.
Jean-Paul Kauffmann, *The Dark Room at Longwood.* Harvill, 1999.
James Morton, *The First Detective: The Life and Revolutionary Times of Vidocq: Criminal, Spy and Private Eye.* Ebury Press, 2005.

Derinda Outram, *Georges Cuvier: Vocation, Science, and Authority in Post-Revolutionary France.* Manchester University Press, 1984.

Simona Pakenham, *In the Absence of the Emperor: London–Paris 1814–1815.* Cresset Press, 1968.

Lord Rosebery, *Napoleon: The Last Phase.* Cosimo, 2008.

LIST OF ILLUSTRATIONS

cheologie, J. Doucet (Paris, 1739).

Page 329: The Arrival of the *Northumberland* at St. Helena From G. W. Melliss, *Views of St. Helena; Illustrative of its Scenery and Historical Associations* (London, 1857).

Page 345: The Pavilion at the Briars From Frederic Masson, *Napoleon à Sainte-Hélène* (Paris, 1912).

ABOUT THE AUTHOR

Rebecca Stott is a professor of English literature and creative writing at the University of East Anglia in Norwich. She is the author of the novel *Ghostwalk* and a biography, *Darwin and the Barnacle,* and is a regular contributor to BBC Radio. She lives in Cambridge, England.

We hope you have enjoyed this Large Print book. Other Thorndike, Wheeler, Kennebec, and Chivers Press Large Print books are available at your library or directly from the publishers.

For information about current and upcoming titles, please call or write, without obligation, to:

Publisher
Thorndike Press
295 Kennedy Memorial Drive
Waterville, ME 04901
Tel. (800) 223-1244

or visit our Web site at:

http://gale.cengage.com/thorndike

OR

Chivers Large Print
published by BBC Audiobooks Ltd
St James House, The Square
Lower Bristol Road
Bath BA2 3SB
England
Tel. +44(0) 800 136919
email: bbcaudiobooks@bbc.co.uk
www.bbcaudiobooks.co.uk

All our Large Print titles are designed for easy reading, and all our books are made to last.

m